The struggle is real...

We'll smile for you.

PART 2:

AWAKENINGS

RECKONING

PJ SELAROM

PJSELAROM.COM

• Available on Kindle, Amazon.com, and other retail outlets.

All characters are fictional unless otherwise seen in a hallucination. The creatures (e.g., unipegon, asegafians, archeornyx; kiradoura; tridras; ditchightl; dicen, etc.) are his proprietary property.

Fantasy/Sci-fi Adventure. Mystery. Romance.

1ˢᵗ Edition

THE JODE: Part 2: Awakenings Reckoning

ISBN-13:
978-1-7340860-0-3 (PJ Selarom)

ISBN-10:
1-7340860-0-9

Printed in the USA. Layout by PJ Selarom.

Special Thanks to the ILLUSTRATORS:

Map: Corey McNaught
Cover: Carlos Villas

<u>Acknowledgements</u>

Thank you, Aristotle, for writing about spectacle in your "Poetics."

General Slowpoke, Beta One and Colonel Misstep, your support and belief in this crazy series raises me up. Dad, you're not forgotten.

Finally, Ms. Doris Works, you always wanted to write a book, but circumstance took you away. This second novel, win or fail, is dedicated to you.

DIALECTS

	Father/Mother	Husband/Wife	Son/Daughter	Day/Night	Year; Life	Death
MAN						
LOREL ELF	Bloodfather/mother	Mate	Bloodson/daughter	Sunday/Moonday	Season	End of seasons
KHUN ELF; SPRITE; GNOME	Bloodfather/mother	Mate		Sunday/Moonday	Season	End of seasons
NIXY	Bloodfather/mother	Chosen/Bonder	Spawn	Sea blanket/Great Pearls	Season	End of seasons
GIANT; FAIRY	Trunk/Stem	Seed/Earth	Sprout	Cloudnoon/Starnoon	Growth	End of growths
DWARF	Jewel/Gem	Brace/Charm	Nugget/Trinket	Great Light/Deep Cold	Ring	End of rings
OGRE	Boulder/Rock	Vitamin/Mineral	Stone/Pebble	Light/Dark	Shift	End of shifts
PIXY	Boulder/Rock	Vitamin/Mineral	Stone/Pebble	Light/Dark	Shift	End of shifts

DIALECTS

	Emperor/ess	Prince/cess	General	Advisor	People	Old Person	Home	School	Doctor
MAN	King/Queen	Prince/cess	General	Advisor	Kin	Elder	Home	School	Doctor
LOREL ELF					Clan	Elder	Home		
KHUN ELF; SPRITE; GNOME	Leader					Elder	Home		
NIXY	Ocean (female)	Lake/Pond	Reef	Tribune	Schools	Elder	Grotto	Ripple	Algae
GIANT; FAIRY	Tree/Flower	Plant/Fern	Thorn	Leaf	Roots	Twig	Hollow	Ring	Chloro
DWARF	Grand Diamond/Coal	Diamond/Coal	Stalagmite	Tar	Ore	Fossil	Core	Matrix	Crystal
OGRE	Mountain/Hill	Butte/Mound	Crag	Sand	Sediments	Dust	Cavern	Ion	Resin
PIXY	Lord/Lady				Sediments	Dust	Cavern	Ion	Resin

MAIN CHARACTERS

Lorel Kingdom (Elves):
*Ygl: General.
*Steadfast: Ygl's unipegon, mount.
*Welbern/Demonslayer: Ygl's broadsword.
*Limbus: Ygl's son.
*Ploone: Limbus's best friend.
*Snip & Winky: the boys' respective asegafian cats.

Forest of Khun (Elves, Sprites, Gnomes):
*Blasmle: male Elvin Leader.
*Rushar: Blasmle's hippogriff.
*Rungna (-Olivia): female Elvin Leader.
*Folcen'na: Rungna's hippogriff.
*Oreol: Sprite Leader.
*Lojstania: Oreol's wife.
*Mitral: Gnome Leader.
*Jinx: Mitral's archeornyx.
*Systoli: Mitral's friend.
*Rube: Systoli's golden cardinal.

Quirmean Empire (Man):
*Rondo: Emperor.
*Werkle: Rondo's brother, Advisor.
*Aman: Shop owner
*Jonas
*E'alor: Jonas' friend.

Giantic estate (Treedom):

***Kute**: Prince (Plant)

*Stonecrusher: Kute's gray pegasus.

*Crater: Kute's large horse.

***Juna**: Fairy Queen (Flower)

***Erosc**: King (Tree), Kute's father.

*Shadocoat: Erosc's ebony pegasus.

***Umbala**: Kute's brother, General (Thorn).

*Slab: Umbala's red pegasus.

***Dionjor**: Erosc's brother, Advisor (Leaf).

***Ood**: Fairy King (Tree), Juna's husband.

***Alduur**: Shield bearer.

*Powder: Alduur's white pegasus.

Ogrean estate (Mountaindom):

***Gravelp**: Princess (Mound)

*Hogar's Beard: Gravelp's kiradoura.

***Smush**: King (Mountain)

*Dune: Smush's gryphon

***Squash**: Queen (Hill)

***Crumb**: Advisor (Sand)

*Patch: Crumb's kiradoura

***Squish**: Crumb's wife.

***Punok**: General (Crag)

*Pillager: Punok's gryphon

***Gasma**: Pixy Queen (First Lady)

***Guisarrio**: Pixy King (First Lord)

***Lady Hoodia**: Pixy

***Lord Vicstusi**: Starrm's husband.

***Lady Starrm**: Pixy

***Lord Zeph**: Pixy

Dwarven estate (Grand Diamondom):
***Ding**: thief
*Red Fang: Ding's wolf.
*Gore: Ding's diamond-headed axe.

Nixy estates (Oceandoms):
***Sama**: Nixy mother (bloodmother)
***Ryl**: Sama's son (bloodson)
***Isoris**: Queen (Ocean)
***Tatenu**: Isoris' sister, Advisor (Tribune).

Miscellaneous:
***Tungloc**
*Dicen
*Tridra
*Ditchightl
*Los & Num: twin suns
*Nus & Anul: twin moons

The Divinity

ELVIN:
ACHAL: Lorellian goddess of memory and history. Wielder of the psionic sword.
MIREDO: Khunian god of nature. Wielder of the bow of storms.

MAN:
ISTRATOS: God of magic and games. Wielder of the staff of power.
WELNA: Goddess of the arts. Wielder of the shield of creation.

NIXY:
JEBLE: God of the sea and logic. Wielder of the trident of waves.
NUMR'C: Goddess of dreams, fertility, and peace. Embodiment of the island.

GIANTS:
LOLUNG-COR: God of war. Wielder of the lance of strength.
PYTY: Goddess of the grain. Embodiment of the mountain. Wielder of the sickle of sustenance.

OGRES:
FALVANCH: Goddess of the earth. The Great Sculptor. Wielder of the club of order.
HOGAR: God of resilience. Embodiment of the desert. The Rock Shaker. Wielder of the pick of chaos.

DWARVES:
HENC: God of wealth. Wielder of the axe of winter.
PARIOT: Goddess of invention. Wielder of the hammer of sacred magma.

FAERIE (including Gnomes):
ETHNEL: Essence of preservation and small creatures; Wielder of the dagger of luck.

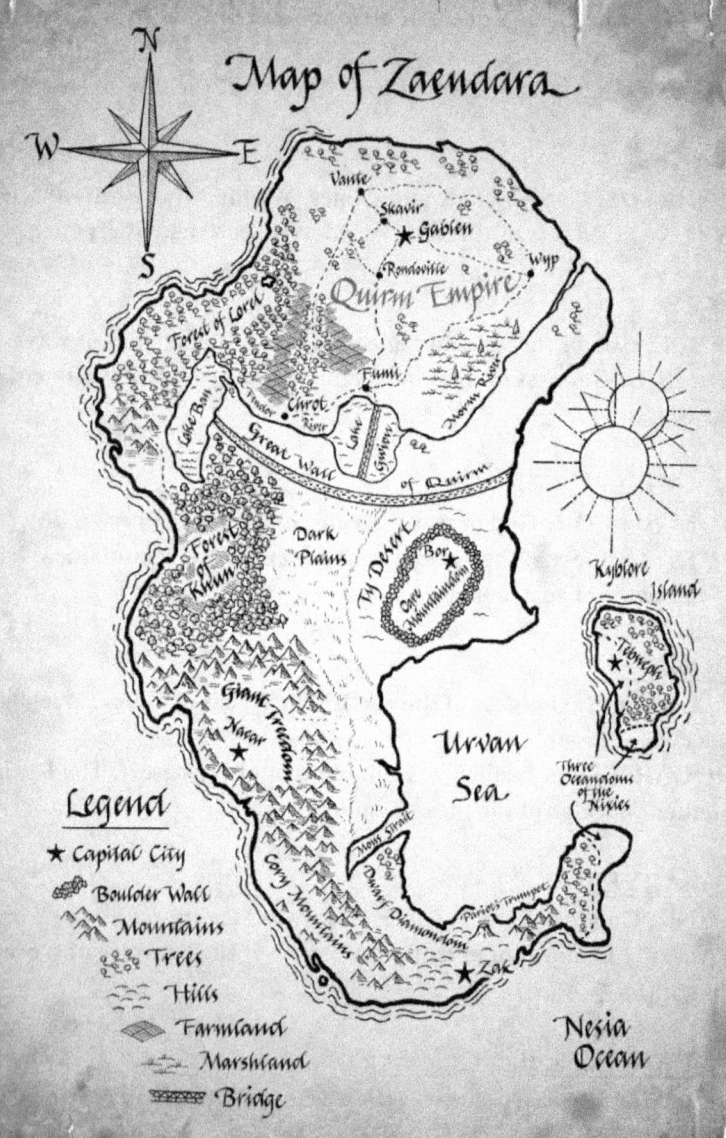

Salutations.
I am Achal, Lorellian Elvin goddess of memory and history.
Welcome back to Inner Earth.

Please accept my profound regrets. I misinformed you in the previous book. I stated I would narrate in the third person while Ygl would narrate in the first; however, whenever Ygl encounters an accidental remembrance, I will narrate his unexpected experience. Moreover, a dialect that does not fit in the preceding charts is the one for "children." Elves merely say "**bloodchildren**," while the Ogres say "**bedrock**." Dialects will be bold-faced minimally according to whoever narrates. Let us resume the tale:

Our heroes and heroines are in a bit of a niche. Evil's influences are emerging and greater existences have been wasted.

Yet, in an unknown residence, a lazy sunlight's circular beam blends with the dusty air through a half-closed opening. The dust particles hum, traveling across the place like a plague of locusts bumping against the blunt, nondescript objects... a corner there... a rising line here. A line of elevation roams with the dusty plague toward a robust, vertical curvature—perhaps a bed's heading of sorts. Along the head's deep shelf, a serpentine crest pokes from the engulfing shadows. A ruse perhaps, if not for light's glint bouncing off a silvery groove. Upon further review, the serpentine crest reveals a spout where much of the dust mingles like moths to a melodic flame. From the spout's hole, the humming dust melts into a more harmonious tune:

PJ Selarom

Thy final goodbye had a hold on me
So I was searching for something to make me complete.
After all the moments in history,
It'll take more than a night to get over thee.

Today, I'll be all right.
I'll make it without thee by my side.
I can feel the suns blowing me kisses from the sky.
Today, I'll be all right.

I'll dance on a mountain and let the moment last.
My future won't be chained to the past.
I'll glide through skyways in a cool summer's breeze
And travel the byways and streets of my dreams.

Today, I'll be all right.
I'll make it without thee by my side.
I can feel the suns blowing me kisses from the sky.
Today, I'll be all right.

My tears of joy won't evaporate.
Thou won't be around, but, I'll see thy face.
That doesn't matter if thou is gloomy.
Don't be sad. I'll smile for thee.

Today, I'll be all right.
I want the whole world to take a look inside.
And hear this chord in my bones
playing a happy song.
Today, I'll be all right.
Today, I'll be all right.

Yesterday thou took my breath away.
Today, I'll be all right.
Tomorrow will be better than tonight.

Awakenings Reckoning
Today, I'll be all right.

The harmonious tune fades. Swen's melodious chanting resumes. The genie endures and endures...

CHAPTER 1: The Tower

Chrot, the slave city.

Stonecrusher's tail submerged beneath the Fendor River's mystic portal, carrying Ygl after Kute and Ding—fugitives of the Quirmean Empire. The closing portal's unnatural molecules clashed, causing the currents to crash inward as if sneaky seaweeds stretched upward stealing the portal's edges, enticing the impressive tides together.

All that remained was the rushing Fendor. Long and majestic, the waterway flourished as the bluish-yellow glow provided a florid appearance with a glittering shine. From Lake Gwion's higher altitude, the Fendor's southern half surged with haste northwest to empty into Lake Ban amid the Forests of Lorel and Khun, and Quirm. The glow rebounded through the unflappable southern half throughout the northeastern waterways, ending at the Morm River's gushing outpour upon the Nesia Ocean... the glow dissipated.

The mystical scenario altered, revealing a gathering band of Quirmean warriors aghast at their foes' method of departure. What had occurred? Did the scum not drown? No. Not them. The warriors noticed one of the three escapees exploited power securing the others within the Fendor's unyielding currents. This was evident, for how did the fugitive destroy a portion of Chrot's defensive wall, massacring several warriors in the process? May Xurchon bless the defenders' wits?

From the distance, reinforcements hastened from Morro Ascension. The exploding wall and massive Giant were not a challenge for them to decline. Another heralding group rode off with messengers who raced to warn the Quirmean emperor, but this group wanted to ascertain proof of his rivals to him. At a lengthy rope's tail-end slumped the wrangling form of a lifeless Elvin maiden. Many blades punctured her, contorting Thalla's alluring features. Her elegant arms jumbled carelessly about the grasses, knocking down a set of rooted arrows as Thalla was hauled off to Gablen, the capital.

The emperor must be warned, promptly and judiciously, of the threesome. Only he could defy this power called magic with some of his own, his divine right. The emperor must be gratified. He must rule all of Zaendara with this Jode. He must be satisfied, or else he'd recede into his chamber—forever locking himself away from his beloved populace. He, most of all emperors, the hand, heart and mind of all Quirm. And so, Emperor Rondo must be warned before all of Zaendara would befall upon them.

Tendrils of snowy smoke encircled the final mystic scenario, replacing the dimming picture, fusing with other smoky tendrils. The snaky smoke rose and diffused with nether, darker levels within Rykon Tower's steep, angular ceilings. Rykon Tower, Rondoville's main worshipping temple. The ivory tower was established ages ago at Rondoville during the empire's birth, self-named after its foremost beloved emperor. Rykon II, Emperor Rondo's father, married Empress Hethomes. Hethomes bore for Rykon II two other sons, Spenz and Werkle, but Rondo was favored.

A unique dominion seethed and pulsated within this sacred temple's ivory walls—magic, but magic harboring malevolent lifeblood to its essence. Black magic, the nefarious arts, was its embodiment, and the titan who wielded such arts was the fetching, unclothed man the award exuded soundest from. "The Lorellian general has escaped thee, Rondo," Xurchon stated.

Ease impressed upon the Quirmean emperor during this clandestine summit. Though he didn't bear the hoary, sleek robes his uninvited priests brandished, choosing to exhibit his customary imperial garb instead, the ease rested comfortably within his velvet folds. This ease confused him, belting him from out of nowhere. Did he really desire Ygl to flee with the others? Was the desire by choice? Was there something about his new god that frightened the emperor so much that Rondo anticipated the threesome's escape to secure his suffering's desire, a suffering that Xurchon promised to rectify? The Quirmean emperor shuddered at such thoughts. "And, do you know how to retain them, mighty Xurchon?" Rondo asked, becoming uncomfortable observing the near-human eyes peering at him through the luminance.

"Was it not thee who stated they were useless? Powerless? Inferior?" Xurchon inquired.

"The Elvin general wields magic, but I sensed none on him when he was sent to the pit."

"Then, it was the pit where he attained the magic. And from none other than his own Lorellian brother could he have acquired the capability to get it."

"Methelo died before Ygl was ever captured. There's no way he—"

"There is a way, my careless apostle." Xurchon's adolescent pupils turned bloodshot; his soothing voice garnered a hateful shade. "Doth thou not notice the glow, Rondo? No other magic emits a glow such as that before it is cast. The Elf has control over a fragment of the Jode much like thou dost. That makes him a very deadly foe, indeed. If he gets the Jode before WE DO," his Unholiness' voice boomed, like the god he meant to epitomize. Oh, Xurchon's wrath, ceaseless. "THEN ALL WILL BE LOST. THY PEOPLE WILL NEVER LOVE THEE. ZAENDARA WILL NEVER LOVE THEE. THE JODE IS THE KEY! I AM THE KEY!"

Emperor Rondo became restrained within the milkiness, performing his best to maintain a level of composure. "You... you are making me uncomfortable..."

"I AM... sorry, Rondo. I didn't mean to frighten thee. Do not worry. The Elves will love thee. The Dwarves will, too. I know this, for I am god. Am I not?"

Rondo wouldn't respond.

Xurchon continued, disregarding his disciple. "We must stop this General Ygl before he diminishes thy rule. His unipegon has disappeared beyond my scope of influence, and he retains his sword your captain failed to retrieve."

A gentleness affected Rondo through his robes. Yes, he must stop Ygl before all was lost, but his enemy, too, warranted control over magic—a magic granted somehow to the general by dead King Methelo.

The Lorellian King harvested no magic upon his personage when Rondo secretly scanned him. For sure, Methelo must have had possession of magic, but why was it not... could Methelo have had assistance from the—no, there were no gods! Or goddesses! They were never real. Xurchon was the one true... Rondo resisted his dilemma.

"I... I am sorry. It... it will not happen again," the emperor stated halfheartedly, bowing his head. He didn't need to, but he felt courtesy as a matter of importance in this instance. Things were happening too fast.

A giddiness evolved in him; he knew General Ygl was to blame. If that dratted Lorellian hadn't rescued Quirm's other enemies, none of these problems would've arisen. Ygl made the emperor's mission more challenging, and Rondo hated the Elvin general for that. "I'll expedite my plans, great Xurchon. I assure you, by the next two days, Quirm will attack and capture the Forest of Khun sooner than they can react. As for the Giants, it'll not be long for the Ogres to fall as our unexpected pawn. Then, both races will collapse beneath Quirm's might."

The Quirmean emperor paused. He could feel another sentiment affecting him. A sentiment that urged him to go into battle, dictating to him to conquer the Jode. He held back the sentiment. "I do hope they will love me," he mumbled.

"They will love thee, Rondo. I know this. It saddens me, though, to witness a fool ride about the country attempting to warn all the estates possible. He is simply wasting his measure, including, since our last hope belies about him. And, if that doesn't work, then we'll personally have to intervene. By the way, hast thou any word about Swen?"

Rondo's hairs strained at an end, but he was pleased the matter, at least, changed. "She has been found and will be returned."

"Good. Good. I cannot wait, but I'll be patient as thee hast been. Let us end our meeting until later, Emperor. The next day will be a better one. I'm sure." Unwavering, Xurchon's fading form reigned within the billowing smoke. His alluring eyes folded, his body emitted smoke as whitish as that which girdled them.

Rondo attempted to retain the inexplicable feeling persisting to nag him. He needed to state something to abate it. "What about your promise?"

The God of Evil's eyelets unsealed, revealing bulbous, bloodshot seeds levitating in the fumes. "It will be fulfilled in due. Dost not worry... and, get me that sword. Retrieve Welbern."

Calmness became the emperor's subsequent grace. Regrettably, he understood why. Every day he'd arrive to counsel with his novel deity and always the rhetorical question about Xurchon's promise. Was it an impulse? Nevertheless, he always received the correct answer.

Rondo bowed his head as a vague tribute. He abandoned the worshipping chamber to the balcony upstairs, ascending the ivory stairs, past the cubic brasier burning myrfran garlic interspersed with pine needles for long life and prosperity.

The chamber launched to soften to a more natural setting revealing an albescent marble statue—the God of Evil erected reverently off-center. The god's selfsame smoke blossomed from his waist's underside like a peeling onion, substantiating as the base.

The beleaguered emperor swung open the hickory doors adorned three stories above the zealous worshippers ambling Rondoville's cobblestone streets. This moment was so enlivening, to step onto the tower's balcony to grace his beloved citizenry's faces and embrace a crimson morning tinged with azure cloudlessness. He hoped they'd adore him as much as he adored their audience. Soon he would seize a more respectful agreement than he expected—but he must secure the Jode to complete Xurchon's covenant. He yearned he could; he would.

What ensued upon his ancestor, Emperor Ryke, he hoped wouldn't transpire upon him.

CHAPTER 2: Labile

The Ogrean Kingdom.

Queen Juna wavered as she struggled to hoist upon her spider-webbed boots. After all, her delicate form did undergo quite a bit of effort while barely ingesting anything. Her prison cell's sloping wall balanced her with nothing else to prop against.

Her recent whereabouts perturbed her, her hopes collapsed toward a state of confusion. Quirmean forces would soon come sweeping across Zaendara overtaking everything encountered, and all the while impish Pixies would be holding custodial duties against a hypothesized incursion from the Giants. Even worse, the Ogres, the Pixies' shareholder in their estate, were not privy to any of these treacherous occurrences.

This miscarriage of the Pixies' findings aroused great concern upon the Fairy queen as she plucked at her tattered dress' threads. Not even the Giants nor her people knew anything of this mistaken treachery. Adventurous Juna, at last, longed to envision the sight of Ood's face, her husband, becoming real.

"'Fun'..." troubled Juna stated to herself almost as if stuck in a dream. She did not like the idea behind the "new fun" First King Guisarrio was planning to partake with his disenfranchised Fairy. First Queen Gasma had already bestowed her taste of "fun" when she dealt the agitated Fairy a taste of Pixy divine right—Juna's payback would be grand indeed if the occasion arose. However, if Juna stayed genuine with herself, being a prisoner was never her intent. This predicament became a little too much undertaking for her noble sensibilities.

Rather odd, her flawless cell's bulwarks were molded out of an auburn glass similar to her dress' color. Juna could have been mistaken for a phantasm. A foursome of lengthy walls surrounded the wee Fairy and pointed outward at ninety-degree angles from the midpoint. The ceiling and flooring, molded of an equivalent sturdy glass.

Through the sharp convex walls, Juna could decipher two of her captors' silhouetted shapes, not much taller than her. A sturdy skirt of moderate length produced one as being female while the other appeared male because his sinewy muscles could be distinguished along his silhouette's deeper orange.

Their quartet of insectoid wings could not obstruct the eager Fairy from peering past her two sentries in an effort to evaluate her surroundings. For certain, the Ogres endeavored as the races' most significant sculptors, as tales told. The items encompassing Juna she hoped did not fool her. From the ceiling, long stalactites pointed downward with stony curves encircling them. From within the curves, rough torches poked fiery heads. Stalagmites fashioned to form legs for large tables, chairs, and cabinets. Everywhere the furniture was molded of various stones but in very enthralling fashions, not even the opaque, auburn glass of Juna's prison could blur such a wonderful vision.

Juna remembered something else—the lamp! Where was Swen? Juna and Swen came here to warn the Pixies about Emperor Rondo and the Jode, but never expected this turn of events. Unease stirred in the queen again. Since being of noble grace, her ignorance could not appreciate others' customs, but a detainee was her current role and so would be the rest of Zaendara if not warned. Moreover, alarming Zaendara would be useless if she wallowed around in this unusual cell all her life. She felt upset toward those who dared be an obstacle against her independence.

With gathered strength, she felt Ethnel's gift, her divine right, boil within her veins. Her gift coursed through her upper appendages and fueled most energetic at her hands. Froths of light shot about her fingers, the effervescences transforming into a brilliance. Out from the brilliance shot the whitest light she had ever released. The immense power collided against her undesired encasement's wall. A loud sound resonated around her, her brightest light blinding her... Juna gathered herself from her collapse. To her demise, the glass did not shatter. Juna slumped to the flooring.

"That was a nice try, your Ladyship, but your attempt did not help you," stated the startled male Pixy. "Are you all right, Starrm?" He bent to assist the female Pixy.

"Yes, I am all right. It was only that she got us by surprise with that power."

"Your divine right is just as strong."

"I know it is; however, I did not even think such filth, as the Fairies, possessed such power."

"I agree."

"Oh, please, dung—" Juna chided, she loved a challenge.

"Do not call me that, Fairy filth," Starrm, the female, retorted.

"Hey, do not let this piece of glass get in your way, dung. Come on! Let us get the show on, dung. Dung! Dung! Dung! Diggity dung-dung!" Bruised Juna fluttered up, revived with a new sense of purpose, with arms outstretched. She could never gauge how to regulate her childishness.

Male Vicstusi retorted, "How pompous you are. Where was it when First Lady Gasma took you down a peg like First Lord Guisarrio did?"

"They were lucky. Now, I am ready."

"Give me a moment, Vicstusi. I want in on that Fairy filth right now."

"No, Starrm. I want you to relax. We do not need to be concerned about her now. You are not hurt, are you?" The male Pixy's tone changed, more caring. He almost reminded the queen of her husband, Ood.

"I already told you, Vicstusi, I am fine, but thank you for asking me twice, my sweet **vitamin**."

"Sshh... not in front of the prisoner," he whispered lovingly. "We will get our replacements soon."

Such compassionate words stated between the two Pixies astonished Juna. Maybe they were not as barbaric as legend had related, for sure their intelligence would not be as great as her race's or as preeminent as the ethereal Sprites. Her bedazzled eyes attempted to peer through the obscured glass at her two sentries, knowing her logic's value needed to overwhelm her urgency at this present moment. "I am sorry for what I did. I possess the power of the white light. My attempt was done only because I am quite upset. Now, please, you must understand, I am not the enemy. Please. I know this may sound stupid, but you must set me free."

"No," Starrm retorted. "You shall not be set free until our First Lady Gasma and First Lord Guisarrio have met with our council, which we are a part of."

"You do not understand. Your estate will be attacked. I do not know when, but if you do not act quickly, the Ogres and your race shall fall."

"By the Giants they would fall indeed if we had not been warned beforehand," the male Pixy responded. Even through the glass, the atmosphere between the Pixy and Fairy felt apprehensive.

Juna continued, "Listen, nothing will be gained if you do not listen to my plea. There is no such thing as an attack from my **roots** nor the Giants."

"I am sorry, Lady of Fairies, but we can only say that what you plea is not true. You are the first of the Fairies to enter our desert after so long. We would have welcomed you if there had not been a rumor of war being aroused between our races. Why you would dare want to attack seems perfectly reasonable," resolute Starrm stated.

"You must believe me. The Giants are not forming any sort of attack. Man is."

"You liar. It was Man who warned us," the male Pixy reentered the argument. "And it will be Man who will stand by us when the attack comes. Now I see that what the legends say are true?"

Juna asked, "What do you mean? I do not understand."

"That, Lady Fairy, is kept secret by my **sediments** and my sediments alone. No other race knows the source of our aversion toward the Fairies."

The situation was getting uncontrollable; all of this arguing gained nothing. If they must be told straightforward, then straightforward Juna's disclosure would be.

"Listen. Please," Juna pleaded. She did not want to censor herself any longer in this argument. If she did, the situation would probably get worse and who knew what would happen to her in adversarial territory.

"It is of great imperative we Pixies struck back at the Fairies. We know—"

"You have got this information all wrong."

"My sediments have spent too long—" The male Pixy's barbarian blood seethed.

Starrm interceded, "Vicstusi, wait. Let us hear her out and see what she has to say."

The male Pixy's silhouette hesitated for a moment, staring back at his female companion. "All right."

Juna felt better. "Well, you see, it starts with the attack upon the Dwarves. Their whole estate is now under slavery. And by whom? Man."

Vicstusi's silhouette backed against the auburn glass. His sinewy dorsal muscles and short-sleeved vest shown more evident upon the opaque surface with the indistinct accompaniment of a quartet of insectoid wings slackened upon each another. Juna grimaced at his fashion blunder, wondering how he could wear leather in this hot weather.

"That does not matter." Vicstusi stated. "Those bulky miners deserve being tamed with the way their **shifts** lead them," he replied.

"Shifts?" Juna could only fathom he referred to the Dwarves' lives. "Would you believe me if I told you the Elves were captured?"

"No." His response, more an astonishment than a disapproval.

"You cannot be saying the truth. We were only told about the Dwarves, not of the Elves. Man would not attack the Elves, would they?" Starrm's urgency was more directed toward her male counterpart.

"No," King Vicstusi answered in kind. "Man has done nothing. They would never attack the Elves. Both races are too peaceful with each other and, as I hear, have always thrived in harmony."

"Then, the Fairy lies to us," Starrm concluded.

"My name is Juna, and if you both are too dimwitted to know that Man is tricking you, then you are in worse trouble when their invasion comes. The lamp I brought with me is proof of their attack."

"Lamp?" Vicstusi and Starrm harmonized.

"Yes, the lamp is the only proof of their attack. Within it lies a genie named Swen who will tell you the truth."

Alarmed, Vicstusi arose, endeavoring to peer at the Fairy queen through the resistant glass. "We... we were not told of a lamp."

When proof's final piece had been misplaced, Juna's shock never halted. "Then, there is nothing left. I doubt you would believe me if I told you of the planned attacks the Forest of Khun will have to defend itself against."

Queen Starrm's thoughts wandered away as she stared blankly into the stony shelter's interior. "And Man is behind it..." Her reticent breath slipped heedless of her whisper.

"Lo, my dear small friends, Lord Vicstusi and Lady Starrm! How does the prisoner fare? Have you gotten anything out of her?"

The source: a rumbling voice increasing to rowdier and rowdier as the voice approached from a hall east of Juna. The voice's accent broadcasted as Giantic, but Juna could decipher a difference in tone, a scrambling boom compared to her fair citizens' eloquence residing in the Cory Mountains. This voice fitted with the Ogrean expression, and the owner was a blurred Ogre ambling through the sculpted archway. He wore what she could recognize as a buoyant, sleeved robe exaggerating his size more.

A most fetid stink accompanied his entrance. Juna's eyes and lips expanded into similar circles, and her ducts started to tear. She covered her nose and mouth in an attempt to hamper the damp stench's lurid path and contemplated the benefits of remaining with the less smelly Pixies. "Oh, Interim no! What is that? That is messed up," she criticized.

"Crumb, the great **Mountain**'s **Sand**."

A "Mountain" Juna already understood as their ruler, however. "I am a little baffled, Lord Vicstusi, why be bothered by a little bit of sand when—"

"Sshh." The Pixy king tapped the glass, acknowledging his visitor. "Welcome, Sand Crumb. The Fairy has done nothing wrong."

Queen Starrm's impatience would not wait. "Why does Man attack the sacred Forest of Khun? I thought you said Man was trying to stop a war from occurring, not starting one of their own? Including on Khun?"

Advisor Crumb halted in his tracks. Juna could not tell whether he was astonished or in disbelief. He stated, "Why no, there was never an attack on the sacred forest by Man. They have no reason to attack,"

"Oh, yes, they do, Ogre." Juna's palm stifled her nose to the best of her ability. "It is there, in Khun, where General Ygl took refuge. He is the only one of his race to escape Man's attack on Lorel. The Protectors of Khun know of Quirm and its emperor's insane idea to conquer all of Zaendara just to have a Jode in his possession. Tell me, Sand Crumb of the Ogres, did you know of the attack on Lorel?"

Crumb peered past Starrm at the squeaky voice emitting from within the obscure glass cell; he scowled. "Who are you to be asking me these questions?"

Vicstusi and Starrm scattered away from the Ogre's thunderous range. Even through her jail's auburn walls, Juna could not resist the raucous effect.

Crumb continued, "You, who are nothing, but a soulless prisoner to the Pixies and Ogres alike—a remnant of the Giants' strategy to destroy our Mountaindom!"

"I am **Flower** of the Fairies, and I demand your answer!" She hoped no one acknowledged her halfhearted approach.

"You-you are a traitor of all Zaendara. You-you are no flower," the Ogre said, chortling. "She-she thinks she is a flower! A flower!"

"You are the traitor. You are the traitor!" Juna understood this was why Crumb had taken so long to answer her inquiry. Somehow the Ogrean advisor was instrumental to this fiasco. He concealed his tracks well despite his heritage. Could his people have evolved?

Impatient Vicstusi swooped forward before the discourse would advance further. "Tell Lady Starrm and me, Sand Crumb. We are of equal status as you. We demand to know, as well. Is Lorel under Quirm's rule?"

Crafty Crumb remained silent for a moment, contemplating what to disclose next. He gave a nervous turn and proceeded to a stony table—a blurry figure fading away from the Fairy queen through the opaque glass. A smirk creased his face as he drummed his fingers on the table's surface, the drumming like a herd of large horses gallivanting. "Lorel has been captured... but only on the grounds that **Butte** Kute, of the Giants, had been found negotiating with them. If Man had not intervened soon, we would have never discovered what those meddlesome Elves of Lorel would have done."

The Pixies and Juna were stunned, impregnating a silence to reside within the shingly dwelling.

"Crumb, dear! Are coming?" A female voice called from atop the stairwell.

Crumb continued, "I will, Squish! My **mineral** calls. I must leave now. I only wanted to see how everything was getting along. Now, I must counsel with those who are privy of the attack."

"The lamp." Baffled, Starrm refused to believe the advisor, yet. "What about the lamp, Crumb?"

"... What lamp?"

Juna enjoined, "The lamp that was taken from me when I got captured."

"Quiet, Juna," Vicstusi ordered.

Juna disliked uncontrollable situations. Once Vicstusi regulated her to silence... she needed to remember her status during the debriefing. She gnawed down a little harder on her tongue.

"Oh, that lamp," Crumb surmised. "Utilize your memories correctly, my Pixies, and remember that there are no lamps anywhere within our Mountaindom. The only lamp in this estate is located in my room.

"If the great Mountain Smush ever does discover a lamp, it will heighten his wits to persist to the past into the legends. This will influence him to gather the Ogres and Pixies about him to attack Quirm when it is actually Man who is trying to save us from the Giants' treachery."

Juna rolled her eyes and snarled her upper lip to his confusing response.

Vicstusi, however, was sold on Crumb's response. "And, only we Pixies know about the Giants, and we shall defend the Ty Desert to the utmost of our capabilities." He turned his attention to the auburn prison. "But if things do get out of hand, our Council shall be warned."

"I could agree with you much better, good Vicstusi," smug Crumb responded.

Juna beheld Starrm's lithe form alight downward in front of the obscure glass. The female Pixy crouched almost in meditation; her wings, double the number of Juna's, collapsed behind her, the second lateral pair stretched less lengthy.

Another thundering footfall descended into the chamber. A smaller version of Crumb appeared, her robe's dangling sleeves alive in the stoniness. "What going on, dear? They are waiting," his wife, Squish, questioned.

"Okay, I must leave. I do not want to get too late." The advisor proceeded out the rough exit.

"Squish, wait! Crumb, please do not leave." Adamant Starrm rejected complacency. "I do not understand. We do not know anything that happened between the Ogres and Man. Excuse me if you will, but your sediments are too slow and ignorant. How could your sediments know something about the legends that my sediments know nothing about?"

"Like the Pixies, there are parts of the legends only the Ogres have knowledge of and will never disclose. Have a good **light**. I will be back to see how our guest is doing."

"But I—"

"Stop it, Starrm," Squish interrupted, hurrying her husband. "I do not want hear anything else. Two sediments met unexpected end-of-shifts since her arrival."

The Pixy Council members were vexed. Starrm almost shouted like Juna's voice. "That cannot be possible. End-of-shifts? Are you sure it was not anything territorial?"

"No. There was no bloodshed. No wounds. No bruises. Just end-of-shifts. Nothing but end-of-shifts since her arrival. That Fairy has brought a curse upon our sediments," stated Crumb, shuddering. He propped himself up against the banister, grabbing his face, his wife holding him.

"Are you okay, Crumb?" Queen Starrm's doubled filaments fluttered.

"I am fine." With that, Crumb was gone in a thudding huff with Squish.

Juna slumped backward, contemplating what happened as the advisor departed. So, the Ogres were simpleminded, but how, in all Inner Earth, did Crumb attain such comprehension and cunning? This shrewdness was not derived from the Ogrean estate—he acquired it from elsewhere.

Quirm... Quirm... Juna began to loathe the word with every ounce of her psyche. Xurchon was behind all this. She understood this very well, no need to doubt the legends.

The Fairy queen's guesswork awed her: Man had elected Xurchon as their contemporary deity. If this contract became effortless enough for the God of Evil to accomplish upon a civilized empire, then how difficult would the task be to corrupt the Ogrean estate?

She must notify the Giants. She must notify them. "Oh, Interim, you roots are about as dumb as the rocks out here."

CHAPTER 3: The Arrival

Deep beneath the Fendor's surface, the undercurrents were much more relaxing, an unusual peace churned in these murky waters the twin suns' shafts sliced through. However, the deeper our mounts carried us, the less frequent Los and Num's radiance pierced the depths, prompting my infravision to come into play. The equines' reddish aura and Redfang, Ding's gray wolf, discontinued their descent and began trotting in an orderly manner along the course of the river's bends. Though we never achieved the Fendor's bed, journeying into the watery depths—with nothing to cling onto—imparted the impression we arrived there. My jodepiece's sentience was somehow unresponsive as well, with no resistance for my telepathy to address. Maybe the ongoing mystical event had a bearing on the fact?

The dense scenery was a beauty with many fish interspersed with strange weeds bypassing, and intruding spikey reefs matting the riverbed. We had to maintain surveillance just in case uninvited visitors made an appearance. No gills needed here—not in this environment, where my jodepiece bended nature's rules to satisfy the imbalance.

I discreetly lagged behind my two companions, distraught with my mate's end-of-seasons. After I saved Thalla at Skavir, she risked her season saving me at the Fendor River. I did not notice I grieved so hard, for the watery currents kept cleansing any possible tears away like a buoyant washcloth, but the cleansing could not undo the horrendous pain within my grieving heart. I still remembered her final words of encouragement biding me to go on, to keep alerting. Thalla met the end-of-seasons for the mission, for my love, for the many enslaved.

My skin bristled against mourning's weakness. I wanted to give up everything and return. Go back and kill all of the Quirmean race with this jodepiece on my left grasp and Welbern on my right... Kill... And kill until I accepted the end-of-seasons myself... However, if I returned to Quirm to assuage my guilt, the magic I enacted upon the Fendor River would cease, leaving Ding and **Plant** Kute to remain trapped in a watery bosom. Plus, Stonecrusher would, in all likelihood, not allow me. He would perhaps bite into my cloak's nook and throw me upon his spine again—smart pegasus.

The mounts' tails and fur swayed with elegance within the waterway. The mounts surveilled this way and that, always mindful they were traveling in the correct direction. I found remarkable their knack to sense their destination while all I perceived was the trees' branches zigzagging above.

Trees? The trees of Lorel.

Alas, we arrived from Quirm's grasp to return to what I referred to as home. Home with humbleness. My reprieve was somewhat acceptable, at this point, the Fendor's segment that flowed beneath these caring emerald canopies cleansed me. The Forest of Lorel's trees expanded us a shade that we could feel welcomed by. The rush of current abated partaking a stillness, a tranquility... we had reached placid Lake Ban's mouth. For a while longer we traveled within the calm currents and verdant canopies' increasing coverage, veering more south in the abysmal lake.

As abysmal as my suicidal objectives. There was, of course, no reason for my **season**'s extension. My goddess, Achal, should just let me end. Why bother to move on? Every progression became an arduous venture into madness. The madness, a testament to hope's frailty. Thalla and I used to play among those trees. I proposed to her when she was pregnant among those trees.

Stonecrusher changed course and trudged up toward the surface. Tremendous strides my Giant mount took, attaining a height in distance. The Forest of Khun's land was coming near. An armor's outlined glare, as murky as the waters themselves, diffused through. Small figures flitted about here and there, separate from the glare.

But what was I doing? I should not brake, for why should I encounter more misery? More shame? As my companions achieved the surface to awaiting hands, I quickly connected to and shut down the watery portal, forcing Stonecrusher to dive toward the fathoms with my telepathy.

The gray pegasus struggled and thrashed; my will was stronger. The water pressure tightened about my head. Within wisdom's darkness, tiny sparks of light danced about me. Stonecrusher shrugged off my feeble kicks' commands, adamant defiance to our aspirant end-of-seasons, and charged upward, wings flapping... my lungs ached with a throbbing burst. The undercurrents brushed roughly past me, their fluidic clutches trying to retain a souvenir as Stonecrusher continued his powered jolts toward a second deliverance.

Darkness flashed within my eyes. My strong grip on the reins began to weaken; I slipped off, not knowing whether my mount achieved the surface's safety. In suspension, my lungs exhaled the final bit of air held within.

****

The Protectors did not save me because they "had to." They saved me because their belief system compelled them to protect whatever arrived within their forest's locale, Khun. Such honor left me conflicted. With my consciousness' every fortitude, I acknowledged what I must do. I must protect every estate, warning them of Quirm's transgression upon the peace we all reveled in as a whole. No matter what obstacles may get in my way or what I may fall victim to during these horrid trials, I must prevail, yet failure's scent never deterred from my wishes.

I found myself in one of the Protectors' indigenous treehouses instead of the tent from my last visit, a young sequoia. Unlike Lorellians, Khunians sought no need to create makeshift treehouses from weeds, leaves and tree limbs. The Sprites were always available to their allies with the gift of tree shaping, creating many a spacious treehome, from sentry posts to my present lodging. Their divine right gouged the pith, heartwood and sapwood, replacing it with residence. And not once did any of these trees fall ill from the reformed inner embodiments. Along the walls toward a vaulted ceiling, fibril sinew shot through fat, healthy rings signifying Oreol's divine right could not be denied—assigning Lorellian trees to bear thinner rings through harsh weather. An obelisk window greeted an apparent, early **sunday** with pinkish skies. Sapwood bedding and a pillow of the softest moss represented a different welcome. Moss clung to the walls with a decorative stratagem consisting of exotic flowers, a calming arrangement from Lojstania, Oreol's mate. An animal's hide, possibly bear, my blanket. The sequoia's exterior was recreated into a fibril doorway with a median, vertical split for flaps.

"Bloodfather...?" An anxious Elvin bloodchild resided at my bedside, wearing his hooded tunic.

"Limbus? Limbus..." I felt throughout my bedding for some means of arising. Oh, how I ached all over!

"Bloodfather, please lie back down. You will hurt yourself."

I did with gratitude. Nothing was communicated between us for a moment... a sniffle, and our breaths' catching would not escape us.

"Limbus, you are..."

He leaped up, giving me a tender hug so as not to hurt me. "Why, Bloodfather? Why did she have to embrace the end-of-seasons?" he cried. "I feel so lonely. Only you are here. The only one to keep me going. Bloodmother was the other half and now—and now she feels so far away." He shivered, weeping warm tears.

I held him close, disguising my guilt's deep pangs and my stinginess forgetting him during my suicidal endeavor. This deed was all I could do. He must never know of my selfish act, "Most of the lineage is gone, my bloodson. We are all we have. Let us try to keep it that way, but do not worry." I held him up, keeping my hold. "While we stand idle in Man's war yet to come, we will eventually get a new bloodmother. One for both of us."

Limbus leaned down, hugging me tighter, sobbing. "Bloodfather, please do not forget me. Please do not forget me..."

"I will not, Limbus. I will not. How can I?"

****

Late into the sunday, my body began to refresh from the hopelessness restraining my will from surfacing, or so I believed. Silent Limbus convened by himself upon a sapwood chair at the far end, contemplating beside a large sapwood table. Snip, his faithful asegafian cat, lay next to him, protruding an elongated tongue providing a desirous bath upon beige fur. Much like a butterfly's mouthpiece, Snip's tongue was useful in attaining those hard-to-reach areas while the asegafian maintained a relaxed posture. The feline tongue was also good for fishing.

My treehouse's lower interior was similar to my last visit's tent, except for size. Plush, grassy flooring exploited a small pit in the center for a fire. Three other chairs accompanied Limbus' table and upon the table a wooden pitcher of water from Lake Ban. Positioned closer to me, a smaller table situated near the hearth. The evergreens' fresh scent carried very well here.

From outside, I heard many Lorellian bloodchildren chattering. Just Lorellian bloodchildren, for Khunian Elves did not have sex, therefore did not bear such a relationship's fruit. The chattering slowly silenced as some were instructed where to go and what to do by Blasmle, the Khunian Elves' male Leader. Metals clashed and arrows thudded into lifeless targets. The noises became louder, making me apprehensive, but they did not seem to bother Limbus one bit. So there must have been purpose for the ruckus.

The treehouse's fibrous flaps opened. Plant Kute strode through with an underbite smile as wide as his frame. "Here you are, Sprout-of-the-General. Everyone was looking for you. We should have known you would be here. I should kick myself for not thinking about looking here. Do not worry. We know how you feel.

"And you, General. I am very sorry for the self-same incident. Just think what would have happened if you would have given your growth as did your lovely earth."

"Growth?" Kute's dialect confused Limbus.

"Uh... uh... what I believe you call 'seasons,' little sprout," Kute corrected himself.

"Please, Kute, let us not start talking about that." Though I understood Kute's logic, I failed to acknowledge how Limbus would have felt if he would have lost me, too. The loss would have been amplified. I turned my head, concealing my distress.

Kute continued, "Oh, and here are your new garments made by the female Gnomes and Sprites themselves. The garments are just like the ones you wear, but sewn of a different nature."

"How?"

The Plant laughed. "By Lolung-Cor, you have never heard of the gift of weed-weaving? They are your neighbors."

"No. No, I have not. Some of the clothes my kin wore did arrive from Khun, but we had no idea of how they were created."

For sure, weed-weaving must be great art because Kute's prior bearskin garments did not yield a cleanly scent, nor escaped tear. Again, he sported boots strapped to tight slacks with strong beltlets—even his jacket sewn of bearskin was anew. Anyone would respect the muscly bulges on his body exposed through the crisscrossing seams bracing his jacket together.

"Neither have I until I witnessed these **roots** doing it last **starnoon**. You see, they take grasses of various colors and patch them together in ways, so as to resemble, let us say, my boots. Then, if the garment is made of the same sort of skin, a small bit of that animal's fur is taken and sprinkled upon the grassy sculpture. This part is completed by the female Gnomes and the rest is completed by the female Sprites, I think. This is great because this is not our real clothes. I mean look." He grabbed a piece of fur and munched on it. "I can eat it because it is just grass. I mean, it is not the scrumptious grains you can get from my **Tree**dom, but if one is willing to survive in the wilderness somewhere, taking a bite out of your boot is not a bad idea at all."

I chuckled. This Giant certainly had a way about him. "You better save some for walking."

"That is okay, General. My old boots are in one of my saddle bags."

"Well, if you still have your old boots, why wear these?"

"Oh, I do not know. It is different."

"Trendy?"

"Yes... you could say that—'trendy.' Anyway, some of the Gnomes give the female Sprites a wider berth to gather around the grasses in a small circle. Then, the Sprites rotate slowly, hand-in-hand, singing the most enchanting song I have ever heard. The Sprites are probably the most enchanting singers in all Zaendara. By Pyty, they are maybe even better than the Fairies and my roots. However," he leaned closer with a whisper, "do not tell the Flower. Suddenly, light came from the center where the grasses were, and in its place lay my new boots."

I chuckled again. I seriously doubt, judging from Kute's bass voice, the Giants could beat a toad in singing. "And, Ding and my garments were done the same way?"

"Correct."

Kute strode to the sapwood table to pour a drink from the wooden pitcher, placing my bundled cloak upon it. My forest green cloak unraveled to reveal my tunic, headband, and shoes all as intact as they were before our capture... Kute shook his head after taking a sip. "Whew! That is a good drink."

"It is willowberry tea with a touch of brown sugar lilies," Limbus answered. "It is medicine for my bloodfather, sir."

"Oh, my apologies. I see it has done wonders on your shoulder."

I felt for the shaft wound on my right shoulder. Fresh skin was the replacement, proving Kute correct, but I did not believe the tea really had much to do with the mending. I rubbed my thumb upon my jodepiece. "I see you have healed as well."

"That, General, is the nature of my divine gift. I could not grow to any height without the capability of rapid healing."

"I see. Where is Welbern?"

"Do not worry. Your Demonslayer is hidden well beneath your bed. Well, I really do not know how well hidden that is, but it will have to do.

"They also made you two new leg scabbards. One for a knife, the other for a pipe and darts."

"Thanks."

"You are very welcome. By the way, Sprout-of-the-General, have you seen the Fairy Flower about lately?"

Limbus did not know how to react, realizing the Plant addressed him.

"Limbus, he wants to know if the little Fairy queen has returned."

Without looking at Kute, my bloodson answered, "The Fairy queen has not been here since you left."

I could imagine the look on Kute's face when confronted with the disclosure of Juna's perpetual absence. I felt sympathy for my new friend since the Fairies were much closer to the Giants than the Dwarves. And now, this uncomforting news.

"We will find her. She is resourceful," Kute responded. His selflessness remained resolute.

Amazing. Maybe there was sense in telling him since he did not appear so upset. "Somehow, I was told by a spirit of her whereabouts."

"A 'spirit'?"

"Yes, Swen."

"Oh, the genie. It is nice to know the genie is still on our team. Well, if you know, General, then please disclose this information."

Resisting the sudden knot in my stomach, I answered, "She is held prisoner by the Ogres."

"Hmm... the Ogres. How did such a thing happen? They were to be warned, not capture her. This is indeed a bit preposterous."

"I am sure it is a misunderstanding."

"A misunderstanding? General, I will have you know that my roots may be warriors and agricultural in nature, but the Ogres are barbarians. Killers of innocents. This is what we were told in our legends. I follow these legends. The Fairy Flower must be rescued."

Feral Rungna, the Khunian Elves' female Leader, bounded in with a concerned look upon her hairy face. "Is all right everything here?" Her array brandished various animals running amok. Tanned Oreol, the Sprites' male Leader, fluttered behind her, sporting a shirt of stringy gold and black slacks. The Gnomes' Leader, Mitral, trailed upon his chirping archeornyx, Jinx. The trusted mount positioned upon Limbus' table for luck's sake.

"The Fairy queen has been captured," Kute answered.

"Juna?" Oreol's quadrupled, bird-like wings swooped around the Giant Plant's head, the fluffy green matching sacred Khun's colors, like any Sprite.

"It seems they are on Quirm's side," I stated. Again, by instinct, I sought for the reassurance straddling my finger. The crystalline artifact's sharp edges nearly cut me. "But I know they are not. Quirm fights alone because they are after this."

In unison, all eyes gawked upon my motley, faceted artifact's allure, including Limbus who forgot the misfortune of losing Thalla. He arose, entranced.

Oreol gasped, "The Jode."

"No, a piece of it. I call it a 'jodepiece,' honorable Sprite."

"This little jodepiece represents the bigger fabled Jode. A jewel bestowed with such great mystic powers that even a god would crave dearly to have it in their possession," Kute added.

"But your legends are not as complete as ours, Plant Kute," Oreol corrected. "True, the Jode has such powerful magic in such a beautiful form, but that form is inhabited by an evil spirit that inhibits possession of the jewel from others."

"Is this true, General?"

"Yes. I struggle with an entity inside, which has so far been kept at bay with my telepathy.

"If you knew of this before, Oreol, why did you not say anything?"

"Simple, Ygl. You did not ask."

"I did not have to ask. You said you never bothered to think about it."

"... There were whispers from the trees. That is all I know."

Rungna snarled with comprehension. "Which is why Rondo Emperor needs it for himself. He will use Jode this to rule Zaendara all beneath his hand twisted."

I concluded, "Starting with Khun itself. Both combined will be ruthless."

Unpleased, Mitral's Gnomic voice boomed clearer than any from his small frame behind Jinx's feathery crown. "Quirm shall be stopped. Animals of good nature have already answered Rungna's summons. Every Khunian Elvin warrior that has protected our sacred forest, even before the season of my birth, must be gathered. Do you hear me, Rungna? Every one of them? Last of all, we shall have to put the Lorellian bloodchildren on more extensive training."

"Not only is the bloodchildren's swordplay better," Rungna commented, annoyed at Mitral for singling her out, "but possess skill great with the bow and arrow as Elves all should. The greatest of all of them is bloodson your, Limbus."

Mournful Limbus paid little attention to anyone—understandable, considering I performed my best to save face before him.

"He will make a fine general in the future, Ygl. We are even deliberating about appointing him head of all the Elvin bloodchildren." Tiny Mitral beamed.

I pulled myself off my bedding with the blanket still wrapped around my nakedness. Bending beside my bloodson, I whispered, "I want you to be all right with this honor. When I was younger than you, my bloodfather, Scall, laid this honor upon my shoulders. You will not believe how proud you will make me. You will make a great general indeed. Come. Hug me."

Limbus looked at me, trying to understand his pain. I knew what hurt him, and nothing could deter him from the acknowledgement. If he would have heard Thalla's reassuring words to me, that may have reduced his discouragement from falling into madness, but who was I to judge? The same pain stirred within me with every recurrent beat.

"I assure you, Limbus, I will find us a new bloodmother even if I have to face Xurchon to find it. You know, your bloodmother told me one thing before she embraced the end-of-seasons. She told me to keep going and to not worry for her because it was our love that would always thrive beyond. Right now, I can feel that love stir within me." I rubbed a single tear from his eyes. *"And it will keep stirring, as long as I believe in it. That is all you need to do, Limbus. Believe in it, and your bloodmother will always be there."*

Limbus' face wrinkled as streaming tears streaked down the bumpy surface. I knew what I said was not true. Emotionally, yes, but not physically. Limbus was too young to deal with such pain... I pulled him tight to me, as tight as tight could be.

"Why, Bloodfather, why? Why?" he cried for an answer I could not bring myself to provide. I held him closer as silent grief stirred precariously within.

Sympathetic Snip rubbed onto his master, his frilly ears perked up with curiosity as his glassy orbs regarded Rungna, licking her hand's backside.

A horn blasted outside.

"Blasmle," Rungna almost whispered. "Horn his, that is."

"But that is not the call-to-arms," Mitral interjected. "Your mate blows another tune, Rungna."

Oreol shuddered sharing the simultaneous moment with Mitral—both in a strange thrall's midst. "By the gods and goddesses. Quickly, everyone, to the main clearing. Ethnel has arrived!"

With tremendous glee, the Faerie figureheads darted out of our little enclave leaving the rest of us in astonishment. Rungna stared blankly toward the plush grasses while Limbus remained ever so more alert. Moreover, I could feel a peculiar energy touch me and felt comfortable with it. A strange cleansing washed over me, conveying a wish to safeguard my very nakedness from unscrupulous evil.

Rungna mumbled aloud, "At last, a god has answered cries our. Maybe the moment of joy is far away not as we thought,"

She beamed, opening my hospice's fibril flap. How exquisite her cuirass melted upon her form... Turning, smiling, she said, "Come, everyone. Let us take glimpse our first of a god none have observed after these seasons all." She bounded out.

My bloodson hesitated...

"Go on, Limbus. Do not worry. I will be all right." I placed my hand upon his shoulder. "Anyway, it will be yours as well as my first seeing a god, will it not?"

Limbus shook his head in agreement. "Okay, bloodfather."

Kute arose ready to follow exiting Limbus and Snip. "Do not forget to hurry, General. At last, a god has come."

I did not answer. The past forays had already caught up with me quicker than I could attain awareness... too many thoughts... one filled with a greater pain than the rest. I thought I could stave off my anguish long enough until left alone.

Alert Kute could not be fooled. "Coming, General?"

I leaned to my side trying to conceal tears, but the tremors beneath my blanket revealed too much. Kute quickly slid next to me, cradling me in brawny arms like a bloodchild, granting soft kisses to my crown's temple, shushing condolences. "Sshh, General. I am here... Sshh... We all are. You are not required to bear this suffering alone... Go ahead, get it off your chest," he comforted.

I swiveled to him, trying to maintain some bearing. "Kute—"

Our lips met only for an instant, a shocking one at that, enriching me with a new sensation... and fear. In an instant, I trembled with a resistance I never experienced. Never had I been kissed by another male. I struggled and squirmed from the Plant's grip, leaping free with all my strength into a forward roll over my articles, grasping my dagger, reclining onto my posterior.

"General?" Kute pursued me, looming over my recumbent forehead.

With an instinct, my horizontal dagger pressed against his throat, my huffing and puffing tagging along.

Equally surprised, Kute dared not glance down. With measured words, he replied, "General, I think you may need to take your root's practice of meditation into consideration.

No matter what, you are my friend, just like that grumpy little thief outside... I am sorry. I meant nothing—"

Gentle, I gripped his arm, lowering my dagger. "I know... friend." I rolled up.

"I will smile for you," he mumbled.

"... Swen said that."

"Yes, I heard her. She is very wise. Do you require of me to leave?"

"No. Stay while I dress. I like your company."

****

Miscellaneous footsteps pounded from everywhere, for no Zaendaran had ever seen a true god. Every Protector of the sacred Forest was filled with a gaiety, expressing shouts of praise to the one being whose arrival proved their beliefs relevant, beliefs that were not proven for hundreds of seasons' turns. Scampering feet strove hard to attain their greatest glee's objective, replacing metals clashing and arrows thudding.

How wrong Xurchon was to think he was Inner Earth's sole deity. Ethnel was here. Here to mark the return of every race's deities. Gods and goddesses who would tear asunder Rondo's dreams from becoming utter reality.

Never had I experienced such joy. Was it because I had gone through experiencing the pain? A god... After donning my garments and rushing out my hospice's doorway, Kute and I became spellbound. In every direction, the Protectors of Khun had disseminated their numbers. The gathering crowd was so thick, Kute and I had to pull our way through the tight throngs to go where every captivated face kept an audience. Even through the vibrant trees' entangled branches, the twin suns could sense the overwhelming awe amid the amassing crowds their rays showered. But the strangest spectacle I ever observed from this crowd of courageous warriors: every one of them kneeling in prayer.

Not very far ahead, the clearing. The soothing emissions grew sounder and sounder... my jodepiece felt colder upon my finger.

"Strong-hearted Protectors of Khun," the God of Faerie's resonance abounded not like a booming hollow, but as the most angelic of Sprite voices; a universal endlessness stirred my senses. "I am Ethnel, Essence of all Small Creatures, Essence of Preservation, and furthermore, renowned as the Essence of the White Light."

Ethnel, a definite and true deity. Like a wisp, his voice traveled true and clear. His overwhelming presence in the clearing amplified the closer I arrived. His presence's pull, admiring and undeniable, tempted me to soak within his allegory—but he was not my goddess... not my Achal. My guilt probably engaged my conscious to deter from such idolatry. Nonetheless, the Sprites and Gnomes gazed upon his visage with great wonder while everyone else speculated with surprise and intense relief.

... Was the Fendor rushing through me...? Currents. I could feel currents, yet not feel them at all.

Ethnel seemed comparable to a slender Gnome in nature, harnessing all the Faeries' features combined in one personage. From his head flowed great emerald hair and a matching beard with fresh leaves budding out of the tresses. An obscured face hid in a cavernous hood, appearing very smooth and cherubic in texture—making me wonder if he was female, or both. Gossamer insect wings popped from his posterior with a feathery scattering here and there, a colorful highpoint reminding me of Steadfast's appendages. A Pixy standing upon another's shoulder would equate his height. Ethnel was, by no doubt, a demiurge; the power emitting from within his shrouds attested to this fact. I could not decipher if I was walking or floating the closer I came to him... Virtue exuded from his space.

"I am sorry none of the patron Gods and Goddesses, the rest of the Divinity, could arrive here to fulfill thy beliefs in us. They have sent me. It would be quite difficult for Xurchon to intuit such a small form as mine compared to a much larger one. Yes, the emperor of Quirm does pose a threat toward Zaendaran peace. Xurchon focuses much of his power through this desire. Two foes, such as this combined, poses quite an existential threat. I am pleased many Protectors have regarded preparation for this assault. An assault that will affect not only Zaendara as a whole, but Khun's holiness. The God of Evil's might is so ardent that it will affect everyone in all Inner Earth. I have arrived to counsel thee of this, my Protectors. The might of the Divinity will not—"

"Please." Guilt was an understatement for my interruption of one so highly regarded, but somehow his message carried a hint startling me more. Sprite and Gnome interests reverted toward me as if I had performed a sacrilege. "I am sorry, great Ethnel."

"That is all right, General Ygl. Thou hast suffered much understood loss. Please, continue."

I should not have been shocked by his knowledge of my name, but he was not my goddess. "Is there any way the gods and goddesses can intervene? If I am wrong in my inquiry, then I am sorry for asking, but if there is no fault for me to bear in my action, then why is it so?"

... Wind... somehow, I could taste the four winds exalting from the north, south, east and west... yet, no breeze stirred.

Ethnel studied me with much patience, then peered at everyone with tender regard: the Sprites, the Gnomes, the Khunian warriors, the Lorellian bloodchildren and the scattered beasts attending. In return, I studied him closer to acknowledge a brief sadness in his face that did not fade away. A sadness his fervent followers would be too blind to admit. Somehow, the knot in my stomach knew what his answer would be.

"I am sorry, my faithful and subjects of the other Divinity, but I shall need to concede to the latter."

Everyone was startled. The Khunian Elves stared at one another, hoping to divulge an answer to this response, but what answer remained when your last hope vanished with what you had wished to happen? The gods were not going to help us! To a force greater than ours, they abandoned us.

Many Sprites and Gnomes' agape faces overflowed with an empathy that could tear a soul asunder. Ethnel lingered on the table like a helpless sow.

Oreol became the Protectors' spokesperson in his stringy gold. "But why, oh great Ethnel?" he pleaded, swooping downward with Mitral close behind upon Jinx's spine. "Why do you abandon us?"

The Essence of Small Creatures placed his hand on Oreol's shoulder. "Because we feared that Xurchon must be stopped internally as well as externally. There is a jewel he searches for called the Jode. If it is found by him, he will utilize it against all Inner Earth starting with Zaendara, for the Jode inhabits a powerful magic inaugurated within this jewel.

"This magic must not fall into the hands of evil. A group must be formed to find the Jode and keep it away from the God of Evil's grasp. It harbors magic that cannot be vanquished. The Divinity calls for the formation of a party. The Party of the Jode must be established, and this Party must go and warn the other estates before they fall."

I could not hold back. "I-I would like to be a part of this, great Ethnel. And, to stand with me in this Party of the Jode, I call forward Plant Kute of the Giants and Ding of the Dwarves."

"General, you must have read my mind," Kute acknowledged. "We have come this far. The journey has been interesting already. Would you not agree, Ding, my friend?"

Surly Ding ambled with a grumble to his step. His ruddy skin and reddish-brown hair, an evident standout in the pale crowd with his faithful wolf, Redfang. His back scabbard could not hide the glint of his diamond, double-headed axe, Gore. "Humph."

"Then, so be it," Ethnel approved. "The Party of the Jode is formed." A great murmur followed as appreciative eyes surveyed Kute, Ding and me.

"And, what of Oreol and I, or Rungna-Olivia and Blasmle, great Ethnel?" inquired Gnomic Mitral.

"Pfft..." Oreol tried to shush his equal. Mitral returned a stern frown.

Ethnel would not condescend to their apparent bickering. "Ye must stay behind to command thy forces. All four of ye are needed more in Khun, as the Party is for great Zaendara."

"And, what of Flower Juna, Ethnel? What of your 'Bearer of the White Light'?" Kute inquired.

Toward the southeast the Essence of Preservation stared. "She is still with growth, Plant of the Giants. Held captive by the unwitting Ogres. She will be unable to abscond unless the Party goes to salvage her there. But I warn thee. Going to the Mountaindom will place ye in great peril, for Xurchon will try anything in his power to hinder the Party. The Divinity remands him at the moment, but if he acquires the Jode, dire tribulations will arise. He covets the Jode for himself. Nothing will hinder him.

"Thou, Ygl of Lorel, must lead the Party. Thou retains that one gift Xurchon most dreads that hinders him from obliterating thee directly."

"Thou do? I mean, 'I do'?"

"Yes, thou dost. And now, I shall take leave before Xurchon can detect my mere presence here. Thus mark my words, subjects and subjects of the other Divinity. We make no assurances. We will do our best to arrive together as one force to diminish the God of Evil's wrath and his threat upon Zaendara. Mark them, for they speak true."

Fainter his words became until what became of the Essence was a hazy image swathing bi-colored eyes staring at me. My body could feel the soothing discharge evading. The power of the Fendor... the galvanizing winds... and the air's lightness was no more—Ethnel became no more.

Funny. I realized I called him/her an "essence" instead of a god. I wonder, why was that? How reassuring it was to know that the gods were real, nonetheless. The "Divinity," as Ethnel and Kute referred to them. My body trembled as if the other Divinity gazed upon me, but the tremor was only momentary. Another soothing sensation swept over me like an invisible casing of warmth: hope. I realized the Divinity was with me to assist in whatever way they could, if they could.

The beautiful, green grasses between the table and me flourished lusher and more plentiful than the grasses surrounding.

"Can you taste that, General? I can actually taste the lingering flavor of the grasses and—"

"Of the dirt."

"Yes. Very fresh and crunchy, but it dissolves with this god."

"Yes."

An unexpected, cool wind passed through the monstrous trees' shade. Strength had been granted me, Xurchon. Neither I nor would Khun fear you. The Divinity would do their part and the moment was upon the rest of us to perform the same. The Party would come rescue you, Juna, and Zaendara as well.

Blasmle arose upon the table with Rungna standing proud and true upon the bench below. His bold smile matched their murky armor's speckled glistening. "Clan my... Gnomes... Sprites... Protectors all, acknowledge words those spoken by the Essence great, Ethnel. We must begin the defense of forest sacred our with rapidity. The defense outer must be tightened so as to be alert more and strong when Quirm dares first to attack. Man will face more of a match than they think. All of Khun must beckon, not at call my, but at the Divinity's proclaiming themselves."

"We are not preparing for a battle," his mate added. "We are preparing for a war. A war that may spread itself throughout Zaendara all."

The crowd hollered in agreement. Such a bombastic hollering that made me squint as beasts and all raised their voices in honor.

Oreol swooped in to speak, but Mitral and Jinx intercepted the miffed Sprite. "No, Oreol. You know this forum is for my divine right." The Protectors' Gnomic Leader paused to absorb the abundancy of sounds. "Now, all have heard what must be said." His booming voice echoed through and about the leafy canopies. "Those who have eaten their meal must go and prepare for defense. Those who have not, go to the Spiral Table and eat enough to grant you the energy needed. Bloodchildren of Lorel, you are needed as much as any Protector of Khun. Your mastery of the sword still needs more practice, but your archery could be an equal to many of our own. Your asegafian cats and you shall be a great match for Khun.

"And most important of all, let us all hope the Party of the Jode will continue their quest of the jewel so named. With good fortune on their side as well as the Divinity.

"Now, let us commence on the path Khunians must take to protect the forest it so sacredly fought to preserve."

One final hoorah of great confidence and the crowd depleted to a lessening to perform as ordered. I spotted Kute in the diminishment, but to my disbelief, he strode in the opposite direction.

"Kute. Kute. What are you doing? Let us get Ding and get going. We have a long road ahead of us."

"I will have you know, General, that the Fairy Flower and I are rather good friends. If I am to rescue the Flower from a race considered barbaric, then I will need all the strength to fight those Ogres."

"But, Kute, we should leave now."

"General"—his wink, empathetic—"I love you dearly. I am hungry, and I am very sure I am not alone. Now, where is that Spiraling Table?"

CHAPTER 4: The Rift

The Spiral Table was a long counter that spiraled toward a central endpoint. Nobody talked here. Nobody was supposed to at this expanding oaken behemoth located within Khun's widest clearing. The Sprites mystically crafted it from available branches, the sturdiest of vigorous oak with sporadic gaps in between furnishing participants easier trafficking. The timber's thick arching underneath kept the ample benches and wide tabling attached. Lojstania, Oreol's mate, created robust pockets of plum blossoms, racajaandoo blooms and lilacs throughout for a nice ambiance. Unlike Lorellians, Khunian Elves were not meditators, however, the Spiral Table provided an area to give sincere thanks to their god, Miredo, for everything he provided. The Sprites and the Gnomes were in agreement with this action. The spoons' smooth tapping upon the marbleized dishware and slurping from hefty mugs were the sole sounds emanating from such an earnest meal composed of mostly plants, and soups put together with gracious rodent involvement.

Most Protectors left the Spiral Table before the sunday would greet a starry sky. The feast done, defense became importance. No resting for these full bellies. Everywhere weaponry and armor's cankerous noise carried with the Protectors' solemn chatter discussing what would be Quirm's initial attack. The final swords' clanking and arrows' plucking belonged to the Lorellian bloodchildren performing their final sunday's effort. They needed the practice more than others. Even the animals were gracious in their assistance hauling what bits of everything they could carry within their jaws and upon their spines.

Among the bloodchildren, Limbus switched blades with his companion, Ploone. The two friends appeared so unique within the midst of the ever-changing plain of blades. Both seemed to hold their own mastery of the sword exhibiting the fortitude granted them all these seasons. Limbus and Ploone must have practiced hard for this. They both made me very proud.

If I took a telepathic joust into Limbus' mind, I would fathom he thought nothing of his bloodmother at this moment. All his thoughts were focused on his new home's defense and his remaining friends. I knew there must be a firm hope secured within him foreseeing a new beginning with a new bloodmother—one he hoped I would find for us soon. He prompt me to remember my protective bloodmother, Rarle. She was so protective of Methelo and me. With her unique psionic gift of retrocognition, past-sight, she deemed it necessary for me to become a general to our bloodfather. My new title was her idea though I did not know how effective I had been since getting it.

Oh, Thalla, how you would have just appreciated watching your bloodson now. You would have said, "Oh, Ygl, our Limbus will take your place very soon and we will be left to ourselves forever."

But you had gone now, Thalla. Limbus had proven to me our mourning's sabbatical had concluded. Prudency declared for it over...

I turned from the foray and strolled toward Kute at the Spiraling Table. His robust cheerfulness pulled me through the winding path.

"You should not worry so much. Quirm would never attack Khun," he bellowed.

"Kute, are you drunk?" The Quirmeans were the only race to ever brew this substance called "liquor." At least, according to my bloodfather, but I could smell the intoxicating liquid escape the Giant's rowdy lips. I had no idea the Khunians created their own brand.

"Drunk? Oh no, dear General. Do you partake in this drink with your neighbors? If I was ever drunk, it would have been before we were captured by Man. No, I am only putting sense in these Protectors' heads."

"What sense? It is you who seems to be taking everything with so much composure."

"What should I worry? It is my race's custom to take war as it comes; not to worry, especially at a feast. The Giants have always been the strongest race. I doubt even Quirm or the Ogres could defeat us."

"And, what if you lose?"

"... None are more superior at warfare."

"And, what of Xurchon?"

The Giant Plant paused once again. He rose and strode up the winding path. "We will not become slaves to such—indecency. I assure you, General, I will do everything in my power to save the Fairy Flower. There is no doubt the importance in acquiring this infamous Jode."

Later that sunday, I went into my treehome to pack things I would take on the quest while Kute and Ding prepared the mounts. Throughout the packing, I experienced the nagging awareness the only force that could be so frightening to a god or goddess would be power equaling or surpassing them. The only influential force upon me equal to this nature would be my jodepiece itself; therefore, Xurchon must be concerned about what tactics I might use to find its main body.

What would be the tactics I would use to search for it? Rondo accesses by way of the Death Mist and his vast army, yet both did not seem to fare him any better. Maybe my motives should be more direct instead of indirect. Let alone, I must not forget the unknown persona who disclosed my jodepiece would lead me to the Jode.

After examining my looped finger, I initiated psychic energy, but before I could, my jodepiece began to glow! A short moment later, an unnatural force tugged at my hand. I submitted to the phenomenon, and with caution, turned in the force's direction. The phenomenon halted me and resumed tugging me toward the southeast—toward the Ogre estate.

The Ogre Kingdom. My jodepiece was pointing me in the Ogre Kingdom's path.

I remembered Swen's riddle:

> Across the sea of sand,
> In a hidden green,
> Lies the powerful Jode

The "sea of sand" could be none other than the Ty Desert. As for the "hidden green," it must be somewhere in the Ogre estate.

"I cannot believe this... it resides where Juna is. My Achal, I will not need to worry anymore." I gathered my things and hurried toward the site we were embarking from. Everyone grabbed most of their belongings and headed toward a safe zone in the forest. Others were occupied getting mounts prepared or making wooden arrows.

"General Ygl?" Oreol inquired.

The Sprite Leader startled me. "Yes, Oreol."

"Mitral is off with his Gnomic warriors, but I am going to speak on behalf of Khun and he. We do hope you find the Jode, and we wish the Divinity will be by your side during the entire endeavor. You will need it."

"Thank you, Oreol. I realize that if Quirm did assault Khun, I am not sure they will attack you with armed might at all because the emperor knows the forest is sacred."

"So, how do you suppose? Magic?"

"By magic. I have hesitated to tell anyone about this, but Emperor Rondo has a piece of the Jode himself. He also has magic of his own, his divine right which is increased by this jodepiece."

The eminent Sprite was alarmed at first. "I think my gift would be sufficient enough against him," he justified.

"Your gift will not. I have decided to give you half of the piece in my possession."

Dumbfounded, the Sprite Leader scanned around, spotting the nearest tent. Tents made of animal hide were always shared in Khun. "Come with me."

We hurried inside. Sunlight permeated from Los and Num revealing the standard oaken tables and chairs for small gatherings. The concerned Sprite flapped about backward while scrutinizing me and the artifact I attempted to twist off my finger.

"How are you to split it?" He flitted around my shining jewel, averting its mystic shine.

"I guess any blade would do." I pulled out the dagger granted to me with my garments. With precision, I ran my finger along the blade, producing a slight sting. Yep, it was sharp.

I stabbed into my artifact—not a dent appeared on the glossy facets.

"Incredible," Oreol remarked.

"Ding would probably know how to break it, but he has not spoken to me for quite a while. Not that he ever really does. I have to break my jodepiece in half."

"Considering it is of magical nature, maybe it cannot be cut by something mundane," Oreol advised.

"So you think I should use Welbern?"

"Your blade is of magical nature, is it not? Use it. Maybe Demonslayer will be able to hinder the magical bonds in this jodepiece that defies your dagger from achieving even the slightest marring."

I slid Welbern from my back scabbard, eyeing my small powerful artifact. "You know, I never thought the tales about Welbern's power were true until recently in an esoteric vision we both may have shared in Quirm."

"Maybe you should start believing in them."

"Even before, when my kin was under assault by the Demons, I could hear the horrible screams of those Demons who cringed at the sight of my blade once they left the protection of their Death Mist. That mist messes with all your senses, Oreol." I compared my blade's size to my jodepiece. "This is going to be a bit ridiculous."

"It is the only way, Ygl."

I raised mythical Demonslayer high above me. The alloyed fuller reflected in the diminishing sunlight, exhibiting cryptic runes.

I swung down with all my might. At the metal and talisman's connection, an instant, colorful luminance sprang forth with mercilessness, flashing out at me. My hands held firm upon Welbern's hilt. I did not—I would not—let go.

Swiftly, the spectrum's tints swirled about me until transforming into a speedy whiteness mixed with streaking layers of... of... cloud.

... Eyes... soulless eyes... whose pupils' chasms sucked me into an arena much like the Interim's haunting depth. Those same eyes pierced through me, forcing me to break my grasp.

Another force, rattling from Welbern... tightened my grip upon my striated hilt. With my blade's emerging feeling and my psionic divine right, I resisted the power emanating from those bleak chasms.

Alone in a black magic's void. Alone in a void...

... Heat... and... cold... heat... and.... cold...

A primitive scream—as loud as the depths I avoided—haunted me. By Achal, I could have sworn I heard two screams penetrate the striped atmosphere... a warmth passed from Welbern through me. The hair behind my neck prickled.

The tent shook. The thick, hearty table broke.

The same wailing echoed again with distinct delivery, "XUUURRRCHON-CHON-CHON."

Never have I felt so frightened in all my seasons. I maintained my courage with a racing heart. My anger grew. I slashed out at the ghostly entity masked in the haunting pattern touching me like a brush of lightning, teasing me. The whiteness wailed, then diminished to nothingness. A nothingness that transformed into a bluish-yellow spark exploding onto me in a sea of hues.

Oreol did not react to any of the happenings. At first, I thought the Sprite was terrified, but his stubbornness made him too strong for this. He probably witnessed more deeds than I had, so why was he staring?

My Achal, his wings were not fluttering. He was floating on air! Oh no, the jodepiece had possessed him.

"Oreol, break the spell! Do not let it get you!"

The Sprite Leader's head quavered. He clenched his fists. Sweat appeared on his forehead. His eyes bulged. "Ethnel... Ethnel, protect me." He toppled upon the abundant grasses.

Several Sprites dashed in to investigate the matter with Jinx hauling Mitral. Kute and Ding, with other Protectors, filled in the gap at the tent's entrance.

"Milord Oreol, are you all right?" a pretty female Sprite cried, almost in tears. Her curly brown hair, embroidered with a cherry wreath of racajaandoo flowers, exhibited olive streaks matching her double-split dress' entrails.

"I am all right, Lojstania," groggy Oreol replied as Gnomes became a part of the gathering assisting him.

Lojstania was Oreol's mate who, with religious zeal, referred to him as any other kind of dignitary, which illustrated the level of love she held for such arrogance. Few of her fellow Sprites obeyed her courtesy. He never referred to her by any other title, but did not punish others for any offense upon his. I guess even Oreol had certain modesty.

His concern did not hide. "I sensed it, General Ygl. There is an evil in your little piece. A presence I had never encountered before. It tried to control me, but... but I sensed... Welbern there... guiding me from it."

"There? What do you mean, Sprite Milord?" Kute inquired. I stood corrected, Kute would be the second person to refer to Oreol as a dignitary with close enough zeal.

"It was a cloud... with all that was taught me, I could not distinguish at all what the persona was... someone was in it... in the cloud... other than Ygl and me. I... I know it."

Lojstania, a little uncomfortable, adjusted her flower wreath while breaking the silence that followed. "Well, that does not matter now. You need rest. Come. It will only be for a while."

The Sprites, in their flimsy outfits, lifted and carried their beloved Oreol out of the tent to the closest hospice. Mitral remained with Kute and Ding. The Dwarven thief stomped out with his typical grunt.

A light's glint caught my attention toward quite a miracle to consider. Upon the lush grasses, jostled between the table's rupture, lay my jodepiece's two halves.

CHAPTER 5: Systoli

Every Protector milled about, readying for Quirm's attack. Word got to me that Oreol was feeling much better and awaiting my delivery. I instructed Mitral on how Oreol should control and avoid my jodepiece's power. As for me, I donned the other half around my neck, dangling from a makeshift chain of resilient weeds like a crooked, lunar crescent trying to touch the ground.

Kute brought the mounts out maybe thirty feet away in the expansive clearing, brushed and prepared for the Party's long journey ahead. Amazing, Kute showed no signs of impatience for Juna's sake. However, he did approach Blasmle and Rungna's stealthy arrival a little farther away, towering over them as if they were wraithlike bloodchildren. In tow were their hippogriffs, Rushar and Folcen'na—winged wild creatures, hybrids with a posterior possessing a horse's features while the anterior exaggerated any bird of prey's resemblance. Russet Rushar's frontal resembled an eagle while Folcen'na flaunted a tannish gold appearing more like her namesake, a falcon. I guess I used to think all hippogriffs resembled eagles because I saw Rushar so much, but I was wrong.

I took an interest in the threesome's dialogue after acknowledging the hippogriffs' hesitant caw to Kute's abruptness. Feral Rungna cawed an order for the hippogriffs to cease, but the Leaders quickly drew daggers from their forearms' vambrace upon the initial discussion. The hippogriffs cawed in defense.

The Leaders' response drew an immediate reaction, not just from Ding and Redfang, but from loyal Stonecrusher and Crater, and the crowds milling about.

47

My perking Elvin ears tried to listen more intently as I struggled through the building throng to no avail. Upon my arrival, Kute maintained a safe distance from the armed Leaders and some Khunian Elves with his palms facing them in an attempt to ease the incident. Ding guarded the Plant, Gore held high. A snarling Redfang and grunting steeds rounded up Kute's defense.

I jumped into the skirmish's center. "Whoa! Whoa, what is going on here?"

"Nothing, General. I simply disclosed to them I was openly bisexual—"

"Kute."

"Leave him be," Ding stated, gripping Gore tighter.

"You are welcomed not here." Blasmle's deep-set pupils flashed unyielding to Kute.

Kute tried to alleviate the situation. "For sure, Elvin Leader, you must understand I align myself in this war with you, therefore, so should those you have shackled. I am sure your same-sex **roots**... clan... you are punishing would love to protect your forest with you."

"Unnatural," Rungna growled, lurching downward with a notched arrow.

"BLASMLE AND RUNGNA-OLIVIA," the familiar echoist boomed from the treetops behind them, above the masses. Mitral scratched his head, tipping his acorn hat, patting a twitching Jinx. The slender, beardless Gnome who held Mitral's hand on our last visit positioned to his other side with a golden cardinal. "I did not know you were a part of the Divinity? I do believe Ethnel stated the Giant was a member of the Party of the Jode. You would go against that sacred decree?"

"Ethnel is not god our," Blasmle remarked. His rumbling testimony, unrelenting.

"Ah, but he/she represented the Divinity. His/her word is their word. Are we not a forest of safety and solitude for those who respect it? The Giant has done no harm but stated his honesty. We should respect it and his Party."

I could not tolerate Blasmle and Rungna's insolence toward my dear friend. "I agree with Mitral. Desist and let us be on our way on a task most sacred. He is what he is. Let it be. We have much bigger issues."

The Khunian Elves hesitated.

Jinx swooped upon Kute's shoulder hauling urgent Mitral. "Yes, let it be, Blasmle and Rungna. Let it be," Mitral agreed.

Blasmle and Rungna gave repetitive glares at the four of us. Blasmle sneered. "No Oreol to keep you in line, Mitral?"

Flabbergasted at first, the Gnomic Leader responded. "I... I do not need Oreol to—we are equals. Much like you and I."

How would this foolish standoff end? With a little more hesitance, the powerful couple lowered their weapons, turned around and disappeared as wraithlike as they emerged. I heaved, gladdened the skirmish was avoided. I did not want to deal with their divine right, especially in my unreliable state.

I patted Kute's shoulder as Ding corralled his friend's safety with the mounts. "Are you all right Kute?" I asked.

"I am fine, General. Thank you for asking. I hoped to reach out to them in this matter of importance."

"What? The ensuing war or your same-sex agenda?"

"... I think I can accommodate both."

"My wonderful Plant, they are very set in their ways."

"Roots do change."

I leapt upon Stonecrusher's spine, a signal for everyone to mount their own. "You do not get it, Kute. The Khunian Elves are ancient. They are even older than my kin. They have much longevity and have experienced more than any of us. I doubt they will change, but I respect your challenge against their dogma. I do not think anyone ever has.

"Mitral, thank you for helping out. Do not forget what I told you."

"I will not, Ygl," the Gnomic Leader responded. "May Ethnel and the rest of the Divinity guide you."

I chuckled. "I was told that already. We should make you an honorary member of the Party."

"Honorary?"

"You know. Uhm, a member selected but not necessarily a member. An honored member."

"Oh, well, if that is the case, I would be honored to be granted this position, but I need to stay here—with beloved Khun."

"Understood."

With a tap upon Jinx's side, Mitral winged off the Giant's broad shoulder upon his archeornyx, prompting his fellow Gnome to navigate downward upon the golden cardinal. "Plant Kute, especially you," Mitral noted. "I want to thank you so very much for your courage. You will not be forgotten, and you have a friend in Khun. You are very welcomed here under my clan's protection."

"Why, thank you, little Gnome. That is very kind of you. If you were not so small, I would hug you," Kute responded.

"This colleague is a dear friend of mine I would like to introduce to you. His name is Systoli," Mitral offered.

Systoli gave an approving nod.

"Well, then that is two great Gnomes I owe a hug to."

With a subsequent laugh, the Party commenced its journey southeast. Protectors alike withheld from their errands to honor our procession's passage.

"Hail the Party," some cried. "Hail the Party of the Jode!"

The announcements reverberated with a fleetness throughout the camp. Soon every encampment in the Forest of Khun hailed us on the task yet to come, whether from tents, from treehomes, from bushes or from flower beds. Sprites zoomed out in all their splendor, dancing in the air as the swords' clashing provided an enchanting rhythm to the praise they sang:

Marching, trekking; traveling on.
For the Party of the Jode we sing this song.
Always searching, seeking; finding on.
For the Party of the Jode we sing this song.

May blood drip dry
and wounds heal quick.
We will not be denied
the end of the conflict.

The Jode, such a mystical jewel,
must not reach wrong hands,

Awakenings Reckoning
for, Xurchon, most dire most cruel,
will use it to break the land.

The blessing of the gods come with you.
A piece of the Jode by your side
to defeat the evil Xurchon,
for good will surely override.
For good will surely override!
For good will surely override!!

Marching, trekking; traveling on.
For the Party of the Jode we sing this song.
Always searching, seeking; finding on.
For the Party of the Jode we sing this song.
We sing this song.
We sing this song!
We sing this song!!
We sing this song!!!

Khun's tremendous tree trunks rung with the Sprites' transcendent vocals no matter how far our Party rode from the encampment. The Sprites' singing imbued inspirational season to the sacred forest prompting small creatures to crawl out of hidden lairs in various pockets. Leaves flittered into the air in rhythmic abundance within a cool, whistling breeze as if animated by my jodepiece. Beasts approached from all corners to the distinctive call of a celebratory howl—yowling and baying in response to our passage. Streaks of lightning passed overhead, mixing with the blue. The grass rustled with season, and a most comfortable feeling washed over me. Were the twin suns' shimmering rays trying to extend, attempting to obtain the origin of so captivating a song?

We neared Khun's perimeter, hurdling over monstrous roots. My Lorellian ears registered upon a buildup of recognizable yipping through the festive din. A sprinkling colony of yipping asegafians teleported everywhere, even upon the tree limbs, the Lorellian bloodchildren arrived waving a final solemn farewell.

My bloodson, Limbus, and Ploone aligned toward the rally's outlet with their respective mounts, Snip and Winky. Winky came from the same litter as Snip, but not as hairy, and sported a squinty eye. The bloodchildren appeared so regal in their borrowed armor. Limbus' hooded tunic imparted a creamy contrast popping from the murky, titanium cuirass, and his leglet shown visible within the flowy pants.

"*Good luck, Bloodfather,*" he praised.

I rebuffed tears. "*Thank you, my bloodson. Be safe, you hear. Make me proud.*"

"*Yes, I will. I love you.*"

"*And I you, as well.*"

He must never discover how I never wanted this rank. A title thrusted upon me by my bloodfather, Scall. A general for no apparent reason. Unknown to my Limbus, I needed to do the same for him—to make my bloodson proud.

CHAPTER 6: Soft Winds

My head swayed back and forth, riveted by the Sprites' transcendent effects. After scanning about, my eyes opened wider. We arrived in a grassy clearing that grew higher as the mounts galloped past our previous cut path leading to where we had been captured. In several areas, dark spots showed where magic had last struck. Some rigorous weeds had been tumbled where the mounts had attempted to escape from the Death Mist's threat. Behind us, Khun's tremendous trees diminished into a facade within the harsh, Dark Plains' exalting weeds. The Sprites' song must have been so charming because my awareness regained with immediacy. No longer did the enriching thoughts saturate my mind. Certainly Kute must have experienced the same drowsiness with simultaneous head shaking.

Our Party journeyed the sunday's better part through the Dark Plains—me first, Kute second and Ding tagged behind so Redfang would not be trampled. The path was rather narrow and well hewed by thick sword and bulbous club, and shall I say, naked hooves as well. The Giants must have created their mounts' razor hooves before the Quirmeans confiscated the special shoes. We would have stopped to break, but we had the urge to keep riding and our mounts felt just as tenacious. My headband collected so much sweat, prompting me to take it off.

"Limbus is the last of my legacy. My lineage will end if he meets the end-of-seasons. I regret leaving him behind."

"General, you are your own legacy. We cannot afford such thoughts' welcoming. Your **sprout** remains with my thoughts as well, as if my own," Kute stated. "Look!" Kute rode toward a dark spot's left, twenty feet away. Unlike the spots our past skirmish created in the previous locations, this one was a smaller smoldered plot.

I realized the plot was more than a burnt area. A mass of brown fur clumped over it. A leg had been burnt so badly, a shriveled clotting replaced the missing appendage below the thigh. This creature had met quite a severe end-of-seasons. I poked at the rodent corpse with my dagger before running my weapon through the unlucky creature to exploit for all. As the remaining limbs drooped, a thin, membranous skin completed another attachment on the other side. "Well, Kute, it seems Ethnel and I were correct. Juna did escape. I am sure Advisor Werkle would not have bothered to shoot down prey such as this, even if he was hunting. This must have attacked her while she was recuperating or something. I will not venture to scan the jodepiece over this beast to prove my theory."

"That is probably wise, General. Your deceased **earth** would approve of your decision. The creature is known as an aerial squirrel. Very carnivorous rodents they are."

"Not after our Fairy Flower had it meet the end-of-seasons," I joked, trying to ignore any mention of my departed mate. "All right, let us break camp for now. We have traveled long, and I think the Party deserves this needed breather."

Los and Num traded places with their celestial counterparts, Nus and Anul. Darkness inevitable blanketed the Dark Plains. Flooding bi-lunar light casted monstrous shadows with the tall weeds. Too many shadows formed in abundance making it challenging for us to perceive where any beasts lay hidden. Well, not for me whose infravision performed best during this moment. Apparently, Dwarves did not have the Elvin knack to visualize blooded signatures in the darkness. We all had our talents.

The Party decided to take turns guarding camp. Ding took first sentry, then he awoke me to go next because of my infravision. The next sunday's arrival seemed fruitless. The mounts corralled themselves around us to make us more secure. If there was anything a predator planned to attack, the feast would be our underestimated mounts.

Twinkling stars, like swiveling icicles, absorbed the sky adding beauty to an otherwise grotesque recess. The tall weeds' fluctuating profiles bended slightly to a simultaneous cool breeze. My dark brown curls untangled in the fresh coolness. The insects hummed to the rhythmic flow.

I shivered... my hairs stood on end... a presence...

My infravision surveyed the field to uncover no blue or red auras, no warm- or cold-blooded creatures—even the insects had dispersed from my view. Could they have sensed the presence before me?

Without hesitance, my thoughts scattered in my mind and clashed together. I reared up from the booming attack. A psychic attack!

No. No, not psychic. A dwindling prevailed within me preparing an emptiness.

The intrusion: spiritual. My assailant attacked me spiritually! Who was it? Rondo? Xurchon? Somebody intruded within me trying to control me, and my psionics used what it could to pierce the ethereal barrier trapping it.

I clutched my head, attempting to regain control of my divine right, to build a defense, but my unknown assailant battered down my spirit, weakening my will. My defense became an unlikelihood.

I shot up still struggling; still fighting. A step forward was taken, then the next; I tripped over one of the mounts, falling upon grass-laden land, wailing my burning agony to the others.

Kute awoke to the uproar and the neighing. "General..." He searched for me, bewildered by my hapless struggling upon the ground, my hands still pressed upon my head. "General! Blast this darkness."

I felt drawn to my tormentor. I had to return to Quirm, to Rondo, and to my end-of-seasons. My tears could not wash away the regret.

"K-Kute, help me." I arose again, struggling. "Somebody is trying to take possession of me!"

The Giant Plant traced my gasps toward my maddening location, grabbing my shoulders with urgency. "General, what do you want me to do? Shake it out of you?"

The haunting being pulsated within me, shredding my spirit's remnants—and soon, my mind. No longer was I myself, no longer an individual. Somebody, something, kept me in its powerful grasp. Nothing would falter my possessor from hurrying me to the Quirmean Empire.

"General?" Kute urged, shaking me hard.

I could hear Kute in my conscience's distant pockets, rattling me, trying to revive the Lorellian, but the other personage retained too much control.

I turned to my friend with glaring eyes. "Take thy hands off me, mortal," the demanding voice, endless, deep and hollow, and obviously not mine. I realized too late my psychic energies had mixed with my assailant's... we became one—focusing upon Kute. "*NOW.*"

The Giant Plant reeled in pain, bracing his head in a performance all too common, leaving me convulsing all over, my true voice returning, pleading, "N-no. Get... get away from me."

Ding? Where, in Achal's name, was he?

I drifted somewhere else, yet I knew the Dark Plains surrounded me. A sudden vacuum pulled at me from an uncertain depth—the frightening Interim. I was being pulled through the Interim! Did Welbern wail? My dizziness softened into a fading... my eyes flashed open and I found myself extracted into a room, a dark room. The images hazy, but I could distinguish two male patrons appearing before me. I recognized solemn Emperor Rondo in a fancy, light robe and spring apparel, but the other? Who was he? I wanted to cherish this mysterious personage.

An instinct alarmed me not to subject myself to meeting this wonderful being because a foulness beyond belief emanated from his enigmatic form. Ashes seeped through me, choking me. A deafening misery became my reverence... Oh, how I missed you, Thalla...

The deep evil touched me, enveloped me, beckoning me from my companions through the unholy aspect known as the Interim. I resisted with scraps of dwindling, psychic energy, calling upon my regrettable final resource: my jodepiece. My resolute battered thoughts combined themselves, slithered through my enemy's ethereal holes and evaded toward my piece. My bolstered assailants' ethereal advance chased me. The events transpired in a flash, but I attained my piece's core.

Anxiety, alas, granted a way of increasing my desire to rise to this desperate occasion.

After my psionics' defiant entry against the core's malevolence, my tiny artifact emitted a familiar glow. The core's glow enacted as a barrier, shielding me from external harm—providing a kind of amorphous cloak, securing me for the moment that was. My resolute psionics whirled, round and round, in an attempt to absorb all of my jodepiece's resources... my piece's menthol coldness shredded my skin.

The crackling of my piece's power shrank to obtain the shape of someone. The energy shimmered, allowing the image I accepted to become authentically me. The menthol coldness caressed and filled me with a resounding joy. Thin layers of glitter wisped about and through me; everywhere a bluish-yellow shine stretched out toward endlessness. Numbness overtook my frame to the mystic frigid.

And, there I, my vulnerable spirit, levitated into the air. The unrelenting power, almost paralyzing, for in this jewel, no surfaces evolved—only a winnowing deepness; and I had no idea how deep I dove. My piece's apparition surveilled my spirit, a voyeur waiting for my defenses to grant an opening to seep through. I focused my lingering strength into the core, harnessing my piece's haphazard power—*divine right, salvage me.*

With the concentrated power, my merging psionics blasted out in an explosion. Our hybrid energy disseminated, darting back into my hapless spirit, adding new strength and vigor.

My physical form shuddered from the internal onslaught. This final attempt crackled within my body's every region. My mental barriers rebuilt again.

The enemy's offense... failed.

Another being arrived within my mental chaos; I somehow wanted the visitor there. I could not comprehend why, but I wanted this new invader there. *"FIGHT ON, BRAVE YGL,"* said the voice, not the same as prior. Its tone was chaste with wisdom and tense, reminiscent of the personage I encountered at Aman's weaponry shop in Quirm. *"XURCHON'S MIGHT IS STUNNING, BUT THIS JODEPIECE IS THE KEY TO THY PREVALENCE. BELIEVE*

IN THE AWAKENING. NO PROMISES CAN BE MADE. WE CAN ONLY HOPE."

A stark rumbling stirred in my stomach. Rondo already turned to the God of Evil for help. I figured Xurchon would not intervene unless matters got desperate, but my judgment was an apparent error. Xurchon did not want the Party's existence known anywhere, so he planned to eliminate me directly. How could I resist the power of a god when the Divinity seemed to surrender? Their abandonment angered me so.

The Interim's strong pull persevered... amber flames flashed... a wailing... Welbern was wailing?

The Interim's ethereal doorway attempted to shut. My jodepiece's mystic glow stretched toward my enemy's portal. Powerful blasts of magic vibrated everywhere with my defiant closure, but the effects would never reach me. Maybe because such magical threats could never harm anyone in the Interim. What did I know?

After appreciating the mysterious Interim's shadowy strangeness below, I observed the dimensional portal encompassing me. Amber flames flickered. Once again, my jodepiece's magic, with my blade's probable assistance, protected me from being sucked into an enigmatic dimension many a race had come to dread.

"General! General." Positive Kute's concern for my safety was, no doubt, appreciated. "What did you see? Come back. Do not let it capture you."

The distant moans surfacing within this dreaded dimension were enough to inform me Kute was correct.

"Thou hast done well, Ygl. Be brave, for Xurchon hast not been stopped yet. Remember to let the jodepiece lead thee, and the Jode shall be ours." My sympathizer faded away with the Interim's expiring portal.

Hard land welcomed me with a cool breeze caressing my body as I materialized. I stood alone in the Dark Plains with Kute and Ding. A part of me remained cloaked in my jodepiece, mentally and spiritually, as an obstacle against Rondo and Xurchon's next attack... but, for how long? My jodepiece's power was a vital blizzard and very little could be done to falter such a storm—next to my own willpower. I feared this haunting power, the unease angered me more, but now I felt tired, and I hesitated to state... helpless. All I wanted to do was sleep. Emperor Rondo had certainly picked the best moment of inconvenience. I needed the rest. I needed it now.

Ding's red aura stared at me in the weeds' parting shadows with his trusted Redfang lying aside him; his facial expression, hard to see. Infravision did not offer such luxury.

The Giant Plant knelt and held me close, repeating a phrase I remembered from another kind heart not too long ago. "I will smile for you. I will smile for you, General. I will smile for you."

Wonderful Kute, your advice in Khun I would need to heed. I needed to adopt my kin's culture. Meditation was of the utmost importance. I scoffed many an elder away, including my bloodfather, Scall, who stressed this importance, wanting only to play in Khun. And in Khun, Scall delivered me.

The basics of meditation were rather simple. Scall taught me, or tried to teach me, what he called "Soft Winds." First, the meditator must release themselves of all stress, not very difficult at this moment. Then, their body needed to submit itself to an inviting influence. Succumb, for instance, to the idea of those who cared: Methelo, Rolando and Sylvia. And, succumb to the idea of those who filled you with love: Thalla, Limbus, Swen; Kute.

Swen and Kute? Why would I think of them? I could not delve into such puzzling matters, not in my exhausted state.

The meditative avenues permitted my supple "soft winds" to initiate their flow from my feet's soles, circulating warmth from toe to toe—from the big one to the pinky one. In gradual procession, these soft, warm energies would then circulate to my ankles, tickling every little crevice that could be found. Nothing escaped the "soft winds." Then, the circulating warmth flowed up my shins into my knees...

CHAPTER 7: Education

Prince Ygl punched his Khunian opponent in the face.

"Ygl, what are you doing?" An apathetic Blasmle picked the wounded warrior up from a midsummer landscape bespeckled with the twin suns' radiant blessings. "What is this about?"

"He cheated!"

The Khunian chief held the Lorellian prince down, whose creamy tunic bestowed a grassy stain. "Ygl, you need to learn everyone cheats. War fair is not. The season fair is not. Honorable it is not."

At the Miredoan Arena, many a Protector, male and female, gathered to hone their combat skills. Khunian Elves mainly attended, but other residents visited often to observe their newest Protector-in-training of one season—with declining fanfare. Elegant Sprites, with their platinum hair and ivory wings, observed overhead like cascading leaves grinding. Gnomes bounced around upon their rodentia, chancing an expedient peek here and there. On the outskirts, the Elves challenged other obstacle courses like scaling clusters of thin vines dangling from lengthy trees or diving into deep creeks for aquatic combat.

Ordinary Khun was not any different than Lorel, except for the abundant sequoia. The Miredoan Arena, however, emphasized Khun's contrasting challenge, being considered the most sacred expanse. Here, battle was most beneficial for the hallowed territory's safety. Chief Blasmle made sure his reverence remained constant, for his divine right was used with highest frequency here. Many appreciated his gift's profit with the overabundant foliage. Dominating shrubberies festooned by fervor flowers marked the arena's perimeter. Fervor flowers, blue/green striped petals encompassing maroon/green stamens, the perfect honor. These flowers' splendor concealed the dangerous poisons essential to their safety.

If a Protector did not combat within the lush arena, strict policy dictated for them to supplicate with raised arms to their blessed God of Nature, Miredo, and the arena's namesake.

Blasmle placed his arm around Ygl's shoulder walking with the boy along the perimeter with much friendship. After all, they retained practically the same stature.

"Important it is for you to learn," the chief stated.

"Oh, I can beat you. You are nothing." Ygl remarked before tripping over a thickened bump on a sycamore's root.

"Ygl little, you can beat barely yourself," Blasmle noted.

Embarrassed and more exasperated, Ygl jumped up, lunging at the Khunian chief again.

Confident, Blasmle sidestepped him, leaving the Lorellian prince to fall face-first upon the lush grasses. "Anger that... You need to work on that, bloodchild foolish."

A regal hippogriff, Folcen'na, golden hide gleaming, landed bearing another Elf Blasmle knew well. "Rungna-Olivia, what brings you here?" he greeted.

Blasmle sauntered off for his engagement with her leaving Ygl whimpering to himself. As Ygl whimpered, the songbirds' twittering almost alleviated his unhappiness. One twitter stood out amongst the rest like a woodpecker's staccato reaming wood. Being Lorellian, the prince could hear anything better than any race, except Khunians who asserted to flaunt more evolved hearing. A microscopic prick could bounce off a Khunian Elf's inner ear at the slightest whisk, prompting sad Ygl to deny comfort from anyone because he feared being scolded. His sadness stayed with him alone.

Ygl slid a shy glance toward the staccato tweet's direction, spotting a scrawny male Gnome mounted upon a four-legged bird on a nearby fervor flower bush. Quite an odd coupling. His skin, very pale. The avian creature displayed a reddish coloring, blue underbelly and bluish smidgeons throughout. The hesitant Gnome modeled mussy, gray streaks in a russet head of hair. *"Who are you? Are you trying to tell me something?"*

The pair sprung off the leafy embankment onto his shoulder. *"Telepathy? Very good, Prince Ygl. That is a very impressive divine right."* Clean shaven, the Gnome sported gray knickers, a brown vest and a quiver of wooden arrows.

"Well, I could not hear you."

"Are you not an Elf?"

"Yes, but they have bigger ears."

"Okay, I understand. Anyway, I am Mitral, Leader of the Gnomes, and this is my trusted archeornyx, Jinx." The creature's antennae plumage twitched. *"We have been observing you since your training's initiation. Do not let Blasmle frighten you, young Ygl. He has no bloodchildren. He would not know how to react to one. Do you have a lover?"*

"No. I-I have a female waiting for me back at Lorel."

"She is your lover, then."

"No. She has a mate."

"A mate? At such a young age?"

"Yes. I am confused, too, but, I guess, that is the way things go."

"You love her?"

"Yes, I guess."

"Hold on to that, Prince. Hold onto the thoughts of those you love. They will get you through the rough spots."

"I do not know if I want to be here. My bloodfather wants me to be the first general. We have never had one."

"I know. I know."

A shadow's flicker passed about them. Ygl squinted through the branches to spot a winged, waxen creature gallivanting below the clouds. The creature appeared to resemble a unicorn, but employed a large saurian's frame and features. The wings, bat-like with scattered feathers. Reptilian orbs scanned in the prince's direction.

"Is that...?" Ygl inquired.

"Yes, that is Steadfast, the unipegon."

"Wow! I have heard stories about him, but to see him in person..."

"We know he is here, but he is left alone to his intents. He is a wild one. Wilder than even the hippogriffs. Rungna-Olivia herself seems to have no command over him. It would take someone special to control that creature.

"It is interesting, though, that he makes himself be known while you are here. He seems to be looking right at you."

Blasmle returned to Ygl as Rungna, Folcen'na and he departed ways.

"Well, Ygl, I must leave. I will be watching you from afar. Always remember the one you love." Jinx hopped his master off their bony perch, swooping beside the adjacent fervor flower bush.

"What was Mitral doing here, Ygl?" Astute Blasmle knew a conversation took place.

"The Gnome Leader only wanted to welcome me."

"Humph. Well, let us start with training your."

"I would rather learn combat from Man. They are better."

Blasmle remained silent for a moment, absorbing the defiance. He asked, "... You have anger much in you Ygl little. Why?"

"I do not know."

"Why do you not meditate like the rest of clan your?"

Prince Ygl hesitated, forcing his answer. "Psssshhhhh... it is boring."

"Man is not to be trusted."

"What? That is stupid. I trust Man."

"Ygl little, there are things you do not—"

"Know? Do not talk to me like I am a little bloodchild, Leader Blasmle."

"We are a race older far than even yours, Ygl little. We know secrets many you do not," Blasmle replied.

"Psssshhhhh... Achal is our Goddess of History. We bow to her and the knowledge we have kept in our scrolls. We know history better than anyone."

"... You do not want to be here," Blasmle noted.

"Yes, I do."

"No, you do not. Get up."

"What?"

"Get up on knees your. You are here for seasons four more."

Stern Blasmle's sudden directive frightened Ygl. The prince never experienced the Khunian Protector in this manner.

Impatient, Blasmle grabbed Ygl's arm. "I said get on knees your."

Nervous, the Lorellian prince followed the directive.

"Hold arms your out," the Khunian commanded.

As hesitant Ygl followed orders, Blasmle found two medium-sized rocks and placed them on Ygl's outstretched palms. "I am going to teach you about season. I am going to teach you about pain. You see, in a while, rocks those will hurt. I require you to keep arms your out until I tell you to bring them down. If you do not do as ordered, I will strike you back into submission... And, while doing that"—he squatted before the laden Lorellian—"I will tell you a secret little scrolls your never will tell."

As the Elvin chief imparted a dreaded answer to the shocked child, a renegade unipegon delayed its gallivanting amongst the cumulus to focus upon their seeming rapport, and with arched, bespeckled wings, swooped downward toward the duo.

Many a Protector beheld the titillating descent. "Steadfast! Steadfast abounds!"

Much like older General Ygl's experience in the Chrotian barn, Blasmle's revelation to the Lorellian prince resembled more than a dream—moreso an elusive memory resurrecting to haunt young Ygl, to taunt him into a new challenge.

A new challenge of awakening.

CHAPTER 8: To a Head

✦

Everyone suppressed their misfortunes. Mitral's, however, thrived deeper than most. The Gnomic chief never tried to heed his self-doubt since being hampered with his duties over the earth. Duties inherited from his deceased parents. He let the other chiefs strut about with their pride over whom was the better guru. He could care less for such pettiness. To him, the sacred geography took precedence above all else. He loved beautiful Khun with all his heart, and he felt his duty to its maintenance a reasonable bountifulness. Where the Sprites maintained arboreal dominion, Mitral presided with his tribe over more immediate, earthen florae and swards.

He buried himself so deep into this sacred venture, he paid little attention to himself and his needs. Something inherent required tending to, but he did not want to face facts, including when he encountered injustices in his hallowed forest. He endeavored to turn away, to ignore, these injustices, these hypocrisies, so much that his methodology became a flair for ignorance and enablement. Ignorance equaled no guilt equaled no shame. The soils' preeminence held sway above all else.

Gardening was never a daily chore for him and required much courtesy. Unlike spacious Lorel, Khun's trees would not accommodate enough sunlight for all plant life, though many plants tolerated the emerald shading. Moreover, gardening undertook several steps. First, clearing the sod covered area was vital to loosen the turf for the seedlings' roots to penetrate more easily. Second, the earth needed a boost. Decayed leaves, old manure or other organic matter would be tilled into the earth to accomplish this task. Last, the seeds would be planted, creating the colorful ambiance that had become the forest's trademark Mitral held in highest regard. In Khun, annuals and perennials were an oddness, for Khun breathed life into everything winter could barely deny.

CrAcK!

The whipping, constant, daily; not too far away.

cRaCk!

Mitral did his best to block it out, the punishment certain Elves received.

CRacK!

He focused on his work, no need to confront issues outside of his scope of influence. He guarded his tribe well. They did not need to fear such reprisal.

The Gnomes followed their chief's orders with much goodwill fostering from their different work stations. They adored Mitral and left him alone to his devices in his favorite place with the delicious, brown sugar lilies along the river creeks. Except one: a rather slender Gnome sporting a turquoise vest with light blue knickers sought to pander to his chief. With a golden cardinal named Rube, the albino Gnome awaited nearby.

"Why are you here, Systoli?"

"You are by yourself always, Mitral. Everyone works together in their groups but you are always alone. Do you not want... a friend?"

Scrawny Mitral ventured not to look at Systoli, focusing onto the work at hand. "I am dirty..." the Gnomic chief muttered.

"No, you are not."

"I am dirty as the soil," Mitral insisted.

Cautious, Systoli touched Mitral's pale hand, the foremost moment the Gnomic chief had ever had such physical contact giving a welcoming shiver. Systoli stated, "The soil nurtures.

The soil takes care of those who have met the end-of-seasons. The soil is the season where I sit. The soil is needed by all."

Systoli grasped his chief's hands with an urgency arousing Mitral from the reverie. "It is happening."

"What has?" Mitral had stolen away onto a nearby racajaandoo's branch amongst the clustering violet blooms with cherry centers. He nestled amongst fern-like leaves to rest from the ongoing preparations. Sprite chief Oreol's prior ordeal was a bit too much for Mitral to handle.

Why were Systoli and he so pale?

"What we have feared," Systoli answered.

Pangs upon stomach pangs erupted within Mitral. This was an occasion he had prayed would never occur. His mettle would be tested and he was not, in the least, comfortable with the occasion. "Where, Systoli?"

"The Miredoan Arena."

"Then... that is where we must go."

"Mitral... I believe in you."

"... I know."

Onward, the avian mounts jettisoned from their perches. The intertwined thick barks and sinewy shrubs displayed a fantastic arrangement of obstacles on this course toward catastrophe. Throughout the rush, Mitral's powerful voice alerted all Gnomes to meet at the arena—with every vocal expression, with every delivery, and with every range. Gnomes surged from all quarters upon small beasts alike, even the smallest child steered upon the biggest damselfly. A multiplying carpet of furs, feathers, and scales ensued upon the Miredoan Arena.

The mini-armada encountered a breathtaking scene to Mitral's dismay. Within the arena, rows upon rows of stockades kept over one hundred same-sex Elves secured within latches. An engorged periphery of trees with verdant shrubberies encapsulated the horrific scene. These Khunian victims of a hypocritical policy maintained postures not of shame, but extraordinary pride and independence.

Behind each small grouping another Khunian Elf readied to take to task with a lengthy whip at disposal while other whips cracked upon the air and upon sinners' posteriors. Off to the side, Blasmle and Rungna supervised their handiwork with sullen approval.

"NO! This is enough," Mitral's voice boomed with an echo far and wide, beyond the cathedral treetops, compelling the tormentors into defensive stances. The resolve upon the same-sex Elves reflected a love he could understand only too well. "Jinx, help put a stop to this. Gnomes block this punishment at all costs. This will not be tolerated any longer."

In an instant, the Gnomes followed their beloved chief's appeal. As nearby whips licked upward to provide another lashing, Mitral's chirping archeornyx flew overhead, causing the whips to knot upon themselves. Onward the rippling carpet of small beasts scurried, hopped and crawled upon the imprisoned Elves' backsides and upon podiums. They protected the helpless bodies from further harm with ensuing masses of feathery allies alighting upon the Elves wounded. Most small beasts had riders in tow.

The resistance's display left feral Rungna in awe. Sunlight glistened off the descending tiger motif on her shoulder when she wielded her sword. She never truly regarded the smaller beasts, deeming them less than her divine right's scope. "You dare, Mitral."

"This is done, Blasmle and Rungna. No more will you punish this clan, these great Protectors of a forest we all love so dearly. A forest I love so dearly. Never will you cause such atrocities anymore."

"This yours is not to say, Mitral. You overstep boundary your." Blasmle supported his wife.

Mitral's compassionate trembles increased with each increasing step toward truth, a disclosure he had denied for so long. "No... no I do not, my fellow Leaders, for, I... I too, am same-sex... and will not tolerate such an injustice any longer. No more! What are you going to do? Beat down the very beasts we swore to protect?"

Rungna flipped upon a maple tree's massive bark, snarling, dangling sideways, her clinging sharp claws dug deep, spurting a slender leakage of molasses. "You have right no," she snarled.

"I have every right. The clan you punish is just like me. What are you going to do? Punish me, too? Are you both prepared to fight a two-front war with my clan, too? You cannot afford it. Yes, your clan is ancient, but your numbers dwindle because of your celibate vows—"

"Unnatural." Blasmle prepared to notch his bow.

"Yes, call us 'unnatural,' but does your statement not go against Miredo? Your 'God of Nature'? Face it, you two, Quirm has millions to your hundreds. What are you going to do, Blasmle and Rungna-Olivia? You need all your warriors. All these wonderful males and females who love Khun just as much as we do. You need us. You need all of us! You cannot afford such prejudice anymore. Stand up for a forest we all love, and defy your intolerance against love."

CHAPTER 9: Possession

Heat tickled my face, awakening me with a start. My gloved hand shielded my eyes from the light; my hood stayed secure upon my head much like my cloak draped upon my body. Up and down. My stomach straddled upon Stonecrusher's spine, the gray pegasus. I found my face rubbing against his gut, some dirt in my mouth.

I surveyed the barren area. The ground, a pure white grit with pinkish specks. The arid landscape was difficult for the mounts to tread upon. Their path's dusty wake stretched out to nowhere anyone could locate fresh grasslands. Strange elliptical trees with spiny skin dotted the landscape with patches of dry undergrowth. This was not Lorellian climate. By the twin suns, we arrived in the Ty Desert.

My mount was being pulled and I did not need to guess who performed the courtesy. My gloved hand angled to shade my vision to my Giant friend's welcoming musculature. A rope in his hand attached to Stonecrusher's muzzle. Not far, trailing to his right, Ding and Redfang.

Good ol' Kute. He must have had everything packed and ready to go when the sunday broke. He desired the Party to keep moving despite what happened last **moonday** to me.

I swung one leg over Stonecrusher's rump to sit proper onto the saddle with a bit of a wobble. "How far are we?"

Kute laughed. "So, you are finally joining us, General. Well, depending on how long you slumbered, we have traversed a pretty long distance into this land of challenging weather. Depending on Ding's knowledge of the levels of land, we should be close to where the barbaric Ogre estate is."

"Barbaric?"

"Well, the Ogres are considered so, but I am sure many are nice **roots**."

Kute, a fascinating person. I had never met anyone so positive about everything. A strange person to me, indeed. As for Ding, well, he made me wonder in another way... even more.

"How was your rest, General?"

"Believe it or not, I had another of those strange memory recalls. The Forest of Khun was looking more like my kingdom, very regular. The Sprites were not the Sprites, and Mitral... well, let us just say he was not Mitral. They were all so pale. No color whatsoever. They were not... them."

"Are you sure it was not a dream, General?"

"No, it was too real. Like an awakening. It was my actual youth I should have never forgotten. When I was being trained in Khun to be a general, but the appearance of the kin and environment is quite baffling to me."

Kute grunted, sending both of us deeper into thought.

Los and Num, the twin suns, reached their peak in a cloudless, light blue sky, exposing their red-hot faces for the desert to bask in. Stonecrusher and Crater's steady canter stirred an updraft of currents to relieve us from the pale sands' heat. Amusing rosy tints popped ever so often from the grits. Our Party did not gallop long before I took sight of a great endless wall to my right.

"Look," I directed.

"Yes, we see, General. It is the Ogre estate." Kute redirected our tiny caravan toward the proper direction. "Ding, did you lead us the wrong way?"

"I most certainly did not. We were almost there. I am no Fairy," Ding argued.

Disconcerting, the thief's answer, however, to Ding's credit we were guided in the general direction.

My instincts imagined where the Jode might be hidden in the Ty. In my conscious, the main jewel appeared sheltered somewhere unfamiliar. A brilliance glistened from its multicolored facets, entertaining a shifting darkness' shades, a large, crystalline webbing, indeed. The jewel possessed numerous, pronged edges demonstrating a Dwarven smith's possible handiwork. Yet, this Dwarven masterpiece remained incomplete because half of this unwieldy handiwork was missing, exposing a huge pit within the webbing. The prongs moved as if the Jode was a sea plant jostling with the currents.

Upon closer review, the prongs were not pointy at all, but tubular.

The peculiar artifact rotated within a space of nothingness, halting at a rupture upon the artifact's jutting scenery. One of the missing fragments to the rupture hung from my neck, tugging in the craggy stone walls' direction. "Kute, my jodepiece on my neck is guiding us to the estate. If Flower Juna is within those walls, then the Jode must be, as well."

"We shall see, General. And, General..."

"Yes, Kute."

"I had no idea that gem was anyone's property."

His statement astounded me. Who was I to state this artifact belonged to me? Hence, another reason I needed to stay wary of this astounding power. The perversion sickened me.

Our mounts sped with more vigor toward the Ogres' domain, marking a dusty trail. The closer our mounts arrived to our new allies, the greater my respect for such a magnificent wall covering such a long distance—a thirty- to forty-foot competitor to a certain Quirmean achievement.

From the craggy wall's summit, a swarm of tiny creatures appearing similar to Fairies descended upon us. They flaunted an extra pair of insectoid wings. Skin-tight leather, mostly dark, their scanty apparel. Their clothing's significance was neither similar to an elaborate Sprite or a trendy Fairy's wardrobe. No, their outfits resembled a rebellion against either extravagance with a sympathy to allowing exposure to the Ty's unforgiving elements. Some females wore high skirts and the shirts' cleavages plunged deep until a leather belt strapped everything together at the waist. The males dressed in the same manner with the allowance of rather loose slacks. Some males were shirtless. Upon closer scrutiny, I noticed strange inked markings painting their bodies in differing amounts. Some markings resembled waves of water, some resembled various circles, and others resembled clouds among the motifs.

"Kute, who are they?" I raised my arm to slow our humble caravan thirty feet before the monstrous walls. Walls exhibiting not just sharp stones but well-rounded ones as well.

"These are the Pixies. They are the barbaric side of the race Faerie," the Giant Plant whispered. "At least, they will hear what we have to tell."

CHAPTER 10: Strategy

The Forest of Khun.

"No, my mate, do not do it." Lojstania pulled onto Oreol, trying to deter him from stepping any closer to the jodepiece fragment lying on the table. Near them, Rungna-Olivia of the Elvin warriors and Mitral of the Gnomes awaited.

The other Protectors of Khun were too busy retrieving their weapons, preparing for battle or heading to their designated posts. In northern Khun, the Lorellian children's male faction buried within canopies, or mounted upon asegafian cats ready to arch their arrows when commanded. With them would stand the male Protectors (Elvin and Sprites) while the forest's interior would consist of the female Protectors, all Gnomes and every Khunian animal.

Awhile before uniting, the four groups had been focused on their errands when the issue changed to the threat of Quirmean intrusion. Many feared Emperor Rondo would employ magic, his divine right, to assist his massive army during this campaign since that tactic was successful during Quirm's invasion of the Dwarven estate and the Forest of Lorel. The Khunian Elves never wanted to acknowledge Lorel as "the Elf Kingdom's other half." However, matters forced their conscience to accept this fact under the belief Lorellians were victims of a detrimental relationship with Man. The Protector's scope of authority would need to spread further to correct a Lorellian error.

In the end, Oreol decided the only way to fight against the emperor's jodepiece was for the Protectors to resist with an equitable response. "I am sorry, Lojstania, but I am the only one with power enough to withstand it." He gently pushed his wife aside.

"He is the one only worthy," Rungna agreed.

"Is he?" the female Sprite interjected. "After what happened with him in the tent with General Ygl? You dare say he is worthy?"

Nervous, Mitral affixed his acorn helmet. Nervousness was always a part of his character, even after asserting himself as a same-sex male—and his community's effective lead. His whispering persisted as assertive. "If you will not listen to Rungna, Lojstania, then listen to he who feels akin to your mate. Oreol is of a very strong heart. I am sure he will do his best to overcome this jodepiece's influence. Come. Let us move away. He already begins.

"Oreol, we are akin whether you like it or not. I am here for you," Mitral affirmed.

The Sprite king did not respond. His palms pressed atop Khun's hopeful, crystalline salvation. With eyelids collapsed, Oreol's head bowed as he rummaged deep within the fragment. Unnoticed by him, an eerie bluish-yellow glow encapsulated his kneeling form. "Ethnel, bear with me," he stated.

Lojstania gasped; but, Oreol did not hear her. The encapsulating spark flickered once or twice upon him, Oreol twitched in response. His strong hands grasped the fragile piece tighter... his body quavered. The glow flickered farther and farther, encasing all participants in the tent, permitting everyone the potential to behold the phenomenon taking place.

The Sprite king's fingers clawed onto the jodepiece's impenetrable surface.

"Someone is there," Lojstania shrieked. She dashed to salvage her husband; Mitral withheld her. "Oreol! Let go!"

Mitral pulled on her. "Be calm, Lojstania. No one is there."

"There is! I-I cannot see whom, but it is there. Oreol!" She warned.

The Sprite king's lips resounded a warning higher than hers. He struggled and struggled, and twisted and turned. The evil specter must not overcome him; he must overcome the specter. The glow flickered more remotely from him... a menthol coldness flailed upon everyone deeper than the past winter.

Oreol's teeth clenched as a tearful stream jutted from his ducts forcing him to press the jodepiece against his chest, holding the gem; embracing it... a final barrier was all that remained... the blank eyes... they wanted him... would they become his burden? The consuming cold beckoned... and... the heat... the heat—burned...

"No!" Oreol could not handle the pain any longer, struggling for any composure. The bluish-yellow glow flickered once more, then dissipated.

Mitral left shocked Lojstania to assist his exhausted compatriot as a crowd occupied the tent. "Oreol! Oreol, we are here for you. Get up," the Gnomic chief insisted.

The Sprite chief gasped between tremors. "Quirm's attack. It comes from the Great Wall."

CHAPTER 11: The Mound

Slaves we were not, but trekking through the fascinating Ogre estate revived an unwelcomed memory of Quirm. Everywhere a Pixy, male or female, soared about with a weapon at hand.

Preposterous. Why invite our Party in such a manner? Did they not realize we arrived with a message of great misfortune? Why did the Ogres not stop the Pixies from enacting this behavior? The Ogres just acknowledged our arrival with a curiosity coming from blind ignorance or utter boredom.

I did not sulk for concern of what possible misjudgments the Pixies may have raised of our Party. Moreover, my respect was too set upon the modest estate's creative stone-shaping skills. From the start, amazing. Their sleek, marble gate was a standout compared to the magnificent, granite attachment's ugly chunkiness. I could not comprehend the workmanship needed to engineer such a secure gate to slide from one end to the other. On another note, I could not comprehend the incredible pungent smell welcoming our senses—a humid puff of rotten eggs as endless as the estate's granite barrier. Once the Party was able to adjust to the distinctive event, we marveled at the system of cobblestone roadwork leading us to our new destination. Quirm had cobblestone streets, but those streets were limited to the major cities, like Gablen and Rondoville.

How fascinating. Two typically different cultures shared something in common.

However, that was where the resemblance ended. Unlike the angular, Quirmean cityscapes, every building, every towering Ogre structure, was shaped by literal stone with such fine detail as if the Ogre Divinity was responsible for such smooth, curvy refinement. These structures' pinnacles, blunt with not a single sharp edge. Every cut and groove finished. Perfect. Possible stones scooped out from the Ty's inhospitable terrain molded curvy surfaces sunlight bounced from. How could a race so barbaric create such fascinating artwork?

"My, my, dear General," Kute whispered. "You gaze upon the Ogres' estate as if you found a new **hollow**."

"If by 'hollow' you mean a home, you could be correct, my friend. I feel a sense of adventure in my blood despite our situation."

Potent moisture thrived within these walls in contrast to the surrounding land, though not overbearing. The desert's inhabitable environment simply was not the case here in this controlled atmosphere of welcoming, yet humble, splendor. A wide multitude of desert undergrowth abounded, yet modest in their placements. This estate, quite an oasis if there ever was. Glamorous statues of the famous among the Ogres could be spied fashioning several streets we passed as well as some random grates leaking gases from an unknown location— maybe the source of the "rotten eggs." Aside from that disturbance, how could such decorum reflect a race as horrid as them?

As big as a Giant, the Ogre's skin exhibited a very dark color, similar to a Fumian; showing off markings as well. These skin markings exhibited more square- and diamond-shaped figures in contrast to their allies. Many Ogres flaunted knotty tresses of hair dangling from what could be determined a scalp. Some sported thin fur garments, but many were outfitted in loose-fitting layers of cottons, silks, or a linen blending of both. Large nostrils and feet were the major features. Many wore leather sandals or small shoes. Several same-sex couples held hands in public—quite a change in environment to Khun, and even Lorel. A rancid smell followed each passerby. I wanted to commend Kute for his controlled response to the stench.

Gryphons, winged hybrid creatures with a raptor's anterior and a lion's posterior, encircled the cloud-speckled skyways with their riders. Interesting how the clouds never drifted from the estate's border. Another mount was even more interesting to appreciate. A hulking bear-like creature bearing a tortoise shelling encompassing most of its body, upper legs and skull. A thick garland of fur draped the outstanding areas.

Two male Ogres, neighbors, argued with each other along the route, forcing our pathetic parade to a halt. Two other Ogres wearing an emblematic ornament on their left chest tried to maintain peace—probably local law enforcement.

A tree hanging over the other neighbor's property, the argument's center. The opposing neighbor wanted some fruit from the tree, but his adversary would not have anything to do with the theft. "Those figs belong me."

The Pixies decided to encourage the two opponents in the only way deemed possible, according to legend. "Fight! Fight! Fight! Fight!" The fluttering instigators chanted.

Farther down a nearby lane, a lone female Ogre worked upon a stony scaffolding chiseling on a ten-foot, darkish sculpture with white specks. The robust statue resembled a certain male dignitary with an outstretched hand imploring to the populace while the opposite forearm belted his belly. The full-figured female donned a wide-brimmed hat indicative of a long sunday's labor. Her sandals' leather straps laced knee-high with opulent, agate beads positioned in the upper and lowermost levels. A brawny bear-creature rested next to her scaffold. Quite unassuming, yet the populace seemed to give her area some distance. She took interest in the racket and sauntered over after laying down her chisel and hammer.

"Calm down," an officer ordered.

"You calm down," the fig tree's property owner retorted in their broken language. "Tree on my property. That my fruit. Go build some road somewhere. This private matter."

The female sculptor hesitated to get involved, but mustered the strength to rise above her apprehension. She stuttered, "S-sorry get involved. C-can help?"

So endearing, her shyness. Such a sweet person... however, the Ogres and Pixies thought otherwise. Immediate fear set in upon recognizing her voice.

Her fear, just as intense. She clasped her hands and bowed her head, waving long, loose sleeves and pants with slits attached to clay bracelets. A thin porcelain necklace with modest agates peeked from the flailing silks. "I-I no mean intrude, but w-why not share fig tree? At least, fruit that dangle on other side. Right... Or, tear tree down?"

The feuding neighbors were quick to agree with a nod and a fruity hand-off before entering separate homes. On the other hand, her presence did not awe the officers. They gave this dirtied female much regard.

"Now, that is a female..." Kute's admiration tickled me, I must agree. "With such **sprout**-bearing hips, I say."

She acknowledged the Giant Plant, but similar to her kin, blind ignorance overtook, allowing her return to her project to avoid the popular, utter boredom. Her tenderness struck me, reminding me of Swen... tender Swen... I love you, Swen.... oh, there I went again.... How could I disrespect Thalla so cruelly?

We paraded through the rest of the estate until we arrived to where the goading Pixies held dominion. Within a lengthy makeshift chasm, little caves were shaped into rock-hard walls like an oversized beehive. From some of these caves Pixies darted out to meet others. The entire chasm was abuzz with the intermingling crowds of these tiny barbarous creatures.

Peering inside each cave became an unimaginable challenge no matter how innumerable the small dark holes; however, my infravision could speculate these caves as being tunnels leading to the actual homes at the other end. Many Pixies turned from their frolicking and socializing to view our Party with contempt, especially Kute.

We entered another stone dwelling's gates with hundreds of our tiny judges-of-falsehood shadowing. Many other Pixies chatted at stony tables and chairs situated atop larger platforms of tables, vertical rounded poles, and shelves. Countless eyes stared at us with despise in this vast clamoring edifice. This structure, larger than any others. As we passed through archways to different well-furnished rooms and many halls leading elsewhere, we were marched into the largest room of all. Statues erected everywhere and very elaborate furnishings set upon the floor coverings of small animal hides. Some statues imitated water in this extremely moist surrounding. Not lost upon me: the idea Ogres would not be found assembled in this chamber. The Pixies wanted to have their turn with our Party before the Ogre royalty received message of our arrival. This room, sacred to the four-winged residents.

At the room's center burned a five-foot circular hearth with a wavy design on the fringes. The same stone used to sculpt the dignitary statue coated the hearth's base. Soapstone, I think I heard someone call it. Ten feet in the hearth's background on a layered stage sat six Pixies on alabaster, ornamented chairs. The two largest chairs rested front and center. A male and female rested on these larger thrones studying us with the rest of their kin. The female leaned left onto the bald male with her leg crossed behind the other. Even as she caressed his arm upon her chest, rubbing her fingers along his bicep, I became more aware of their contemptuous looks toward our Party. No matter what, my... this... jodepiece would be a last resort. Reasoning must be of importance. If my telepathy was not so wrapped with this artifact, I think I would have taken a peek into our hosts' minds.

"Well, well, Giant." The chuckling male scratched his graying, black stubble on his chin. The echoing chamber assisted his voice, prompting all to silence. I noticed the markings on his arms reminded me of Swen's gases. "And, who may you be?"

"I am Plant Kute of the Giants, hailing from the Cory Mountains, Pixy Leader."

The congregation giggled at their ignorance to Kute's title.

The Pixy Leader joined in the laughter. "They are getting braver these **light**s. And, who may your companions be?"

"I am General Ygl of the Lorel Elves."

"I am Ding of the Dwarves."

"A Dwarf and an Elf, eh?" He scrutinized Ding further. "You look like a miniature Giant who has been in the Ty too long."

How could there be some sort of grudge against us? "We are the Party of the Jode. We have arrived to give you a warning of great misfortune," I ardently stated.

"Oh, so you have? Come, tell us. Is it that we should surrender before the might of the Giants rules us?"

Okay, I must admit we were stunned. "No, it is nothing like that, Pixy Leader."

"Oh? Then, please tell us what it is?" the female challenged. I noticed the markings on her arms, uneven circles. "My name is Lady Hoodia, by the way, and this is Lord Zeph. You need to respect us as such."

I scanned left and right at the many small faces evaluating us. No doubt, many more were gathering behind us.

"I apologize, Lady and Lord. The Ogre estate is in danger of being captured by Man—"

Another hearty laugh aroused from our tiny listeners. "'Ogre' estate? 'Ogre' estate? What the Interim is an 'Ogre' estate?" Many guffawed.

"By Man, you say? And who may I say has sent you with this herald to the Ogrean estate?" Lord Zeph inquired.

"Ogrean? Oh, I apologize. We have brought ourselves."

Lady Hoodia laughed. "You are a good liar, General Ygl. Did you know that? By the way, what does that mean, 'General'?"

"And, did you know you are an ignorant stubborn fool?" Okay, and there goes my anger. The roguish Pixies were not keen about it.

"You dare speak to me that way," Lady Hoodia retorted. She glanced behind at another pretty female with long tannish hair flaunting tints of blonde, relaxing. Firm, tanned legs sprung from beneath a turquoise silk tunic ending at pointy shoes. Something about that particular female told me she was the one—their true Lady. The ordered markings on her arms: taut, curvy lines.

Kute tried intervening, "General—"

"Our **sediments**' enemies." With gases fizzing from his hands, Lord Zeph retorted at Kute while regarding the male sitting behind him. That male called to mind the same bossy impression as his female counterpart—a regular 'Blasmle and Rungna-Olivia' except their gift was shared with the other four as demonstrated by Zeph displaying his divine right. This true broker had piercing black eyes matching his small beard and mustache. His arms' markings, similar to crazy waves. He wore a red leather vest, small boots, and gloves with tight slacks.

I would not relinquish. "I have you know that we were formed by your god, Ethnel."

"Ethnel. Ethnel would never come before those that are not his converts," the true Lady revealed. Their ruse may have been a bother for her—all business and not afraid to go to extremes to get answers.

"He came before the Sprites."

They were speechless. Stonecrusher's restlessness clopped upon the marble flooring. Kute gave an affirming nod in agreement, but did not unsheathe his club. Ding gripped Gore tighter.

The true Lady remained calm. "I am First Lady Gasma. To my left is my **vitamin**, First Lord Guisarrio. You expect the Pixy Council to believe in Sprites?"

"Why not? You did not believe in Elves, First Lady."

"Do not listen to him, First Lady of the Council," the voice aroused from the doorway. Two Ogres mounted upon lumbering bear-creatures, both strapped with double-sided picks along their backs with knobby heads. I recognized one of them, the female sculptor we met earlier. Her older male companion and she wore silky cloaks draped over one shoulder; however, the female used a much larger agate pendant to keep hers attached. The speaker was shorter and, well, more unattractive than Kute. Prompted by soft kicks, their bear-creatures, plodded toward the Pixy Council's stage.

Lady Gasma fussed, perturbed, "You are disturbing our meeting, Crumb."

"Through his lips he speaks lies, Gasma. Please forgive me. He plays tricks with your minds. Tell me, have any of you seen the gods with your own eyes? Not even the aged **dust** has perceived the coming of our gods and goddesses. And you know why? Because we feel our holiness with our heart, not our eyes."

I kept a clear view of the female Ogre examining our Party and her Ogrean opponent's uproar with a profound interest. "But we have seen him with our eyes," I responded. I wish you could come, Ethnel, to prove this fool wrong.

The female Ogre took further interest in me, moreover, I think, her attention may have been drawn to the jodepiece hanging from my neck.

"This is impossible. The insane would be the ones capable of such an accomplishment."

"Then, they lie," someone yelled from the crowd.

"Kill them! Deceivers of peace!" yelled others. Many Pixies unsheathed swords and notched arrows.

"Enough. N-no draw weapons. G-Gravelp see no harm in visitors. Leave alone." The female Ogre struggled against her shyness. Her hand, the size of Kute's, swung up suggesting a sign of ultimate authority. This female must be of great royalty in the estate—even the Pixy Council withdrew any more discussions. Could this be the Ogrean queen before us?

"We apologize, Mound Gravelp, but it was you who has entered uninvited," Gasma challenged, fluttering up. Guisarrio and the rest of the council followed suit as the throng cowered.

"No mean n-no harm, Gasma. Was c-curious when see them earlier," Gravelp answered.

Crumb tried to intervene. "But, Mound, do you not see the danger behind those three? They are the ones said in the legends to bring great danger. Remember the curse coursing through our Mountaindom. For sure, the might of the Giants and Fairies is of great danger—"

"Silence, Crumb. Gravelp hear no more."

Crumb pointed a finger at her. "You do not know what you lead our **boulder**'s estate into."

"One word more..." she interrupted again.

Crumb fell silent. He apparently understood the effect of Gravelp's threat. Incredible. She was a person of much power, yet in all her noble stance and gestures, her language sounded poor. Nonetheless, my gratitude she could have.

Gravelp steered her bear-creature around, nodding toward our Party. "Follow Gravelp."

"What a female," Kute muttered again in admiration.

And with gratitude, we did with Lady Gasma and her council close behind following like hungry dragonflies. Most of the Pixies beyond the council's chamber left their cave dwellings to observe our procession out of the Pixies' dominion. From our exit's point, the Pixies and Crumb halted.

Mound Gravelp proceeded to get acquainted with us during our procession to Bor, their capital. She learned of our capture, of Lorel and the Dwarven estate's capture, of the Party's formation, and most of all, the Jode's threat upon

Zaendara. For her part, she taught us about her dialects. As it turned out, she was an actual princess while older Crumb ranked as a royal advisor, or "Sand."

I even learned something new: "'Giantic' estate? Not 'Giant' estate? Why did you not tell me about this earlier, Kute?"

"I did not think it was important at the moment."

Nobody ever thinks "it" was important. Gravelp informed us her bear-creature, Hogar's Beard, was known as a kiradoura whose draped white fur had brown tips. Why would anyone want to ride such a bumpy spine?

"Touch this," Gravelp directed me, nodding to the shelling.

Fascinating! The kiradoura's shell felt rather cool. Her mount's fur somehow collected undercurrents that transferred to the shelling, hence the ideal mount for anyone in this environment. Finally, the markings on everyone's body, tattoos, represented the respective culture, the desert environment and were individual. Her tattoos appeared as orange and white speckles frothing on her neck's sides, circulating down her arms like a waterfall peeking through her sleeves' slits. Her continuous shyness tickled me. How could anyone fear this female?

"Gravelp not understand well what you speak but have idea. Ogres keep themselves. We go tell me boulder."

"I do not understand, Mound. Why are we going to speak to a rock?" Kute inquired.

A bit confused, at first, Gravelp caught onto his ignorance. "Oh, Boulder is one who sired me," she answered. "He Mountain of Mountaindom. He Mountain Smush."

"Oh, like Lords Zeph and Guisarrio. He is your king. Smush is your bloodfather and Lord," I concluded happily.

"Yes, Mountain Smush. I need to know what Jode again," she inquired.

"It is a very unique gem with great power. The small charm hanging from my neck is a piece of it."

Gravelp scrutinized the jodepiece marveling at the beauty... catching me by surprise, she touched my charm. I shivered as her face became paralyzed as hard as stone. The Ogrean Mound struggled against my jodepiece's evil. I tried to pull her hand off but her grasp was too firm. I knew my artifact would overpower her if I did not act. By instinct, or luck, I allowed a telepathic blast to slice between her psychic link and the piece—her hand popped off. She tapped on Hogar's Beard to halt as she gulped deep.

"Are you all right, Mound Gravelp?" Honorable Kute asked.

Some Ogres had noticed the emergency, but hesitated to comfort Gravelp. She encouraged the bravest kin over, reached into a pouch on her belt and awarded each potential rescuer a clear crystal. "Yes, Plant Kute... Gravelp all right... and Gravelp understand."

We hurried our mounts faster to Bor, the capital. Through the elaborate cobblestone streets we galloped and plodded, leaving behind rows upon rows of the most fascinating stone-shaped structures I had ever seen. The Ogrean kin, or "sediments," as Gravelp referred to them, was quick to move out of our path in respect to our urgency. More than likely, they were really respecting or fearing Gravelp. I did not have a problem with that at all. Every so often, we passed elaborate poles hoisting semitransparent, swollen orbs aloft made of quartz and an unusual, black crystal swirling in the mixed design. For the season of me, I figured the objects must be some sort of torch for the streets, but how the torches worked, I did not know.

Gravelp explained her government wholly serviced her sediments, her kin, at all costs despite the works her sediments provided in return. Hers was an estate truly of the kin. A kin that did not seem to respect their leaders and wanted their own territory. Quite fascinating. The good thing was the Mound understood our trip's importance after her experience with the jodepiece's power, and prepared to inform her bloodfather of our crucial news.

Gravelp motioned our Party closer together for a moment of privacy. "Friends, before meet me boulder, Gravelp need to tell friends thing. Crumb only tell Pixies and Gravelp about Giant attack. Crumb say no want Ogres to know anything yet. Crumb say Man help us against attack, but Gravelp think Crumb lie. You tell truth. Gravelp can tell. Crumb lie. He have no purpose for what tells. He only use legends and Man's words."

"You mean your Sand stating our Party would bring danger?" Kute asked.

"No. More than that. Legend say we left behind by Giants. I know no more, but still no right be skeptical about stupid Giant war."

At the street's end, looped a granite archway above the Party's head. In and out Ogres sauntered, but fewer in number since many congregated within. As we rode through the archway, wonderment bedazzled our eyes. Thirty-foot, enigmatic spires extended, lining the pathway's borders. Each spire inhabited a mixture of many lustrous stones: quartzes, agates, opals, jades, obsidians, and what-not. The twin suns' rays shined brighter upon these edifices of colored stone.

Colonized behind the spires, massive homes, and each home exhibited a different shade of color swelling into other darker shades. I took interest in one dwelling because of the multitude of green hues. Gravelp instructed the stone was malachite and the building belonged to Sand Crumb. Could that be the "hidden green?"

Rectangular flags with rounded corners waved high with various stones' images tumbling about in the soft breeze. No doubt, this was the capital. This was Bor.

Still we traversed inward until encountering the tallest and widest spire of all. A forty-foot edifice of magnanimous size, however, equal to every other building in Bor. I could not understand, but something told me Mountain Smush resided here. A good indicator could have been the carved marble statues assembled around the edifice like gatekeepers to a forbidden portal or maybe the building's intricacy of design. Though formidable, the statues presented a pious impression to the public with an outstretched hand in appeal, like the statue earlier.

No matter, along the way Kute and Gravelp carried deep dialogue. They related to each other as if their acquaintanceship lasted throughout the seasons despite this being their initial encounter. Both races' beliefs had vanished in the couple's instance. I tried to respect their privacy for the sake of my being a general, but something interesting stood out about this conversation between the Plant and the Mound.

"You could be my beard, fair Mound," Kute flirted.

Confused, Gravelp stated, "...You have beard."

"... And, so I do," he said, chuckling.

Confusing indeed, nonetheless, they discussed their kin's dialects. Interesting enough, I had forgotten how a "trunk" meant to a Giant as a "bloodfather" meant to me. To Man, "trunk" and "boulder" would sound rather distasteful. Then, amidst the idle talk, I remembered another reason for our arrival. Kute had kept himself so involved in diplomacy with Gravelp he had forgotten as well.

I knew telepathy would be a challenge under the circumstances, but a psionic sending was imperative. "*Kute,*" I felt my psionic call flash from my mind to his awaiting invite. He winced but remained amiable. "*Ask Gravelp about Juna. We need to know. Sorry, for the intrusion.*"

"Oh."

The cobblestones crossed between a pair of looming monuments. Near there, Gravelp halted Hogar's Beard, acknowledging Kute's change in demeanor. "What matter?"

"Oh, nothing, Mound. I need to know if you have seen or have been told about the whereabouts of a small Fairy female here in your Mountaindom."

"By means, friend Kute, no speak things out here where Pixies' ears well for Sand Crumb," she warned. "Come to me boulder and **rock**'s courtyard. None allowed entrance."

"I thank you for the warning, Mound."

Within the monuments' fencing row, we traveled through the pathway into a courtyard unimaginable compared to Quirm. In Quirm, the ground was as luscious as Lorel's where many kin lectured or played games. The courtyard here shown a bit barren with minimal spiny trees displayed with shrubs of sage accompanying them. Moreover, this was quite an oasis with some fruits and a small pond adding to the scenario. Though some Ogrean nobles presided at random marble tables providing lectures, only awake audience members entertained them. The softened dampness even followed here making us a bit drenched—but what a welcoming drench, indeed.

We stationed ourselves at a table closest to the dwelling. Several Ogres did acknowledge us with passive prying.

"Here we talk," Gravelp whispered. "Now, you say Fairy here?"

"Yes, we were told by Ethnel that Juna was separated from us when we were captured by Man in the Dark Plains. She is supposed to have a lamp with her," I continued.

"A lamp? Ethnel, Faery god?"

"Yes. It is supposed to house... ugh, **cavern** a genie in it named Swen."

"Strange. You speak like legends true when nothing but tales."

"Remember the power of my jodepiece—"

"General—" Kute warned me, noting my slip.

"This. This jodepiece. Remember this jodepiece's power you have just experienced, Mound Gravelp. I am sure it was all too convincing."

She thought for a moment. What a phenomenon, not a single race believed in the legends—not even those who held sanctuary over Khun's sacred grounds, but these tales' slinking fragments were proving their disbeliefs erroneous. All the estates had to have knowledge of the danger threatening Zaendara in the legends. Many believed Zaendara a peaceful continent. No two races had ever disrespected another's independence. But what happened before this? How were the estates formed? Where did our gods originate from? Was there ever a war?

"Gravelp understand," she confirmed. "You speak true and Gravelp sorry, but if lamp here, then only Crumb have it. Lamp be no use to Pixies."

"And, Flower Juna, friend Mound?" Kute inquired.

"Gravelp sorry, but know nothing about her. Only place she be is with Pixies since they only ones know of supposed Giant threat."

"I see," Kute noted.

There must be something in Giantic legend relating to the Pixies, for concern replaced Kute's gallantry—a first for me to witness. Juna must be in danger, and we must save her with Gravelp's hopeful assistance.

"Come. We must tell me boulder. Opportunity enough be wasted." Gravelp called for a noble to corral the mounts as we promenaded within the Ogrean Mountain's spire past a series of marble stairs and halls decorated with alabaster windows and what-nots leading to places known to Gravelp. Like the entire estate, everything was fashioned out of some form of stonework.

Of course, the bountiful, desert shrubbery added some beauty to the gloomy interior as well as the intricate relief popping off walls. A relief, according to Gravelp, was a pronounced carving embedded into walls. The relief could relate a story or simply reflect a personage. In a repeating motif, many reliefs reflected apparent governmental officials entreating the public and performing charitable acts. Quirm barely had reliefs to my knowledge; and if the empire did, I doubt the carvings would be so humbling.

The palace's glossy floors reflected serial flashes from sets of torches hanging from ceiling encasements. I had never experienced such places or public humbleness by royalty. I hid my discomfort from the Party and Gravelp. A lithe, minty residue wafted from the central carpeting.

Unlike the palace halls at Gablen, these halls flowed a bit busy with some workers reviewing small boards riddled with figures, rushing past us to engage an estate needing new touch-ups. The closer we arrived to our destination, the more active the hustling and bustling.

A welcoming archway appeared not far ahead where the busyness initiated. A looming pair of opposing, alabaster windows uncovered a vast chamber beyond. Within, groups of Ogres congregated at separate granite tables discussing plans for the estate's improvements. Once noticing Gravelp and her entourage, they concluded their business, gathered their essentials and paraded out the chamber with their slates, leaving behind a solitary male and a female with blooddaughter.

Fatigue sapped any refined sense from this pairing, yet a purposeful spirit seemed to motivate them. The trio proceeded to convene upon a couple of elaborate chairs three feet away upon a dais. The male, a very hefty Ogre with a very shaggy beard, shown maybe a foot taller than Kute with massive legs poking out from his hefty granite seat like brunette attachments. He slouched upon the chair much like his messy tunic upon his body, probable results from many seasons of public service. Heavy dusty hands acted as a pillow under his chin. Next to him, on a beige marble chair, the female swaddled her small bloodchild on her lap. All were dressed in simple threads, weightless linen.

Cylindrical columns scattered about the chamber. Silent sentries fifteen to twenty feet in height, these thick pillars erected snug within the domed ceiling. They displayed cryptic etchings of symbolic, fiery portrayals jutting through the alabaster light and bolting into a shadowy, lower level.

"That me boulder and rock, Mountain Smush and Hill Squash," Gravelp whispered.

I could not blame Smush for seeming bored, since he could never experience season's joy as we Lorellians had. Very few guards roamed the sparsely furnished area.

Gravelp continued, "Be careful. Me boulder not understand things well. The **shifts** must be having effect, though a dust he is not. Be glad we get to boulder before Crumb. We have advantage."

And, an advantage it was. With Crumb working behind the back of Ogres and Giants alike, we could work behind his. Mountain Smush turned out quite welcoming; excited to see what an Elf, Giant and Dwarf looked like. His voice grumbled deeper and rougher than his **pebble**, his bloodchild. He listened intently to the Party of Jode's tale about its beginning and the two estates' capture. Like Gravelp, he studied us with an eagerness as we related our arrival to the Forest of Khun and how the end-of-seasons of those dear to me broke my psionic bond. He may have attempted to find a flaw in our unwoven tale. He would find none. Hill Squash moved uneasily, holding her blooddaughter tighter as we described our capture and escape from Quirm, and the loss of my mate's season. I trembled during my testimonial about my suicide attempt in Lake Ban, realizing how near a victory Xurchon would have attained.

The Ogrean Mountain puckered up when I concluded with our reunion in Khun and the appearance of Ethnel. "Wait. Say a god in Zaendara?"

"Yes, and it was he who formed our party to acquire the Jode for all the Divinity before the God of Evil could procure it."

Gravelp interceded, "Boulder, believe Party of Jode, please. Gravelp sense they speak true."

Mountain Smush turned to me. "What Jode?"

"I wear a piece of it around my neck." I held up the small shiny artifact for all to admire but sure to keep.

Like his blooddaughter, Smush studied the jodepiece, then me.

Gravelp tensed with earnest. "Boulder," she pleaded.

Smush's voice scraped, "You Leader of party?"

"Yes, great Mountain, I am. I also have some control over this artifact." As I stood on his powdery rug, my psionic senses dug deeper into the faceted surface. I knew my sense's counterpart embedded within the design persevered as a kind entity constructed within the jodepiece's magic. Either I must attain my psychic half, or at least let that portion bridge toward me.

"Demonstrate," Smush instructed.

Kute noticed my struggle. "I am sure, Mountain, that the general is doing that right now."

My closed eyes could not perceive the bluish-yellow glimmering surrounding me, but I could feel the unyielding coolness pulsating... contact was made... the mental bridge connected. An easing overcame me with an honesty superseding self to a new worth... Mountain Smush and Hill Squash gasped in awe.

"Come, jodepiece. I yearn for the skies. Lift me. Lift me high."

Oh, Interim, I began to sound like Swen. No matter, I had not budged, yet. The jodepiece would not allow me to command it, but the enchanted pulp could still be wielded— that dimension the jodepiece would not deny me.

My fingers uncurled for a ceiling swirling with clayish colors, feeling and extending to the air overhead. The enchantment was there. I knew this truth. I just had to feel for that truth.

Menthol coolness and the glow itself upheld as expressions of the jodepiece's magic. If I just concentrated more on the glow... the urge to fly... the want of touching floating's enticing taste... I no longer commanded this with my mind. My heart cried out within my chest, making my body crave for the strips of air teasing me... the very space about me wailed with a pain. The sorcery, too potent for shaky air particles... the menthol coolness ascended from my hand and pulled at me... the glow rose.

I... I rose! My full concentration focused on this powerful summons with the aches and pains that came with levitation. My shoes no longer connected with the fine flooring. The gap with the ceiling lessened. The space beneath, solid, yet there was no ground. I clawed and clawed with every fiber I could muster. My frame shuddered and fatigued until my forehead tapped the swirling clay. With that success, I allowed myself to a careful landing... too much energy had been spent for this task.

Why did I not choose something simpler? Maybe because I thought this would be? I should not have been so determined to show Mountain Smush proof of power undeniable. The coolness dissipated, leaving me limp, relieving me the need. "Kute..."

There was no need to search for my friend. He held me up so I could lean upon him. "That was an awful lot you put there, General."

"Thanks." I gave a wry smile.

The Ogres were speechless, agitated.

"That, Mountain Smush and Hill Squash, is what our Party and allies call magic."

"What me Mountaindom do about this?" Smush asked.

Kute took up my mantle. "Do you not see, Mountain? All estates are in danger of this jewel's power. We need to use all our divine rights. Two estates have been crushed by its might, and one steadily commences to the point of rebellion. The Forest of Khun is, more than likely, under siege by now, but we were able to leave a piece of the General's gem with them so that it may assist in defending their estate better. A risk we have taken obviously not likely again."

Gravelp agreed, "B-but, their force not all. W-we need to rise against M-Man, Boulder. Man's estate massive, but if all estates rise, th-then equal."

Mountain Smush sat silent for a moment, contemplating. Elder eyes sized the Party and me with an unflattering passion. Could his glare peel anymore knowledge from us?

"Boulder, w-what matter?" Gravelp could feel Smush's scrutinizing scope including her.

"If Ogrean estate get in battle, what you do, Ygl?" Smush asked.

"The Party of the Jode plans to rush to the Cories to acquire the Giants and Fairies aid. Our main intent is to seek out the Jode. The Quirmeans and Xurchon have been trying to get a hold of it for quite a while."

"Who Xurchon?"

"He is—"

"Hold your tongues, deceivers." At the arching entrance, Crumb arrived and a female Ogre accompanied him. Both plump intervenors dressed in soft linen apparel, open robes of sorts exposing the abundant tattoos. Their sleeves' hems, long and droopy. I guess he sweated too much in that last outfit.

Gravelp shoved her shyness away. "Y-you dare, Crumb. And, why you bring Squish? Your **mineral** nothing to do with this. Out from our boulder's—"

Mountain Smush slammed down his fist. "Silence, Gravelp. Crumb speak. Are you fine, Crumb? No more ailments?"

"Thank you, Mountain, I am fine.

"I, as your Sand and **stone**, must warn you lies slither from between their teeth. Listen to me, my Mountain. If you do not, that error will lead to our end-of-shifts. Has my word ever failed you? Remember the Spring of Nesia."

The Spring of Nesia? Well, I had never heard of this before.

Gravelp whispered, "That is spring Crumb found within Mountaindom. Spring eternally spurts, but Gravelp think gods put there."

So this Crumb wants to sway Smush's thoughts by reminding his bloodfather of a different past. "I am sure, Mountain Smush, the magic of the jodepiece I wear has proven my point of impending war."

Crumb glared, strolling around the Party with his droopy sleeves wrapped between his arms. "If war approaches, Elf, then it is the three races standing before us who are the perpetrators.

"Boulder, I implore you. Why should war, or even the mention of it, involve an independence or an estate as peaceful as ours? There is no right. And, who is this Xurchon? A myth. That is what it is, Boulder. A fantasy is what he is, just like everything that spills out of their mouths. Lies, I say. They want war, Mountain Smush. They are the barbarians."

Kute chuckled at Crumb's mysterious motives. "Sand, I believe it possible you may want to reword that opportunity."

"See, Boulder. Have I not spoken true? The warrior Giant begins to boast."

My Achal, Crumb twists our words.

Gravelp challenged, "And, the gem's magic? Prove that, Crumb."

"Simple, Mound Gravelp. It has been known by our sediments that Elves were legendary about their magical nature. His magic is focused from him through the gem.

"Tell my boulder, tanned Elf. It is said your sediments never speak lies. Tell him, if there is a war, how can any great army pass through the burning heat of our Ty Desert just to rule an estate as humble as ours?"

"I agree with my vitamin." Squish wheezed while adjusting her white outfit. My sharp vision noticed her dark locks shrouding a small tattoo behind her neck.

"Why she-she here?" Gravelp demanded.

Mountain Smush assessed his bloodson's mate. "... Please leave, Squish," he ordered.

With a huff and frown Squish obeyed.

I could sense Crumb trying to play a trick upon me. Did he not perceive what misfortune he led his kin into? "There is a war. I am sure you know of it. We have already related our story to the Mountain. The Party has traveled far and come too close to the end-of-seasons. Too much has occurred for any obstacle to falter our mission. Man and Xurchon must be stopped.

"If it is war our three races seek, then, why would such a peaceful race hold Flower Juna of the Fairies captive?"

"What Flower?" Smush asked.

His eager blooddaughter answered, "Like Rock, Boulder. Like Hill Squash."

Smush fumed with anger in his seat.

I stole a quick glance to the side. Kute flashed a slight smile. He realized I ensnared this so-called advisor in a way that would influence Smush not to deny us.

Ding, on the other hand, could not disguise his frown underneath his unkempt beard's heap and lowering head. Was Ding frowning because of what was transpiring or of me?

Any judgment about the thief's withdrawal would be pure conjecture at this point.

Smush rose from his throne. "Party says their Hill here. Speak haste, Crumb. Is Hill here?"

"Boulder, I might say." Crumb measured his words. "The Elf may have breathed in too much of our sulfur. I understand. I state this upon the mighty Club of Order of our goddess, Falvanch, and my burial, that there is no sign of any Fairy in all of the Mountaindom."

I could not take his falsehoods anymore. "I cannot believe this! Mountain of Ogres, you rest upon your throne of royal stoneware and listen this mockery of your... your sediments mislead you and mislead you! I tell you—"

"Temper, General," alert Kute mumbled.

Too late. Smush stepped from his throne toward us. At first, I thought Smush's abruptness startled me, but then a slight rumble merged into the earth initiating a quake. "You dare speak that manner." Smush's words, just as measured.

Crumb held the upper hand because of my ridiculous temper. "I move for their immediate end-of-shifts, Boulder. Who would dare speak of our beloved estate—?" Crumb challenged.

Again, sweet Gravelp entered the argument with arms upraised, impeding her bloodfather's path, halting him. "S-Silence, C-Crumb! Boulder, I beg of you..."

The quaking dissipated with Smush's advancement. "Speak."

"I question Sand's allegation about curse."

"No care hear, Pebble. Crumb is Sand because very intelligent. He say curse. I believe curse."

Crumb, emboldened, proceeded. "Yes, Gravelp. A curse. We lost a rock and her stone this light. How many more must meet such mysterious end-of-shifts? As a matter of fact, the stone's poor little body was shattered, Gravelp. Shattered beyond belief. Would you have any knowledge of this?"

"Of course not."

"Are you sure, Mound?" the advisor pressed. "I mean, his end-of-shifts was so similar to the incident."

"Curse n-not me."

"Oh, so you agree there is a curse, then?" sly Crumb pressed.

"No, you play with mind, Crumb."

"Maybe you are a part of the curse, Mound, and do not know."

"No."

Well, this was not a good turn of events. Not a good turn at all. The tension was as thick as this chamber's etched walls, eerily filling every crevice. I could not comprehend why but I peeked at Ding again—his constant smiling made him unaware of my interloping.

Taking a delicate chance with my internal protection within my... the piece, I allowed an instant telepathic sending to seep through my comrade's mind. Intrusive? Yes, but rules could be bent as far as I was concerned... I shuddered... the sentiment in Ding's psyche was just as disturbing as the one coursing throughout the room. Sinister evil. I did not doubt the sentiment being Crumb himself but why our Dwarven ally? My companion was very stubborn, I must admit, but Ding could not be in league with Xurchon. The Dwarven thief was an atheist, for Achal's sake.

Kute broke the silence. "We mean you no harm, Mountain."

Gravelp shared a rapport with bewildered Kute—she actually peered past him. "C-Club."

"A club? You want to go to a club, Mound? I would be flattered, but now is not appropriate."

"No. Club on your back."

"What about my club?"

"Club royal. That royal c-club of my Mountaindom."

The throne room's lighting was not the best despite the dual alabaster windows' looming presence. Nonetheless, beside the granite throne leaned another club much like Kute's with a bear claw handle. Oh, my Achal!

Aghast Smush stayed calm. "Where you get club, Plant Kute?"

"I do not know, Mountain. I have had this club as far as I have known."

I enjoyed seeing Crumb be silenced. Everyone focused on Kute's club. Gravelp came through again.

Gravelp continued with her support. "His club s-symbolic of trust between races. It is royal. This is good harbinger. I move f-for end of meeting until next light. Will provide quarter for them."

Her bloodfather sauntered under a window's soft light pondering with much intent. "So be it. Ogrean estate not war for long. Smush no want any of it. Tomorrow meeting at midlight here. Pixies invited. Leave, but Crumb stay. Come to quarters, Crumb."

"Mountain," Kute interjected. "I would love to give you a hug."

CHAPTER 12: The Tattoo

Gravelp broke the extended silence we shared down the cavernous halls. With very few workers and guards around, she felt safe within the etched walls. "You lucky, friends. Gravelp save you from Crumb defeat you. Very tricky Ogre. Gravelp no like change in him. Strange. Crumb once was wise and thoughtful, but, now..."

Mound Gravelp seemed to have a lot of trust in Crumb until recent. What could have triggered Crumb to turn against his own kin? I hoped that eerie feeling I experienced was not a mystic insight into Xurchon's influence touching an innocent's soul before salvation.

"Mound Gravelp, if you sensed the change in Crumb, I am sure Mountain Smush certainly must have."

Gravelp contemplated. "No. Me **boulder** more trust Crumb than me."

"He is older? Uhm, does he have more **shifts**?"

"Yes."

Kute intervened via telepathy, *"General, I think he pinched me..."*

"Who? Crumb? But, he is married..." The two epiphanies hit me at once remembering Thalla was bisexual. "...*Oh... but, he just got done ranting against our Party."*

"I know. The strange wonders of the heart."

I did not want to comment further acknowledging my surprising confessions centered upon my feelings for Swen and him.

Gravelp shook her head in disappointment. "It be hard the next **light** for you when meet. Gravelp give advice. You leave earliest can before meeting. Sand Crumb surely figure new strategy. He very cunning."

"And, the lamp and Flower Juna, Mound. We must get them before we leave," Kute reminded her.

"No worry, Plant. Crumb probably call it Elf magic—"

"Elves do not have magic. That is Man's divine right," I interjected.

"I understand, but very hard to convince Ogres about legends, including me boulder. He almost **dust** and lost wisdom. He take too much advice from Crumb. Gravelp rarely believed."

"Is it because of the 'incident'?"

Gravelp paused answering me, pondering the proper response. "I-I no w-want to talk about that. As for lamp, Gravelp know much within walls of Mountaindom. Friends, Crumb considers not one, but two estates within walls."

"... The Pixies. Juna is being held by the Pixies."

"Correct. We spoke about before. Remember Ogres fear Giants as Giants fear Ogres, but Ogres know nothing of rumored war. Gravelp tell you Crumb very cunning. I think maybe third estate. But, no worry, you get lamp. You get Flower."

A third estate?

Kute smiled at her. "I am sensing we are going to receive a great aid?"

"You do." The Mound returned an almost toothless one. "Me. Come. I lead to rooms."

"*General Elf...*"

I almost did not recognize the wheezing timbre. "*Who is this? Squish? Is this you? Why are you contacting me in this manner?*"

"*Please. I do not have any opportunity ... I need help...*"

"*Where are you?*"

"*In west side foyer. Please—*"

A curdling scream bounced off the darkened, cavernous halls' etched walls, perking everyone up.

Kute readied his club. "What is that?"

"Squish!" the frightened princess answered.

"Quickly, Gravelp! Where is the west side foyer?"

"Follow."

We hurried below the palace floors heading toward the same huge foyer we had passed through to obtain the stairway leading to the throne room. We detoured to the right into another spacious lobby with high vaulted ceilings and a quartet of alabaster windows permitting Los and Num's rays to disturb the static darkness.

At the tiled floor's center crumpled Squish, motionless. The closer our arrival the more evident the end-of-seasons' messy, crimson kiss became. Someone... something killed her.

Gravelp gasped, "Oh... no..." She knelt down sobbing, touching all over the corpse of Crumb's mate concealed within the shuffled robes. "... Oh... no... no... her bones... they completely shattered..."

"Who could have done this?" Kute knelt beside Gravelp, holding her.

"I-I.... I n-no know."

Upon the perfectly tiled flooring, near Squish's corpse, I noticed something different—earthen matter. Not noticeable to everyone else, but my Elvin vision. How could there be such an imperfection upon something so perfect? Shattered earth? What could that mean? A gruesome growing pool of blood approached it from underneath her.

An immediate memory flashed of my deceased Thalla replacing Squish upon the bloody spot, forcing me to turn away from Squish's speckled carcass. I stared into the shadows. The guilt of my disrespect to my mate's remembrance overwhelmed me because of my resurfacing fondness toward Kute and Swen—these damned feelings!

The issue at hand needed more immediate attention over my confusion. I shuddered, connecting with the nearby shadows in the pristine chamber searching for answers... the shadows? The shadows were moving? Mingling...

"Hold," I gasped.

"What is the matter, General?"

"Do you not see it? The shadows in the perimeter. They want to engage us. Quickly! Everyone to your weapons!"

The encroaching, thickening shadows quickened into a bluish-yellow roll. A roll that did not hesitate to transform into a familiar milky mist—the Death Mist!

Kute and I aligned back-to-back, guarding a trembling Gravelp while Ding sauntered to our feeble defense without a care in the world.

"Ding, hurry up before you are attacked," I warned.

He replied with a grunt and a sneer. The lithe mist kept rolling in its slow and sluggish way.

I concentrated on my jodepiece whose phantom rushed through my body like a band of icy, barbed threads despite my essence's protection set within. Much of the power culminated upon my eyes, stunning me. I could feel the power's force attempt to overwhelm me through this most vulnerable of areas. The menthol coolness beckoned me to stop, but the insufferable heat reemerged. My eyes watered as the heat became more overbearing. My resistance must persist... my jodepiece must not control me. Heat... heat... dreadful heat... harmful heat... terrible heat...

My eyes. They hurt. They burned.

Burned! Burned...

The agony stopped. The coldness dissolved. Only the heat lingered, jostling within my hampered sight.

"The mist, General. The mist is upon us."

My eyes flashed open like glimmering, bluish-yellow coals in the bedazzled paleness. A paleness that no longer baffled my senses. Matters had changed now. I could visualize my assailants much better.

They positioned around us in small powerful enclaves. Each assailant of its own resolve. Some stood small; others, large. Several were hunched while others erected straight. Some stood on two feet next to those with four. All displayed dismantled skin, grimy skin or a mishmash of both. Scales sheathed many of them. Each wore armor of a sort, though many of the grotesque heads appeared uncovered.

Close, and closer they encroached our vulnerable Party.

"W-what surrounds us, friend Ygl? I see n-nothing," Gravelp whispered.

I motioned urgently to my Dwarven friend. "Demons surround us, Ogrean Mound. Many of them. We must keep our guard.

"Ding, hurry!"

The smirk on my fellow's face shocked me. Why did he smirk? Did he hate me so much still?

Impatient, Kute refused any of his close friend's behavior. "What is the matter, Dwarf? Do you desire the end-of-growths so badly?"

"My **rings** are fine, Plant," gruff Ding remarked.

Kute grasped his knobby club tighter with a mutter, "It appears the God of All Evil wants us to meet the end-of-growths as soon as possible. Let him try. Let him try."

A Demon charged at Ding from behind, a twisted defect limping sideways, almost noiseless across the tiled flooring. Opaque eyes' hateful lingering considered the Party, but the sidling monstrosity did not seem to notice me. The creeper was almost upon Ding. With no difficulty, a thin scaly arm raised something small and shiny.

"Ding, watch out!"

Startled, the creeper glanced, glaring not at me, but at my arched Welbern striking in its direction.

<hum...>

"Demonslayer!" the creeper's hiss crept as insidious as its originator. Crooked features fell to meet the end-of-seasons. Demonic blood seeped within the spaces between the tiles. A crooked smile creased the Demon's horrid features.

I could feel my blade's yawning hunger for more. Welbern, rumored in the legends, a true mystic sword. A craving sword hungering after all evil anywhere.

<hum...>

The other Demons fumbled away in disgrace, from the warning released from their bloodbrother's crackling throat.

Shocked into amazement, Ding immediately joined us with Gore's diamond-head at the ready.

The Demons readied, cautious yet certain, as their Death Mist chose to encircle us as if to toy with us. The plan of attack had been changed. If I understood my legends right, these defiled creatures would have already pounced us with all their hate and evil pouring from them. Welbern and my jodepiece provided us a token of hope.

"The sword! Take it!" was their culminating mantra.

My sword had never reacted in such a manner before, to my amazement. Not since Lorel's invasion had I experienced such a humming. The Demons could sense the influence my blade held within its metal bosom. Now, they felt and feared more of Welbern's influence. My blade trembled in my grip, acting upon its own merit. A vacant wave of gluttonous desire washed over me with a need to quench a never-ending thirst for nefarious blood. Could this sign be evil's foul scent returning to Zaendara, bringing my legendary blade back to season? I remembered what happened in Oreol's tent at Khun. Could my jodepiece be the offender?

<hum...>

"The sword! Take it! Take it!!" the Demons cackled with bravado.

Despite their defiance, the Demons practiced a cautionary approach near me, hunching and snickering. Many veered closer to my companions. Crude swords and other weaponry slashed out from everywhere. Claws scratched and clattered.

Fiendish laughter echoed about the chamber, challenging my companions' struggling hearing, masking our opponent's next movements.

Nervous Gravelp positioned herself side-by-side to Kute, brandishing her pick next his club against the bleak lightness. They received little response as the enemy's chitter-chatter grew wilder with every little strike marked upon the hefty royalties. Again, Kute's bulbous club broke through the pale screen... by miracle, a scream aroused of pain and anger. Kute struck again with haste, ending the ordeal.

Another Demon charged Kute from the sideline. The opportunistic adversary rivaled the Plant's size, wielding a huge axe in two of four hands. Like desert shrubbery, furry puffs jutted from various parts of the monstrous body.

I ran to Kute's aid. The Demon did not notice me. Ravenous Welbern sent out a telepathic moan of hunger, horrifying me. My blade actually craved the Demon's blood? The hulking Demon's weapons were raised. I rose in a manner I knew was not my own, delivering the blow my ravenous blade intended.

"Demonslayer!" The Demon's massive body fell upon the smaller ones. A smile contorted the defeated opponent's tortured face.

Other Demons scampered away from him—from Demonslayer's gift. A gift Welbern tried so hard to make me understand when we telepathically melded in Quirm.

"All right, Demons! Demonslayer is here and will send you to your end-of-seasons. Every last one of you if you do not leave!"

The wild chatter rose past a climax. More weapons appeared out of nowhere in the frenzy. Some even charged me with much force. I blocked many of them and returned the same attack. Many screamed; others ran.

"Kill the Demonslayer's wielder! Destroy the Party!" Their hissing grew and grew.

A cry came from behind me. "Gravelp!"

The Ogrean Mound lay wounded. A large spear had punctured her leg.

"It is too late, Elf. Even if you do wield the legendary sword, there are still too many Demons to our so few," Ding warned.

"My Dwarven friend may speak true, General. There may be little advantage when they can see us and we cannot them, but oh the glory of it all."

Our adversaries agreed with sadistic cackles. Kute and Ding guarded the wounded Mound while their own bodies withstood any bludgeoning. The Demons became wilder with their measured blows. Kute grew a little bigger, an attempt to even our odds. His equipment reacted jointly.

Welbern slashed out with justice. The encircling paleness answered by swallowing each smiling fiend as their end-of-seasons welcomed them into oblivion.

A spark—my jodepiece's magic caressed Welbern. My startled blade shuddered uncontrollably against the unexpected, harsh assault. Welbern slashed out with a madness slaying more Demons than before. Those opponents attempting valor's grace found themselves fleeing. Welbern sensed their evasion and repelled some of my artifact's magic into me to attack further. However, the mystic onslaught gushed into me too fast... I could not control such an influx... such numbness. My body shivered... I must let go before the onslaught destroyed me... I gasped in pain as my jodepiece's magic exploded from me in an enormous burst of bluish-yellow energy.

Demonslayer, relieved of the mystic burden, pulsated its legendary fury's power. The constant amber light I witnessed within our telepathic melding appeared in utter truth, blending with the bluish-yellow illuminance. The Party watched in amazement as Welbern's amber brilliance tore into the Demonic hordes, forcing the decrepit monstrosities to scramble.

I collapsed, fatigued, upon the ground next to Gravelp, having worked so much magic in one instance. The Demons scattered farther from my piece's magic splashing from my body.

Welbern swished and swished—its amber light pulsated everywhere; then, my blade faltered with a clatter next to me.

"Kute, prop me up so I may attempt to use my jodepiece's magic at an intensity."

"What... Oh, sorry, General. I am still not used to your telepathy. What the jodepiece's magic did to us... our wounds are gone."

Frightened, Gravelp clambered on guard, holding her pick in front of her. "Demons not gone. Demons not gone! Gem magic just keeps them back until you drain."

I spied weakly at my friends' evident health at my weakened expense. A telepathic sending, the best bet at this point. *"Not so, Gravelp...*

"Please, Welbern. Please... Fly above us and give these Demons the justice wielded within you. Show them that justice, my blade. Give them the dreaded kiss of the Demonslayer. Show them your awakening's reckoning."

<Hum>

Throughout my weary form a soothing seethed. Somehow, I could sense my quivering sword's humming pleased before Welbern whizzed toward the vaulted ceiling. The unwelcomed power Welbern redirected into me allowed my jodepiece's mystic ambiance to extend longer.

The Demons cackled with hysteria. Aerial weapons whizzed toward us, my jodepiece's beaming aura disintegrated them.

Kute bellowed at the fiendish shrieks' fear and hate. "Ho-ho, Demons! It seems you no longer mock us but we you!"

All around our Party the ring of paleness pressed. Shrieking louder, the Xurchon's bloodchildren tried to breach our defense with monstrous claws and jagged teeth. Their unpleasant stench overpowered the sulfuric scents. My jodepiece persevered as the perfect obstacle against such dark magic, leaving Welbern to perform a last act.

"Now, Welbern... Now," my telepathic sending included the Party. Shrewd Kute shrunk his size to normal. Ding and Gravelp moved in closer to avoid being struck. Gore's prism teeth dripped of an indigo goo. Demonslayer swung low, almost striking Ding's hood.

"Hey!" the thief snarled.

The amber gemstone on my blade's hilt shimmered. That shimmering transferred to the first coiled rune on my blade's fuller as a gleaming dot sliding along the rune's roundabout route etched within. The dot saturated passing edges with a yellowish-brown energy. When the amber dot reached the route's end, it disappeared, gleaming a bit onto the nearby runic dimple like a fading star, only to reappear onto the next rune repeating the sliding cycle until the final rune's conclusion. An amber flame erupted from my blade: a result of the awakening.

Welbern swung higher, directing a beam of pulsating power into a section of the besieging mist. Fiendish footsteps tripped over each other in horrific evasion. A brilliant burst of tawny light exploded upon its target. Within the burst, other Demons evaded elsewhere into the Death Mist while a trio lay upon the tiled flooring facing their end-of-seasons. How ironic.

Welbern arced wider and spun faster, emitting more vengeance upon the shrieking Demonic hordes. The milky mist faded away into a quickness drowning painful screams and defiant cries, yielding the spacious lobby to our relieved gathering.

Kute propped up my fatigued form. "General...?"

Welbern clattered upon the ground near me, depleted. Kute reached to grab my blade but pulled away from the smoldering hilt.

"I... I am all right. I need to be careful using this power. It is not meant to be," I stammered.

"I understand. Your blade is hot. We will pick it up when it warms."

Opposite of us, Gravelp held Squish close, cradling her.

At the lobby's entrance, Mountain Smush and Sand Crumb rushed in with a small crowd and a squad of ten guards.

"We heard sounds. What happened?" Smush clenched his silky cape.

Horrified, Crumb ran to his crumpled mate upon seeing her in Gravelp's arms, yelling, "No. No! No! Unhand her!" He snatched Squish from the frightened Mound who stepped a few feet away. His loopy sleeves' hem soaked up dripping blood. "No... no... come back to me..."

Unkempt Smush and his lumbering squad caught up. "What happened?"

"... Her... her bones... they are shattered..." Crumb continued. He held Squish's head close, sobbing, pulling the hair in the back of her head up and further revealing the mysterious tattoo to me: a hood with a bowl-shaped scoop below, a dot on either side.

How strange. Her mark's uniqueness. What did it mean and why keep it hidden? And, even moreso, have I seen it before?

Crumb twisted toward Gravelp, pointing. "You. You are the only one capable of this."

"N-n-no. N-no. Not me. Not I." The trembling Mound felt helpless.

Kute hesitated leaving my side to assist her. "General..."

"Go... go to her, Kute. I will be fine." Welbern cooled enough for my retrieval.

He obliged. Ding stayed put, but lowered Gore, sensing the danger.

I composed myself as best I could, attempting to intervene. "Gravelp did not do this. We found your mate, your-your **mineral** this way—"

"I do not believe you. They have brought the curse, Boulder. And now they affect our **cavern**. Someone must be punished!"

Smush did not know how to determine the situation. Remaining calm, he evaluated the Party and his blooddaughter. "What happened?"

"Boulder, we-we were attacked." Gravelp held up her pick to show him the evidence.

"I see nothing, **Pebble**."

My Achal, no blood could be seen on her pick!

I scanned my sword and the others' weapons. Every trace of fiendish existence—gone. Not an indigo drop was left. We found no need to tell Smush about the Death Mist, for no evidence was left to the contrary. How could I explain Demons performed the heinous act when even I found the idea absurd? But Demons tore and maimed. They could not possibly crush their victims to meet the end-of-seasons. Could they? What a dilemma... "I promise you, Mountain Smush. Squish was like this when we found her. We had nothing to do with this."

He did not look convinced.

"Boulder, please..." Gravelp whimpered.

Her bloodbrother leered resolute. "Someone must be punished. My mineral has met the end-of-shifts. Someone is to blame. They are the only ones here and Mound Gravelp is the one capable of such a heinous deed. My mineral's blood is all over her."

"N-not me. Not me..."

Kute chimed in, "The Mound had nothing to do with this."

Weary Smush eyed the Plant, then, his club. A club Ogrean in nature, yet in the possession of Giantic royalty. "Guards, take Mound to royal prison. Our guests—"

Gravelp struggled against her seizure. "N-no. N-no."

"Do not." Smush's stern warning wrenched as searing as the Ty's grains.

Startled, Gravelp stopped and allowed her arrest.

"For sure, Mountain, I believe you could see the error of your way." Kute did not plead.

"How could you be such a fool!? She did nothing wrong!" I belted with exhaust, Welbern still at hand.

The keen guards wielded their picks and clubs.

Kute recognized the danger I placed us in, so he maintained calm. "General..."

After a weighty pause, I controlled my dismay, sheathing my weapon. Squish's blood soaked up more earthen matter. A flying gryphon gallivanted past one of the windows. An unexpected chill pitched from the north.

CHAPTER 13: A Chance

Quirm.

The swirling paleness melted, intermingling with the bleak surroundings. Each ring of the enchanted spiral whisked away, one by one. The pale smoke's thin entrails, residual testimony signifying black magic's practice within Rykon Tower, the main temple of worship at Rondoville. Myrfran garlic still smoldered from the cubic brazier off the wall trailing with the scent of pine needles.

"Dost thou see, Rondo?" Xurchon's voice, a syrupy froth, "Ygl of the Lorel Elves has absconded. He still proves a threat to our plans."

"He has a very strong mind and it gets stronger," the emperor noted. A velvet robe covered his daily garments. His mussy hair reflected his worrisome demeanor.

"But his mind did not protect his companions and him from my offspring. It is the jodepiece and Welbern that aided him." The albescent statue substituted the God of Evil's physical presence.

"Great Xurchon, what if our plans do not go as we planned now that Princess Gravelp addressed her doubts about Crumb?"

"Have no worry. Crumb is cunning enough to deflect any of the Ogrean princess' judgements."

"I do not understand them. Do they not see that all I ask for is their obedience? You have led me through this, Xurchon. I have captured two estates and soon another, but they do not seem to accept my viewpoint."

"This is why we must locate the Jode."

"The Jode. On occasion I think that dratted Ygl is getting closer to it than we are."

"He is not. In fact, I believe, his search may be needless in the Ogrean estate. Remember we checked there before him. The Jode is elsewhere."

"The Giants? The Cories?"

"No. The Giants would have long given it to the Dwarves, hence, making it your soldiers' procurement."

"The Dwarven estate is labyrinthine with many hidden underground passages."

"No. I believe it is in another location."

"Where?"

Whatever plan they conversed about within the unholy stillness, even the Divinity unheeded Xurchon's great advantage. Rondo's heart palpitated with excitement as the answer became disclosed. The Quirmean citizenry loved their emperor, he hoped, and soon all the races' heads would genuflect with great esteem to the solitary individual who arrived to deliver Zaendarans from their destructive paths. New paths would be adhered to.

Though Rondo and his novel god communed with the thought of their newfound discovery in privacy, a race resisted against them in similar silence. Each night while the twin moons, Nus and Anul, graced the skies, the Lorellian slaves at Chrot let down a rope outside their window. Each night, a couple absconded into the darkness to alert others of Xurchon and relate the message of Ygl's threat against the God of All Evil. How these valiant envoys avoided being detected by Chrot's guards none comprehended, but many content spectators recognized not one envoy had been apprehended.

This courageous race commenced to work from within while their courageous general worked from without. They had been stricken, deprived of their elders and loved ones, and most of all, their right to be free and alive—their right to life. Yet, they still resisted with a rekindled strength only the surviving, Lorellian royalty could grant them. A self-deprecating general bequeathed them hope and a prospect to regain what was theirs despite his ambivalence. He bestowed them an opportunity to rebel.

CHAPTER 14: Trinity

The Forest of Khun.

Twice the Lorellian plant life's size, many of its trees' branches would be comparative to a multiple-lane bridge to any Faerie. Sprite chief Oreol situated himself upon the racajaandoo's lower branch, squatting next to a bagged item as if the item was a recent pet he did not want to associate with. The item's wrapping, a weed weaving handiwork, was tied well with vines. He had the best view from his perch surveying the vast clearing. A length of three hundred trees measured the clearing; two hundred stretched the width north. United with him positioned four Protectors who meant everything to him. Lojstania whose divine right was almost equivocal to his, the closest. Her chartreuse wings rested easy, the lengthened, tail plumage swayed ever so slightly.

"Are you sure you are all right, my mate?" she whispered gently to him, frightened for him because a while ago his body and soul had been subjected to the fragment's thrall.

The racajaandoo's clustering, violet blossoms with cherry centers, was his preferred respite because of the tree's reverence by Lojstania. He felt at ease in these trees, close to her whenever she left. He used to entertain resentment toward Mitral who favored the racajaandoos, as well, until the recent disclosure of the Gnomic chief's sexuality and attachment to Systoli. "I am fine, Lojstania. It is Khun's protection I have concern for," he stated.

Humble Mitral revealed himself beside Lojstania, settled upon four-legged Jinx. "It pains me to hear such words, Oreol, as much as I admit they are spoken truer." A bow he held came complete with a wide quiver of arrows strapped to his back, tips dipped with a poisonous concoction brewed from the fervorflowers. All the Gnomes at this site were also equipped with such weaponry, many owning swords coated with the selfsame poison. The swift-flying Sprites and they wore no panoply, no titanium-based covering for their battle readiness.

The Lorellian children, concealing themselves within the treetops, wore some armor provided to protect their chests and heads. Asegafian cats, their mounts, readied for any means for their masters' exodus into the serene wilderness.

"Yes, Oreol, you are needed very much in struggle our." Blasmle rested beneath them upon Rushar, his brunette hippogriff. Within his uniformed helmet, his sharply slanted eyes retained a vigilant probe into the welling foliage a northern mile yonder. The looming Great Wall of Quirm punctuated his trajectory. Laser-sharp eye sight, better than a Lorellian, would not miss anything, combined with a hearing endorsing Khunian supremacy. The Khunian regalia's obscured glistening glinted on either side of Blasmle, along and beyond the neighboring glade's southern boundary. Each and every Protector equipped for the threat to come, and all retained belief for their forest's victory over the uninvited. "If the attack is magical, you the sacrifice must be," the Elvin chief instilled.

"How dare you speak so threatening to my mate, Blasmle?"

"No, Lojstania," Oreol interjected. "If I must sacrifice my season in protection of a forest most sacred, then, so be it." Oreol's arrogance did not permit him to touch her shoulder in this moment of needed comfort, a regrettable contract she obeyed too well.

Rungna-Olivia, the Elvin chieftess, abided away, silent. She felt ashamed for having urged Oreol to play so close to death just because Khun needed so fortuitous an iniquitous gift. If they survived, that sinful jewel would need ruin as its next metamorphosis, if possible. However, Oreol's prudent words made her feel better. No need for a hand on her shoulder.

"Are you sure you can take another chance with the jodepiece, milord?"

"I am sure, Lojstania. Before, I felt I was close to the last point of the gem's defense. My divine right aided me. I am sure—" He observed Blasmle moving Rushar forward. "Blasmle, is anything the matter?"

The Khunian Elves' chief took hold of his horn shaped like a stag's crooked antler. "I see movement ahead up," he stated.

Those who heard him scanned for his purported target, but only the warriors at the front lines with Blasmle could observe well.

Through the deified forest an eerie chill crept from no more than a half mile away. The unnatural miasma's lithe presence boiled silently over the Great Wall, prompting every Protector to brandish their weapons before Blasmle could sound the command. The meandering intruder's shifting mists pressed farther and farther into the forest to reach a most desired goal; the unnerving passage disturbed not a single leaf or grass.

"It is the mist white Ygl told us about when he came first here! Everyone to weapons your! Quirm is upon us!" Blasmle put his crooked horn to his lips and blared a bellowing call-to-arms. Aquiline Rushar galloped through the ranks as the call resounded throughout, every warrior prepared for the Quirmean invasion, stalwart enthusiasm formed a powerful defensive barrier running the arboreal length. The Protectors were going to assure Man did not annex another forest again.

"So, Man brings their magic against us," Oreol commented, snuggling the wrapped bag tighter.

"Why should they not, dear friend?" Mitral questioned, stroking Jinx. Though still far away, the building mist seemed ever closer. "If they can attack an estate as sacred as Khun, why should they not try to impose such obscenity against the power of the gods? General Ygl was correct to leave that jodepiece behind."

"This fragment cannot be of the Divinity. Believe me," Oreol stated.

Lojstania leaned against the racajaandoo's bark clutching her dagger. "But, to the cost of what, Mitral? My love's season or Khun's safety?"

She peered at the ever-shifting entity for an answer. She hoped Oreol would touch her lower back, rubbing her sacrum with assurance, agitating the flimsy, split dress she wore with every stroke.

"We make our sacrifices," Mitral rejoined.

As if the reply miffed him, Oreol yielded his wife a peck on her shoulder, obliging her a rare moment so desired. "Only my endurance of it can tell. Only that can tell."

Her bare feet stepped closer to the Sprite chief, her soft hair falling upon his shoulder.

Mitral's lover, Systoli, perched upon the branch with Rube, his golden cardinal. The slender Gnome dismounted Rube, ran to and embraced Mitral, demonstrating an unequivocal public display of affection.

Being the first Khunians to observe the persevering union, Lojstania bestowed her highest respect to them as both couples pondered about the mystic mist's procession. Yes, everyone made their sacrifices.

At vanguard, the tight ranks separated. Rushar barged through with a squawk, pleasing the male warriors acknowledging their chief's arrival to head their resistance.

Displeased, Blasmle's voice rumbled, "What are you doing? Man solely is not who we fight at the moment. Lessen your defense. I will not lose so many on this attack initial."

Along the fortified line the order passed from one Protector to the next, culminating in rank and file breaking from the frontlines, disappearing deeper into their leafy sanctum.

Blasmle scrutinized the Death Mist's silent descent picking up a pace, no more than two hundred trees away, filling the vast clearing, boiling over the surrounding chlorophyll.

"Blasmle." Mitral and Jinx came upon the scene. "What is your plan? Can we attack? It is only a mist."

"No, not yet. What I fear is within the mist's being. If it is what Ygl General says, what genie his showed us, power and strength is not what we need."

"If you would like, sir, me and my friend may be able to shoot some arrows to see the results," a youthful voice inquired within the foliage.

"Suffice that will, Limbus of the Elves Lorel, but first allow me to resound the order so we can hear the sound of the enemy," Blasmle answered.

Khun's Protectors had been trained to adhere to different resonances from Blasmle's horn. Throughout Khun rang staccato blares. Blasmle desisted his call and anticipated. Soon a volley of arrows shot into the air heading straight for the mist, penetrating the ambling envelope... not a sound was heard from within, no arrowhead struck any surface.

One hundred and fifty trees... the primary defense's forces shifted a bit restive.

Blasmle addressed Ygl's earnest child. "Quickly, Limbus, get some of friends your on asegafians their. Teleport to the rear. Warn everyone to stay upon ground their. I am going to try an offensive."

"Against that?" Limbus popped his head out from within the branches' camouflage. The Khunian armor fit the Lorellian children quite well considering they were the same height. His creamy tunic's hood clasped snug around the form-fitting helmet.

"Just do as ordered. This is for Khun's protection."

With elegance, Limbus leapt down from the branch onto Snip's spine and yanked the shaggy fur—the duo vanished. Blasmle waited while he observed the pallid silence's descent.

One hundred trees away...

The Khunian chief resisted impatience. Limbus and his friends took too long. For sure, they were not riding their asegafian felids through the wilderness on a romp. Confident Blasmle hoisted his horn to puckered lips.

"It is done." Limbus and Snip reappeared with Ploone and Winky. "The others sent your warning to the very ends of your defense... sir."

"Good." A secondary blast blared forth from the woodsy, angular horn, reverberating from the wilderness' four corners. Trained since youth, the Protectors identified this strong blast as the call to charge. Where the front defense had once aligned, rustling grasses and leaves remained. The image of Blasmle raising his sword and blowing another battle cry was a prospect none had seen for a long while, if ever they did.

Beating hooves, scraping claws, and flapping wings' thunder overwhelmed Khun's northern territory as the frontline sprinted forward through the field and beyond to meet what many referred to as death. And, what a splendid death, indeed.

Blasmle searched within himself to retrieve the gift the Elvin god, Miredo, granted him. No one, in this consecrated timberland, considered themselves royalty, however, he was his race's chief. No other proof needed. During his younger years, many eons ago, when governance's mantle was placed upon him, he sensed the divine right surge from his core. Once he used the gift, but decided his supremacy in battle the better, and so the gift was seldom exploited. However, as the lacy menace evolved into a monumental horror before his closing forces, he acknowledged his divine right must be adhered to.

A thought. A simple thought partook. A small white cloud billowed about the Khunian ruler's eager forearm. A gust of wild wind blustered forth from his divine cumulus ahead of his vanguard creating an opening into the monstrous milkiness, pushing much of the mist apart, revealing creatures of immense defect with vulnerable surprise. Some creatures dripped a strange goo from suspicious apertures. The Demons leapt at Blasmle ready to rip him asunder, but a rapid bolt of gilded lightning claimed the twisted horrors' existence.

An unfortunate case developed, though, when the strength of Blasmle's gift appeared inadequate against the mist's innate potency, for all warriors that charged within found themselves fighting for their own lives. The Protectors sustained minimal options when striking a foe even the Elves could barely detect despite superb senses. The hippogriffs aided in the floundering defense with hooked beaks and kickbacks from unrelenting hooves. The Protectors slashed with their weapons in every direction but found their attempts nearing futile against a foe flashing in and out within the curling mistiness. The airborne warriors stayed mindful not to journey too deep into the burgeoning dewiness to avoid being harmed by their own comrades. No matter, nobody knew exactly where they found themselves at any point.

Blasmle dispatched many a Demon with his gift of divine lightning and gusty turbulences, creating a wide hole. He tried repelling as much of the dewy disaster away, but his winds kept losing strength the longer he battled within the lithe invader's hollow space. Nevertheless, many Demons lay slain while others retaliated against those Protectors who charged into the manufactured clearing to exterminate them, regrettable choices either way for those Demons revealed by his stormy cataclysm.

The Death Mist, with a slink, enveloped its main opponent in an attempt to deny Khun's advantage. Blasmle struggled to maintain his assault's steadiness, but the monstrous milkiness' inherent power was becoming unrelenting, the nefarious dew closed farther and farther in. The stoic Khunian, focused on maintaining his position, did not notice the one-eyed offspring developing from the dewiness behind him—jagged teeth gaping, jagged blade held high.

"Blasmle, behind you!" A tiny, poisonous arrow's shaft pierced the unwitting, cyclopean pupil. The fervor flower's neurotoxin seeped into the vulnerable eye's optical passageways, rendering the creature blind, helpless, and fraught. Flanked by Systoli and Rube, Mitral leapt off veering Jinx's spine to drag his polluted blade down the belly of another smaller Demon who stepped into the scene from the nefarious dew, his weight seemingly heavier than before.

The Gnomic chief landed upon the distressed field, awaiting the return of his archeornyx. A scaly hand reached down toward him within Blasmle's fabricated funnel. Mitral noted its gnarled middle finger and focused upon his divine right: his feet firmly placed upon sacred ground, he sought what power the earth's soil could imbue him. A primordial rinse coursed through him, a rocketing pulse of quintessence—roots, dirt, mulch and grime throbbing through his very being, a soil's blessing, of the garden.

Mitral caught the scaly finger with mountainous strength provided by this pulsating energy, crushed the foremost joint and flipped his assailant back into the Death Mist's other side before bounding onto Jinx's awaiting spine.

Amazed, Blasmle neglected to express any emotion to his fellow Protector's feat.

Mitral flew by the Elvin chief's side. "We have to get out of here, Blasmle. Compared to this, our divine rights are not strong enough. The Demons maintain the advantage over us. Who knows how many of us have met the end-of-seasons."

"Correct you are, Mitral. Mist this attempts to seduce me. There is nothing we can do against it. Even my right divine slowly ebbs. This magic dark is too strong, but we are the handpicked..." Blasmle dug deeper, casting the strongest gust he could, creating a much larger funnel.

They witnessed as Protectors and Demons strove to overpower one another. Many of Xurchon's deranged offspring leapt in to seal Khun's defeat. Sprites darted about seeking the most vulnerable areas for their poisoned tips to exploit.

Aquiline Rushar trampled two opponents with his mighty fore-claws while his master compelled another spiraling gust to widen the diabolical arena. The surrounding mistiness pushed away but not as far as prior.

Another bolt of gilded lightning hurled from Blasmle's eager palms at a group of assailants. Most met demise; others were simply dazzled.

Overhead, Mitral guided chirping Jinx to swerve along the funnel's fringes, manipulating Demons to accidentally fall upon themselves, most interlopers toward fatal results. "BACK, DEMONS!" The focused Gnomic chief's trouncing echo boomed, devastating a gaggle of deformed interlopers he noticed in his periphery, showcasing his vast oratorical skills. A defiant narrator with riotous reverberance. His voice, a missile of destruction. "BLASMLE..."

Blasmle did not respond. His ego already accepted the need for plan adjustments.

Oreol and Lojstania had not acknowledged velvety night's befalling. Their confidence was set upon the primary defense's whereabouts. Who would be the victor? Every now and then, they discerned parts of the Death Mist fluffing into the air here and there, for no discord could be heard. The silence unwelcoming. The bigger fluffs they observed they knew could only have been Blasmle's undertaking. The secondary defense would soon need to prepare for any fallout.

The meandrous mist floated twenty trees away, a tasseled bump of miasma above. A horn blast blew from a seeming distance.

Lojstania gave a squeeze to Oreol's hand; he hesitated to reciprocate. Both would not dare look away from the oncoming threat. Their feathery wings wafted in the slight breeze as the pair awaited another blare to command the secondary defense to charge, but the valuable signal did not emerge.

"What could have happened?" Lojstania queried. "Wait. Look."

The dewy disaster's anterior length separated, a powerful windstorm buffeted the opening's fullness, permitting the remaining frontline to scramble out in every direction. Sprites, Gnomes and Elvin warriors whose hippogriffs could be salvaged, popped out of various misty pockets racing along the foggy border toward the evading blares of Blasmle's horn as he continued with his recovering gales. Everywhere the scampering vanguard flooded under the wilderness' coverage, mounted or not. Some of the Elvin Protectors coaxed their hippogriffs downward to rescue any stragglers.

"Back, Protectors of Khun!" Mitral boomed. The second defense heeded his alarm to stand down deeper into the wilderness estate. "We are in need of Oreol."

Lojstania's heart throbbed faster and faster, its pounding, unrelenting. Not long ago, she had seen a strong and valiant defense's charge sweep across Khun's entire northern region into the milky miasma. Now that company of two hundred evaded into a dwindled phalanx of half. Each warrior tried to keep as much distance as possible from this overpowering enemy. What could have happened within for such irony?

Oreol took a breath. "Lojstania—"

The Sprite female unclasped Oreol's hand. She knew what he was going to say and did not want anything to do with his disclosure.

She fluttered toward the silent invader to a higher branch. "You do what you need to do, lover. I will do the same."

She wept with frustration. Her husband kept his emotions in check, baffling her instincts. Was he relieved or not? Oreol always liked to stay in control, which is why Lojstania never appeared to the Party these past days until she sensed her lover on the brink of collapse. If not for this invasion, she would still be accompanying him on that branch he kept sentry on, but Lojstania knew more than one life was endangered this evening. She comprehended Oreol would not be alone sacrificing for a forest all held so sacred. She had an appointment with service herself.

Alighting upon the racajaandoo's upper branch, the size of a two-lane bridge, she hoped her wings' lengthened plumage dangled over the side enough, through the slender leaves, to reap any respect from her distant spouse.

Lojstania fell into a deep trance, her tanned fingertips feeling the bark, she sought the governance her divine right permitted, what she permitted to never allow Oreol's ego to acknowledge. His scope of influence may have been the spruce, the oak, the cedar and the hemlock; but hers was quite different. The dogwood, the crabapple, and the magnolias answered her call, but her favorite flowering tree would always be the racajaandoo.

The flowering trees were just as grateful to her as the evergreens were to Oreol and the male Sprites. Maybe moreso because Khun's trees never shed their flowers during winter's passage, unlike Lorel's deciduous foliage. Lojstania and the female Sprites would absorb this shedding, in turn experiencing brownish to blackish discoloring in their verdant wings with Lojstania experiencing the greatest downturn— resembling a gathering of parched leaves.

A deep chartreuse glow encapsulated where her fingers met the fine wood. Her favorite tree's violet clusters quivered about her like silent cymbals. Countless blossoms widened, using their anthers' sentient clapping to emit a chalky substance: pollen. The anthers clapped and clapped. Clapped and clapped. The racajaandoo's pollen gathered and gathered into a crowning cloud floating above the crowded treescape; and, much like that treescape, it grew and flourished with more chalky clouds throughout, defying the rampant squalls. The loyal racajaandoos heeded their warden's pleas, obeying her. All the shedding trees were reimbursing her in kind.

The milky terror meandered ten trees away... Blasmle's antler horn blared a new command.

"How did you do that, Lojstania? I have never seen you with such strength." Mitral observed Lojstania's fine-grained cumulus' rapid trek against Khun's flagrant trespasser.

From the outskirts of Blasmle's belting breezes, amongst Khun's bending grasses, Systoli and a group of Gnomes marshalled behind their chief beholding Lojstania's chalky nimbus caking against the white, salacious sloth. They bore witness to Blasmle's thrashing gusts and gilded lightning assisting the frontline's final passage. Lojstania's massive, pollen cloud seemed successful, but bluish-yellow sparkles began to project through its caking... eventually the Death Mist would not succumb.

A different blaring from Blasmle's crooked horn: the secondary defense's battalion united like a swarm of mosquitoes rising from an unsealed vessel against a sinister spray. They stretched along the dewy disaster's length, hundreds primed. A flocking of arrows struck the building squalls' exposed Demons.

"I need to help out." Resolute, Mitral adjusted his placement within the whistling gusts his tribe found themselves struggling against.

"What can we do against a force so fatal?" Systoli inquired.

"You believe in me, Systoli?"

"Of course, I do." Mitral's companion hugged him so close from behind, nuzzling his neck. "Always have. I never thought I would see you perform such a feat as you did within that mist."

"It is power I have never felt before. We have never felt before."

"Can you tap back into it?"

"Yes. Yes. I... I know I can. I sensed something more... guard me. I need to help out. I need to focus."

"Stand back. Give Mitral room!" Systoli ordered the others.

The Gnomic chief peered up at the two higher branches knowing his comrades were performing their best, granting him a chance for his race to attest to his new awakening.

"The soil nurtures," Mitral stated, repeating a lost memory awoken.

Stunned at first, slender Systoli smiled with a warmth. His tear swept in the shrilling winds. "The soil takes care of those who have met the **end-of-seasons**."

The winds increased. The thunder rolled.

"The soil is the season where I stand!" Mitral responded to his lover, his friend, his husband.

"The soil is needed by all!"

"BY ALL!" From Mitral's toes to his crown, the primordial energy's cascade pulsated. He could envision Inner Earth's bulky, dense humus, rich with moisture and preserved nutrients, devoid of any biological possessions. His skin darkened, blackened like the humus, stunning his lover again, but Systoli held on tighter. Mitral could sense the ignored humus' many purposes, but he required gracious need of one.

The Gnomic chief beckoned the humus to encourage its plush grasses to grow west to east of the meandering madness's fringes. And so, an extensive lattice swelled into gargantuan, entwined heights. A dismissive fencing of florae bracing between the Protectors and their foe. His floral barrier, with Lojstania's pollens, would flourish, matching the mist's might.

Death's herald fought to pass.

Oreol, astounded by his comrades' actions, untied his bagging's vines, the weed weaving bloomed into a carpet, revealing the jodepiece fragment.

"Do not fail me, great Ethnel. Give me strength." The Sprite ruler rubbed a shiny facet, attempting to procure the energy secreted within. The bluish-yellow glow flailed him without pause.

Oreol's eyes bulged; he refused to accept the terror trying to own them, his fingers raking and raking upon the crystalline gem. He tried to stop his limbs' tremor but to no avail. Again, he wrenched the fragment to him and clasped it with all the stubbornness he could muster, forcing his eyes shut... his pure lips dribbled blood from multiple bites.

No matter the amount of divine right any noble displayed, Oreol knew this jodepiece's magic surpassed superior. "Ethnel, where are you? The pain is too much to bear..."

No reply. No words of comfort telling him to be more direct. No phrases of encouragement. Loneliness became Oreol's friend. His divine right, his best friend.

He thought he was quite versed in his gift until Lojstania proved him wrong. He professed himself the spiritual head of Khun because he assumed he retained the sole gift controlling arboreal life, but error reigned. No, the scope of his divine right's influence belonged to the evergreen; and, from there his power sprang from all segments of the Protectors' sanctum, bombarding the fragment and him like infinite needles of ancient energy.

And, then the menthol coldness arrived... and, oh, the unbearable burning... nothing could be more unbearable...

Oreol grunted...

Lojstania, her forehead drenched with sweat, peered over her branch down at her spouse, hoping his third attempt would not be fatal. The forest's gristly and pollinic barrier would soon collapse to Man's nefarious magic. If so, nothing would persist to impede Quirm, except every Protector's courageous will to meet a gallant demise in battle.

Obstinate Oreol held firm to the vestiges of his divine right against the fragment's final defenses. Any soothing advice from Ethnel would be valued, but soon the iciness reentered—not even the Essence of Preservation could hinder that.

The fragment's power erupted without hesitancy, a strobing without a screen, bluish-yellow sparkle flickered untamed about him. Trumpeting thunderclouds bundled and stretched; the brightest albescence illuminated the oncoming nightfall.

Mitral's hulking fence's fibrous skin could not withstand the corrosion any longer and decomposed toward a murky brown... deafening thunder boomed... splendid forks of ebon lightning zig-zagged against a gilded sky and building flurries.

"I-I cannot hold it. Man's power reaches to possess me!" Lojstania fainted. Several Sprites and Gnomes aflight dashed to assist her, others protected their hearing from the ear-splitting ruckus.

The Lorellian youths, retreating upon yipping asegafians, prepared to dislodge more arrows at all costs.

Oreol beheld all these happenings through a birthing view sparkling mystic energy. He recognized what generated the uncanny storm that strove to resist the Death Mist in place of Khun's loyal vegetation, for his divine right enhanced to defy Man's enhancement—an achievement belonging to the fragment. The jodepiece against jodepiece, Oreol hoped with Ethnel's blessings.

Mitral's unwavering barricade's links began to submit. Oreol's emerald wings quivered. Other fibrous links began to succumb in procession as gaps splintered amongst the entwined flora's deteriorating cellulose. More winds buffeted the eager, lithe mist attempting to squeeze between the gaps created. Oreol could barely hear Mitral's booming screams through the howls.

Resolute, winged Oreol ascended with the bluish-yellow glow tethering him to the enigmatic fragment, his fists illuminated with the crystal's multiple hues. Dual energy from his eyes and hands dazzled brighter and brighter, resulting in the motley dazzlements' merging. The energetic mixture exploded forth into the decaying barrier, igniting into brilliant colors. The sparkling colors swathed the browning decay causing the vegetative fibers to mesh with each other. The enchantment persisted, permeating the wilted plant skins, bandaging the mincing mist's damage. The sparkles persevered, replacing the plant/pollen fusion with consequence.

The dewy disaster could not pass. Demonic claws slashed and tore at the innovative barrier formed, at the very medium that enabled their trouncing of the primary defense.

"I... I c-can see all of Khun. I... I am omniscient..." Oreol exclaimed. He surveyed far into the east. Blasmle's blustering winds accompanied Oreol's enhanced gift in denying the milky monster any further entrance.

But, Man's magic was stronger. All the Protectors braced; the cunning evil exploited an access.

Oreol raised his arms east and west, his incorporated energy emanated livelier. Immense forks of azure lightning lashed outward from the evergreen fashioning latitudinal lines of chlorophyllic fire to sweep across the battle line's endpoints toward southern borders. The salivating flames ascended higher. Before the mist could reach over to relinquish the flickering adversary, the dewy disaster met again another rousing barrier replacing Oreol's incendiary spell.

Khun was secured, but at what cost? Mitral and his entourage alighted upon Oreol's location. The glow had waned from the Sprite chief, yet he sequestered upon the jodepiece unmoved, eyelids ajar, seated proper in a petrified daze seething with vigor.

The storm had cleared. The lively barrier surrounding the sacred wilderness endured.

As the Protectors grimaced at their important victory, a Lorellian boy, a stoic warrior and a newly determined Gnome comforted a lamenting Lojstania, her every teardrop created a new cherry bud on the racajaandoo's bulky branch. The real victor convened within reach of her kneeling form, entranced. She dared not touch him... no one did. To have overcome so much...

"... I have felt the Sacred of Khun," weary Oreol uttered. "They have spoken."

Yes, we all made sacrifices...

While much of Khun's defense sprawled throughout the northern and eastern territory, feral Rungna led the female Protectors and every beast to the western end. The female Sprites brought word that the Death Mist did not attempt to appropriate this region. Puzzled by this behavior, Rungna led her forces there to grasp the message's truth... some other force must be preparing to invade the hallowed land.

She peered across pulsating Lake Ban at the tall grasses carpeting the sandy pathway's edges the Elves had come to label the "Road."

The maiden warrioress sneered, admiring the barrier surrounding her sacred home replicating an aurora borealis. "Well, Quirm, it seems plan your has failed," she muttered within the locks of her unkempt mane.

CHAPTER 15: Black Market

Skavir, Quirm Empire.

Several days passed since Aman lost his servant and an extra night had passed since he found out she died. He didn't want any of this to happen, if not for the interference of that dratted other Elf. Pretty soon he would need to travel back to Chrot to purchase a new slave. He admitted the last one, Thalla, was quite feasible despite the circumstances.

The old shopkeeper browsed over every weapon in his shop. A probable sufficient amount to serve a portion of the Quirmean army, but clients felt prudent to trade them in for a couple of gold trinkets or have them repaired. He fostered a good living with this trade being an expert in such a fortuitous field. And why not? A veteran serving under auspices he could not remember, he could kick himself for not identifying Welbern early enough, too greedy for a feasible sale on that diamond axe. That club was unique, too.

The picture, an oil painting at the back, had fallen off the wall with an abruptness that startled him... he smiled. Yep, it had been too long since that gift had fallen years ago since his service. He stepped over to pick the painting up when he caught movement at the rear entryway. "Who's out there?"

Aman crept closer to the oaken door. The door swung ajar with a deliberate creak. Several soiled faces peered in, a peek of pointy ears became more revealing. Aman gulped—Elves! "Wh-Wh...?"

Two pricks intoxicated his exposed skin. He slumped to the ground with makeshift wooden darts stuck on his neck, gripping his painting tight.

The young Lorellians snuck in, pillaging the arsenal.

"Why do we not just stab him?" one whispered.

"It is against our nature. We are not Khun."

"Do Khunians kill? But soon we will have to kill if we are to have our freedom."

Groggy Aman could perceive the clanking of weaponry being acquired in the available burlap sacks.

"Hurry, get as many as possible. We must get out of here," another whispered. Many scampered through the doorway into darkness' enfoldment.

"Here, take these so they will not know what has happened."

In his evolving stupor, Aman deciphered a female's high timbre in the voice. When she stepped into view, she retained three lanterns and a torch in her possession.

"No, bloodsister. Do you not see? We do not kill." The apparent leader of this roguish group was male. "This Quirmean is an elder and helpless."

"Then, we will pull him out. But I insist this place be burned down."

"... Very well... Pull him out."

Delicate fingers grabbed Aman by his arms and dragged him out the egress into the alleyway's far end. He could distinguish the oil from the lamps being discarded somewhere, probably at the front ingress. The torch's set crackling was expected. The lingering scent of pine ablaze confirmed his life's work crept to a ruinous end. Silent, tipping-tapping heels scampered through the rear entrance with the scent of trailing metals.

The final lamp smacked upon the doorway's panel. Licking crimson flames crawled and crawled, searching for more and more material to corrode. Soon the rogues' sizzling work would be smelled all over the Torture House's residential city.

The lingering Lorellian bent to the old shopkeeper with a light tap onto his shoulder. "We are sorry... sir," the male whispered, melting into the shadows hastening after his impulsive companions.

Grogginess came near to claim the shocked Quirmean, his painting inert in his tightened clutch. Upon the picture's oily slick, the flames' casted silhouettes revealed aspects of a younger Aman knighted before his beloved Empress Maxis.

CHAPTER 16: Consequences

The Forest of Khun.

Rungna glared down the Road's shifting gloominess. Man had certainly selected a strategy that could have destroyed Khun, but Quirm's promptness left little desire.

She led her company of an approximate one hundred fifty down a good stretch of path with modest rests, excluding the Sprites and Gnomes' assistance. A battalion of four hundred stayed behind for her reconnaissance force. Many beasts prowled through the weeds with some Gnomes safeguarding against Man's attempts with the same idea. Rungna-Olivia ordered the beasts not to stray too far away.

A scouter Sprite fluttered frantic to her, landing on Folcen'na's head. "Rungna, the enemy is no more than thirty trees away. They are about seven hundred in number. We should begin our attack now."

"Thank you." Her infravision had already established the Quirmeans' distance up the sandy trail. She just did not know their size. For sure, Man's hubris got in the way during this excursion, believing the Death Mist would have ensured most of their work. The Elvin warrioress turned to the rest of the Protectors. "I want Sprites and Gnomes selected to attack through the weeds with the animals. Let attack your be swift. Remember the mode attack. The rest of us will follow when it is sufficient. We must direct Quirm back to the mountain's side other. Let words my pass onto them who cannot hear me. The rest of you go. The Divinity will be with us."

Movement in the weeds enhanced quadrupled wings' faintest fluttering. The Elvin maidens' infravision detected red silhouettes slinking farther away from them.

A Khunian company against a battalion—such odds.

The Quirmean battalion was very ambitious for a unit with their impressive armory. For sure, their direct mode would be a prospect to Man's advantage, therefore the ethereal Sprites agreed to Rungna's current attack strategy. Onward the miniscule army aviated, with every Khunian beast spearheading to ensure Khun's efficiency persisted grander, denying the company's weakness to the enemy.

Weapons brandished. The primary line of Sprites swarmed in descent, initiating the onslaught, biting swords slicing into the vulnerable areas of Man's panoply, infecting their adversary with the fervor flower's neural poison.

"Gnats!" a soldier yelped as he slapped where a swift soaring Sprite pricked him. Ahead, another soldier experienced a sudden fall from his stallion.

Another Quirmean ran to his comrade's aid. "What is happening?" He rolled the unconscious warrior over, gasping at the upturned eyes. "He-he's dead!"

Wings' zealous fluttering slivered the nocturnal air, veering over the alerted Quirmeans' helmets. A volley of arrows unleashed from Gnomic bows. With a snarl and neigh, the animals assaulted in their own fashion. The Protectors' preemptive offense was underway.

"Weapons!" the captain ordered. Swords, maces and all manner of Quirmean steel slashed out at the diminutive aggressors, forcing the Gnomes and Sprites to dodge about avoiding the blades' bites. Birds and insects dived into the fray, pecking and stinging Man's warriors.

Quirmeans fell dead everywhere upon the sandy terrain, unable to spot their assailants within the nightly umbras. However, some of the minute defenders could not avoid falling beneath their foe's steel. No matter the casualties, the assumed weaker force had performed their purpose of the plan: the Quirmeans faltered in disarray.

A more potent wave of darting wings with rushing hooves and paws charged onto Man's anterior phalanx as the rest of the minute female warrioresses strove to weaken the battalion with their bestial companions. Quirm's anterior phalanx whose strength focused on the primary assault bowled over. Like a battering ram, the reinforcement tore through the phalanx's center to accompany their fellow Protectors aviating about the airspace and scuttling beneath the horses' bellies. The Quirmean mares assisted their masters in keeping the predators at bay, but squirrels and other rodents slunk past the defiant hooves to nip at the steeds' legs. A buck rammed gnarly antlers upon a footman. The secondary force's incessant wave permeated the weltering Quirmean ranks.

Rungna blared her battle-cry, her horn a wee smaller than Blasmle's. With glee the Elvin females charged onto the scene. The Lorellian daughters shot their arrows prior to the Khunian maidens' arrival, infravision provided the edge needed for the juvenile archers' wooden shafts to target the red glowing marks in the darkness. Khunian metal's reflecting shine brandished high.

"They're female?" one combatant proclaimed.

"No matter. It is the threat they pose that needs to be addressed," another yelled.

Quirmean steel struck upon the Elvin maidens' opaque armor. Khunian arsenal slashed back in kind. Though valiant, the male battalion became quite overwhelmed and unprepared for the numerous onslaughts performed upon them.

From either side of the Road, Khun's loyal animals pressured the enemy. The Protectors airborne dived down and throughout the whole line, wounding many an oblivious opponent. Asegafian cats teleported the inexperienced Lorellian offspring where the youth could dagger a Quirmean or his steed without collateral damage.

Rungna's diligent warrioresses fought with all their lives to weaken the invading infantry's will. Their duty. What they prepared for. Protectors united!

Hopelessly paralyzed on three sides, the Quirmeans defended as best they could, but the constant, arising assaults kept their ranks from reforming. Their battalion retaliated harder and harder, but the Khunian company's surgical strikes would not relent; and soon, a number of the baffled infantrymen fled back down the Road while other soldiers grounded themselves and tightened their defense to allow their comrades' exodus.

Several of the beasts hunted the escapees—some of those predators became oblivious to the warriors behind them wielding Quirmean steel.

"Gnomes!" immortal Rungna bellowed. "Command the animals smaller not to attack. Let the enemy run."

Her hippogriff, falconine Folcen'na, bit along the fuller of her opponent's sword, the upper bill's toothlike notch cracking it in two, as the Khunian chieftess drove her blade to rest with abundant howling growls.

A profusion of bodies scattered around her, predominantly Quirmean, as the enemy retreated. She could let them flee, but they were liable to reform and resume another attack from the mountains' confines.

A female Sprite glided past her, the flimsy skirt decorated with spatters of blood.

A multitude of bestial responses accompanied Rungna-Olivia's growling howl as she raced Folcen'na through the ranks, barking more orders. "Hide in the mountains we will not let them! So foolish we will not be. Half of warriors my come with me to the front with shields raised. Lorellians, also! The others take to the skies! Gnomes on the Road, lead the animals through the weeds so no Man could escape onrush our.

"Do not lose sight of the quarry. To the mountains! Let none have quarter! We chase the enemy!!"

Her horn touted the battle cry again. Much like the pale mist, the entire female battalion's might surged through the stretch of land. The Quirmeans glimpsed behind and saw nothing but a flickering blackness following them through the western mountains' overcasting peaks. From Lake Ban's southwest shore toward the Nesia Ocean's northern shore, the estrogen-laden mettle of Khun overran the land, smiting any straggling enemy. None escaped the Protectors' scrutiny. From one side to the other, the rain of arrows rocketed. Quirmeans fell in line along the Road.

In view up ahead, the tremendous mountains. A copse of trees, like a pair of fuzzy footwear at the stony behemoths' base, was entered. Sprites and some Gnomes scoured the branches while the Elvin maidens upon hippogriffs rifled along the treescape.

Rungna and Folcen'na's curiosity flitted about for any dubious movements. Screams echoed from the small forest's bosom with the swishing of swords and the growling of beasts mixing with pine scents and sullied sweat.

Rungna spied a red silhouette in the bushes a short distance away. With lightning speed her arrow notched, but a startling "twang" reached her ears. She twisted to avoid any calamitous demise, but... nothing struck her. Bewildered, she glanced back. The red silhouette did not pulsate, the Quirmean quarry met his death.

Her benefactor revealed himself to her lower right wearing a creamy hooded tunic popping out of titanium array. The dark brown face of his asegafian cat bounced up and down with every leap amongst the females, its lengthy tongue whipping the air, its translucent eyes searching.

"Limbus." She stated.

He had another arrow notched and ready, his right hand held firm to Snip's beige fur. His best friend, Ploone, sped to his side upon Winky. The Lorellian prince's chocolaty, curly locks beheld a certain elegance in the ephemeral breeze.

"You would look beautiful in chases our through the Plains Dark, bloodchild," impressed the Khunian chieftess.

Ygl's son looked up at her with innocent keenness, and then, stared ahead. "I want only to be with my bloodfather and new bloodmother. And, if we have to kill for that, then I do hope the Divinity guides my aim."

"It seems you have them on the run, Rungna." Mitral and Jinx flocked to her left with Systoli and Rube.

"Get away from me, filth," she snarled. The Gnomic chief's blackened membrane took her aback a bit. She inhaled spring's moistened air.

Unfazed, Mitral continued flight with Systoli. "My fellow Protector, we are of the same pedigree. I cannot be any filthier than you, but I can see the difficulty when dealing with someone set in their ways."

Rungna growled, startling Limbus.

"Keep the enemy in your sights. I know I will." Mitral and his entourage jetted forth.

So many males entering her battalion's venture perturbed Rungna, however, she was pleased to see her companion honoring his side of the bargain to stay behind.

Her thoughts drifted to the young Lorellian prince keeping pace to her right. How strange the situation was to have youth such as these—with such courage and... and, love. But, why should Rungna acknowledge Limbus when no Khunian Elf had ever regarded children? Once, in the past, word had been rumored Khun reigned as a stalwart forest impregnated with many warriors, but every Elvin Protector, for unexplained reasons, felt the excess was sacrilegious to the hallowed wilderness—or so she recalled. With her ancient memory, the references became difficult for her to grasp. As life transpired, all Protectors experienced the gradual diminishment of the faithful race's population by hunts, weather, and other consequences because of this indoctrinated celibacy. One thing remained certain: Rungna-Olivia's tribe disliked and distrusted Man for reasons eluding her.

The Khunian chieftess shuddered imagining her tribe's beloved forest evolving into a dwelling for those evil denizens of the Dark Plains. Though eternal, she knew her race faced demise. Immortality did not supersede death. Hardened, the Khunian Elves persisted with their existence until the instance King Scall arrived with his two sons, Princes Ygl and Methelo. The Lorellians' arrival introduced to the hard-pressed neighbors such youthful, yet alien, joy since the sanctimonious teaching's birth. Yes, the Faerie Protectors beared young, but the tiny compatriots were considered too inconsequential to Elves more engrossed with combat and nature.

What important information did Rungna forget?

Rungna's toiling reminiscences returned to the pernicious battle on the Road. Some of her tribe did suffer maybe because of same-sex punishment's consequences. When this war concludes, no doubt many more would welcome passing away to a hopeful, heavenly place in the Interim, decreasing their tribe further. Yes, these youthful eager faces were needed to keep Khun's existence thriving. How nice it would be to have children.

The mountains' rising gradients hastened to encapsulate her forces. Man's forces, culminating into a ragged battalion, was in her clear view not too far away. Khun's reconnaissance units above alleviated concerns to any attacks from the slopes. The Khunian Elves may have been a small race by comparison, but fierceness coursed in their veins, including with their allies.

Another scream aroused from beyond. A Quirmean sentry tried fending off a coatl's attack with his bow. The winged serpent lunged at the warrior's arm. With a yelp, the sentry slipped from behind the gravelly enclosure hiding him, the ten-foot coatl in hot pursuit.

"Bloodsisters, keep shields your up. Look sharp."

The thickening evening ran long. The chase still bore on through the narrow winding passages between the mountains, hundreds of feet high, hindering the twin moons' luminescence. Everywhere beasts corralled around the hillocks, seizing any Quirmean prey going astray, harboring some wounds themselves. Always, those aloft made sure the intruder's infantry could not split up into wayward avenues.

The craggy peaks moved away from a focal point, producing a starry firmament in between. The narrowing passage commenced to widen inviting cool atmosphere, welcoming the blaring of Rungna's horn.

"Hold back." She led her growing brigade at a full trot. "Do you see it, friends my? It is a valley they cross. At the end of valley this must be the Forest of Lorel."

Mitral and Jinx swerved near, booming, "Yes, Rungna-Olivia. There are trees."

The Elvin chieftess bit her tongue. "A forest?"

"One as great and grand as Khun."

Rungna smirked. She did not need the Protectors' throaty cheers to know that a powerful empire's invasion had been diverted, plans foiled. Sprites swirled in the revealing moonlight intoning songs of praise with the Gnomes. Animals howled, neighed, chirped, hissed, growled and buzzed in delight underneath the overture, intermingling with the Lorellian youths' stern faces roving about.

Their strategy led rather simple. Khun's vanguard needed to confuse Quirm's forces in a way to have the Quirmeans believe the Sprites were the true attack. Man would not comprehend until late that the mighty Protectors of Khun proclaimed an equally ambitious army to match despite slighter numbers.

Rungna picked one child up, a female maybe eight years of age. Rungna almost teared-up caressing the small head, she knew Quirm would be prepared with greater brigades, more challenging brigades. She leaned to Folcen'na's right, rubbing Limbus' hood. "General little..."

Limbus permitted the maternal care. "Yes, mam."

"Those younger than you stay cannot. They must go back to Khun. Tell them."

"Yes, mam."

"Here." She handed him her antlered horn. "Blow, general little. Blow loud and clear. Let all of clan your know the Protectors have come to save them."

Prince Limbus' vigorous lungs inhaled a mouthful of oxygen.

The ranges reverberated with victory's honeyed sounds. The female Khunian, yielding the divine right to command animals, spied an eagle wheeling overhead. As she imparted the raptor a measured cry, she could not help but remember the real Lorellian general whose name resonated synonymous to the soaring wonder, and hope his Party performed just as well.

CHAPTER 17: Rose Opal

The Ogrean estate.

The cobblestone streets remained stiflingly quiet, late at dusk. All manner of revelries always concluded early enough during the twin moons' reign of the firmaments for citizens to get their needed slumber.

Pervasive streetlamps provided enough lighting for drunken wayfarers to locate their residence, or pedestrians to venture on a needed walk, or riders to relish a favored kiradoura or gryphon. A most underappreciated contribution provided by Queen Squash and her spouse, King Smush, to a thankless populace. During the day, the shining streetlamps' quartz orbs absorbed Los and Num's rays. A blackened crystal within the orbs reemitted the stored energy at dusk. These eventual emissions replicated solar illuminances upon the orbs' elaborate, granite poles, a helpful assistance against the sulfur gases' mild fogginess. Gases that spilt from the patchwork of grates throughout the estate connected to the Spring of Nesia's underground sulfuric baths. Incredible engineers Ogres were, almost on par with their sculpting mastery.

Of course, the evenings stirred brisker compared to the more arid days. The impatient twin suns soon rose, replacing Nus and Anul for new occasions in a somber estate where citizens wanted little interference in personal matters from a government wanting to perform every service possible.

To both factions' disappointment, this night would not be one of those occasions. A disquieting scream filled the foggy atmosphere, adding to the inexplicable murders occurring while the populace slept. A curse brewed afoot, some believed.

General Punok dispatched more sentries to protect the public and investigate any occurrences with better efficiency. Nonetheless, a louder scream arose from the small village circle adjacent to the royal family's Grand Spire—challenging his directive's accuracy.

Another scream blended with the madness...

From amongst those aristocratic domiciles, a lone figure snuck about, not too far away from a malachite building. The cloaked figure, too small for any Ogrean adult, dodged about nervously. Who would not be tense after hearing a preponderance of screams? Maybe the ample desert undergrowth would provide better coverage for this nervous person hiding from the squad of warriors rushing to their emergencies.

A pink opal building erected not too far away, almost two stories in height, emulating an energy signaling peace and harmony. A side wall exploded from that mineraloid home, prompting the cloaked figure to produce a diamond-headed axe from within silken folds against the cascading diffusion of colored silica and hydration.

CHAPTER 18: Dicen

Los and Num's early rays brightened my room in the guest house holding us.

I squinted at the hot sunlight. Feeling beneath my thin furry blanket, I sought assurance I rested upon the same porcelain bed I slept in from the last moonday. I exhaled. Three small dents still poked from the same spot. Every safeguard was necessary when dealing with a god of evil. My weary memory could have sworn I heard an explosion.

My Elvin hearing detected whispering from the outside hall... a rapping on my door. "F-friend Ygl, it M-Mound Gravelp with others."

Perplexed by her surprising visit when she should be in prison, I slid from the hard bed. That bedding felt nowhere near as comfortable as the plush pastures I used to nap on at Lorel. Smooth stone felt nothing like grass.

Lorel... I wondered what Man had done to my kingdom.

After donning my garments, minus my cloak, I marched to the marble sliding door, strapping on Welbern. I made sure my double-edged sword stayed tucked underneath me during my rest. Unlatching the door's hook, I slid the gate open and stepped back. "Enter."

The bluish-yellow aura still adorned a trio of surprised faces. Two greeted me with a nod.

"My, my, General, are we getting conspicuous," Kute mocked me, mussing my already messy hair.

Ding and Gravelp slid the marble door closed... everyone sported a silk cloak.

"I am being defensive. You know how dear I am in the eyes of Xurchon."

Ding scoffed, "You are?"

"Yes, Ding. I have a piece of what he wants."

"No fuss," the Ogrean Mound demanded. She pulled up a chair crafted from spotted stone, placing her royal club down. "See, Gravelp bring." From her hooded silk cloak's confines she pulled out—

"The lamp..." I gasped at the boxy item resembling a beaten teakettle.

"Sssssh. Not so loud, General," Kute joked. His massive form leaned against a grayish table molded to the wall. "You never know the large ears the God of Evil has."

"All right, but how were you able to get it?"

"Not hard. Know when Crumb wake up. Just sneak in and take lamp.

"Boulder decide to send me to my cavern instead of prison until figure things out."

"You got it from that green building... the cavern?"

"Yes. That Crumb's cavern."

"And, you did not see anything else in there? A big strange jewel, maybe?"

"No."

"You find the lamp, yet no Jode. I do not know. You did say Crumb is very cunning," I noted.

"Wait, General. Could the Sand have meant for this to be a trap? After all, the lamp was not hard for the Mound to find. Was it?"

Gravelp gave Ding an uneasy look, half muttering while observing the boxy lamp's unique features, "No. Not hard. It was near Crumb bed. Looks broken."

Kute and I, too engaged in strategizing, did not notice the dull rune trickling out of the dented lamp's serpentine spout trailed by nebulous gas.

"Anyway," I continued. "We should get started out of here fast before Sand Crumb decides anything else drastic. Secondly, there is also—" The building vapors nearly obscured my view of Kute giving Gravelp a quizzical look, alarming me. "No matter what you do, Gravelp, do not drop the lamp.

"Swen? Where are you? Is this you?"

Through the shifting gases my genie floated, resurfacing deep-rooted fondness I held for her on the Road to Khun. Her cosmic eyelets produced golden tears similar to newborn stars, her contoured hands encircled me portraying misty arms where none could be seen. "Oh Master Ygl, if not for thee and thy friends, my life would be met a most undesirous end."

Her gaseous entrails began to fill the room. She leaned upon my shoulder, tiny wisps of perfumed breath puffing. When her breasts pressed against my jodepiece, a spark jumped up, forcing Swen to glide away from me. "Oh, the Jode is such a powerful jewel, yet for any it is a most deadly tool. Oh, handsome Elf, I envy thee to have such a gift as humanity."

"Wait a moment, Swen. What is the matter with you? Are we near the Jode? Is that what you are trying to say? Or has Crumb done something to you?"

"No, none of that I must say. Thou must find out in thy own way."

"General, is anything wrong? I can barely see you."

"No. No, Kute. Swen, can you take us to where Juna is being held?"

"Tell thy friends to gather round. To the Fairy Flower we are bound."

"Everyone, here, quick. Gather your articles. Kute, can you get my cloak?"

"Of course, General."

After we assembled into a small group, Swen's delicate hands floated up farther than her abstract arm's length, spiraling a yellowish glow in their wake. "Gases floating in the air, take the Party in safety and care to where Flower Juna, so small and noble, is kept a prisoner within the rubble."

Her mystic chant concluded. Her vapors turned about us faster and faster; somehow, I could not feel the wind's onrush. The smooth marble below us disappeared, leaving us suspended in nothing more than a spinning cloud.

"Everyone, no matter what, keep your hands together," I instructed.

"Wh-what she?" Gravelp whispered.

"That, my friend Mound, is a genie," Kute boasted.

How puzzling. Swen knew about the Party's formation? How? I guess spirits can sense anything. And, to observe her hovering above us all, she really did not have any legs! More of her billowy gases flushed out from that flapping void, but not a shin could be perceived.

I, alone, heard a tingling sound. My Elvin vision peered closer through the vapors. A female, much like my genie, materialized in full stature draped in a beautiful dress of gold. She modeled arms. She had legs. "*Swen?*"

The entity rushed beside me in a flash. Her hair, no longer a silvery fibrous mane, shown the color of snow. A violent blurriness upon her face's veiled eyes flashing the color of the jodepiece's magic.

"General, what is the matter?"

"Nothing, my friend." I glanced back to see my genie had already slipped into her lamp's warped features…. the female vanished as well.

Between the fading thin layers appeared a room similar to my current residence, except much larger. From the ceiling, pointy granite structures dripped with stony curves encircling them. From within the curves, granite torches poked their fiery heads. Similar stone extended upward, fashioned to form legs of large tables, chairs and cabinets. Everywhere, captivating furniture stylishly molded of various stones. A sculpted archway loomed behind us with a handrail leading up stony steps.

"We at Pixy estate? This where Ogrean royalty meet underground," Gravelp noticed.

"Look there!" Ding exclaimed. His rough finger pointed at a pair of green hourglasses, maybe a foot tall, resting on a granite table connected to the wall in a shadowy, adjacent room through a secondary archway. In front of the murky glasses were two Pixies, unconscious, piled upon each other?

Behind us, we heard footsteps coming, fast. Three burly Ogres barged in armed with picks.

"Stop! This Mound Gravelp." Even at their princess' command, they would not halt. An Ogre with a crooked nose attacked her.

"Kute!"

"You do not need to shout twice, General. I will save my beard."

I needed to ask him what "beard" meant later...

The next Ogre's hefty pick blocked my friend's club. Every strike Kute placed upon the Ogre proved foolhardy. The Plant's brute strength was the only thing giving him a winning edge over his adversary.

The scared Mound, on the other hand, could never be a fighter. She dropped the lamp, not knowing what to do, especially when fighting her own kin. With her forearms up avoiding repeated strikes, she kicked a passing chair at her would-be assassin, striking the stinky Ogre fully on the knee. As he keeled over, the frantic female hurried past to get her club.

Kute punched his opponent square in the chest after disposing the Ogre's pick to one side of the room. Blood spurted from the tremendous wound, but the Ogre did not flinch once as the Giantic Plant hoisted his dazzled opponent overhead and heaved his victory upon his "beard's" assassin, disabling both for the moment.

Ding circled his larger adversary with Gore's threatening wave. His adversary exploited a vacant stare—the bulging spheres did not move.

"*Ding! Everyone, they do not act upon their own volitions! Do not hurt them.*"

"By Lolung-Cor's lance of strength," Kute gasped. "I have hurt innocents?"

"Yes, innocent, but remember they have immense strength," I reminded him.

Kute charged into Ding's challenge anew, leaving me to take advantage of the disposed lamp. "*Swen. We are in need of you. Save those Ogres from their possessor.*"

"*I cannot help thee, my beloved master. A stronger power is the matter. Thy sword must be used, and remember my riddles not misconstrue.*"

The riddle? I glanced at the two emerald glasses, remembering some of it. "'In a hidden green, lies the powerful Jode of unusual entity.' Those glasses. Ding, come on. Leave Kute to apprehend that last one. We have to reach those glasses."

With a grumble, the thief hurried with me through the secondary archway. Torchlight illuminated the hourglasses in the dimness.

A subtle shuffling arose from my right, a bluish aura bounced around in the dimness—a cold-blooded creature. *Ding, be careful. There is movement in the shadows.*

"Ygl! Ygl, is that you?" the small squeaky voice emitted from both hourglasses.

"Juna! It is I. Which glass are you in?"

"This one," both voices answered.

"Which one?"

"This one. What is wrong with your hearing?" the voices' baffling synchronicity responded. Another trap. How could I decide which glass held our Juna, or the Jode, when—

"Elf, watch out!" Ding attacked the shadowy creature, Gore's diamond bite tested the gnashing; then, out gleamed a crude sword.

In the torchlight, the tall creature's form became clearer. From craving forearms and tensed calves, furry tufts popped. Its skin color, darkish brown with small white spots. Long wild hair flaunted as a black crown on a horrid head. An unclear garment hung over a shoulder. Warped, ochre eyes stared down with menacing delight.

The creature's long claw reached out...

Gore wavered against the new adversary. "A ditchightl. Its touch will mean the end-of-rings probably into the God of Evil's unending bowels."

"Is it afraid of light?"

"Why do you think I know of it?"

"They were in the mines?"

"More. They used to haunt the mines and kill my **ore**. They thrive on darkness, but, even with this dim light, it should have fled."

"In other words—"

The ditchightl attacked us. Welbern blocked the crude sword's swing. My blade sensed the unnatural being's essence and vibrated with a voluntary swipe into the creature's path, placing a scar on its horrid forehead... the ditchightl melded into the shadows with a terrible scream.

"It is mad now. If we do not be careful in the frenzy, an unwelcomed touch will surely get us."

"But Welbern's bite should have killed it."

"The ditchightl has no **rings**, idiot. It is one of the worst of evil creatures."

A horrifying scream, the icy invitation to Xurchon's bowels, arose from behind. I turned to block the falling blade. Ding swung again, but the lithe creature leaped over Gore, forcing my Dwarven friend to stumble in the aftermath.

I grabbed the ditchightl's wrist before Ding would experience its unwarranted touch, shivering from the coldness of its skin. *"Welbern!"*

My hesitant blade complied happily; I shared the glee Demonslayer felt. The glee to tear into any evil creature's soul. But, a soulless one would be another matter... a low arc upward and the ditchightl fell back howling with anger, for its arm had lost a master... from the shadows, the ditchightl glared, hateful, as a new limb's bluish aura reformed.

A rabid foam oozed from the monster's jaws.

In the other room, stone crumbled and busted as Kute attempted to overpower the revived duo, falling against one of the tables. An Ogre grabbed his throat with rough fingers. In a felled sweep of both fists, my Giantic friend broke the grip, cracking his opponent's jaw with a hard left punch.

Gravelp, on the other hand, found the courage to use her club after dodging an object thrown at her. She busted her opponent above the knee cap with much regret, forcing the possessed Ogre to fall.

"Use your stupid magic," Ding warned. "The ditchightl will soon come at us."

"I cannot. Too much of my psionic energy was used on the jodepiece when we fought the Death Mist. Swen said to use Welbern."

The sneaky ditchightl's attack was swift in the shadows for such an awkward creature. I barely brought my blade up to obstruct the blow. Welbern ripped through its depraved heart's outer layer, a long murky liquid trickled with iciness down my sword arm's sleeve. Noticing the blood, I blocked the next attack with a quickness. My double-edged blade rebounded to slash through the ditchightl's abdomen. A slithering howl accompanied Welbern's pointy snout sticking out of the spotted spine.

"Well, kill it! Send it to its end-of-rings!" Ding ordered. Gore slashed off an offending claw before Ding kicked the lopped prize away.

"Welbern will act on its own accord. I have no say over my blade's will."

Demonslayer's fuller shimmered and glowed a familiar amber shine, the strange shimmering dot traveled along the runes' curves. The ditchightl shivered and tried to pull away, but Gore was quick to chop off the sword arm, both limbs' regeneration surged slower.

I sensed my blade's confusion because the soulless monstrosity did not meet the end-of-seasons; then, Welbern recognized the new quarry to be different... the amber shine became orange and fiery.

The ditchightl hissed in terror, "You shall pay, Elf." The black crown burst aflame. The granite floor steamed with the melting of soulless flesh. "Xurchon whispered for our help now, but it will be the ditchightls who shall triumph in the end. Mark my... words..." The creature's eyes melted, the ooze dripping over disfigured lips. "Ditchightls... will... triumph..." A puddle smelling worse than Ogrean odor spread upon the floor, leaving the stench of untold end-of-seasons.

I ran to the emerald glasses. "Juna, which one holds you?"

"Which one is adjacent to the royal family's Grand Spire?" both prisons remarked. "This is the only one glass here."

"No, there are two and both have your voice. One should have the Jode. I am very sure of it."

"The Jode? I see. Are Starrm and Vicstusi there?"

"If you mean the two Pixies, they are seemingly out of commission."

"Oh, my wings. I do not think that is them. Tap the top of one of these cases."

I tapped the one on the right. The left one harmonized with my tap.

"You tapped the right one?"

"I know I did, but the one on the left made the same sound."

"On the left? I see. No matter what you do, the other jar will do the same. So..."

"Break the glass," I concluded, relieving my dagger from my leg sheath. The sharp point slowly wedged a crack into the glass. "Now, all you have to do is fire your white light at this weak point and it should—"

A milky smoke emerged from the tiny hole.

"... Juna?"

"What?" asked the jar on the left, "I do not see any hole atop? Ygl, what is going on out there?"

Two pairs of sickly eyes sized me from the smoke. A grouping of crude swords replaced the vanishing fumes.

"You have done well, Elf, but our plans are not foiled." A stubby Demon jeered, its flesh of oily scales meshed and changed colors without a thought. The meshing forced him to bend over onto enlarging arms and feet.

I charged at him, ready to strike, but a tentacle ejected from the oily backside, grabbing my wrists while another tentacle wrapped my waist.

A second Demon rose upon the serpent half of her form rising with the dissipating fumes. Gore chipped away at ominous scales.

"You should try harder, Dwarf. After all, you know your sin," she hissed.

Her coarse swords turned out to be ten menacing fingers... dripping a substance from their tips. Oh my Achal, those were not blades. She produced fangs!

Her two-pronged assault swung down, shattering earth, forcing Ding to fall back onto his defensive to spare any wounds. The snaky Demon reared higher and struck down again with lengthening finger-fangs, the blades jutting up and down once with a "click," leaving a bitter ooze bubbling from the damage. "I am of the Dicen. You are out of luck."

I attempted to get away from my opponent's slimy tentacles, but the slimy suckers held me in place, biting into my skin.

The greasy Demon growled happily as his face's fabric rolled back to form a carnivorous hole of mangled teeth reminding me of Quirm's manticora. "Now my lord may continue his reign without your interference. Is it not ironic that someone with the Demonslayer and a piece of the Jode must meet the end-of-shifts so easily?"

A thousand end-of-seasons' scent filled me, my anger welled. "Not so, Demon."

Welbern hummed with voracious and distasteful content. The mangled jaws towered toward my head, providing an opening for a bright beam of Welbern's amber light to shoot through "Greasy's" looming throat.

"Aaaiiieeee!" Greasy's gargling scream seethed through the burning wound.

The Dicen turned to see its companion rolling on the ground with reformed claws on a reshaped neck.

Kute and Gravelp ran in and gasped at the sight of the new visitors. "How?"

Amber flames doused my opponent, but Welbern just kept blasting and blasting as if warding off any potential assault from my jodepiece.

I turned to assist Ding who struck again at the Dicen before it could double-up on another attack.

"No, General. Let us take this prey." Kute obliged allowing me to marvel at his use of his divine right granted to him through royalty. He grew big. Huge! His new size grew so immense and looked like the Dicen's bad ending.

The Dicen hissed in shock, aghast with disbelief as the once-smaller opponent equated its size. She reared and attacked with dripping venomous fingers.

The Giantic Plant's club thundered against the chain-linked scales, prompting Ding to join in while a nervous Gravelp kept away. The overwhelmed Dicen began to crumple beneath decisive blows.

In a final effort, the Demonic snake coiled itself around my Giantic friend before he could provide another blow; with savagery, its venomous weaponry sunk deep within his chest.

Kute bellowed an anguished cry, casting the writhing serpent against the nearest wall with all his strength. "I have been poisoned!" The unimaginable pain forced my Giantic friend to shrink to his normal size. "It runs fast through my veins, friends."

Gravelp grabbed him before he would topple over, pulling him upon her seated lap.

"Swen! Come out quick! We are in need of your aid."

"I-I cannot, Ygl. Something holds me back. I will not be able to accomplish the task."

"Try!"

"The Jode. I fear its hold."

I stared at the lamp, trying to comprehend her. Throwing my last chance aside, I approached the Dicen. Half-closed reptilian eyes examined me with impish delight. Welbern's pointy snout hovered near its heaving throat, "Save him, Demon. Can you feel Demonslayer's lust? If you favor your end-of-seasons better than what my blade will do to you, than do as I say. Save my friend."

Indigo drops dripped from reptilian lips. "Do you think I would yield to your wishes, underling? Xurchon and no other is my sire. Your companion's slow end-of-shifts is not the last." An unexpected giggle produced more droplets. "Oh no, we will keep striking upon your 'Party'... much like your

rock." With a final serpentine writhe, the Dicen froze, cracking a smile.

"Rock? Rock? What did it mean?"

"Rock is female that bore you. Nurtures you in my dialect," Gravelp answered. "She speak in my dialect?"

"Boulder. Boulder is your bloodfather. Rock is your bloodmother." I shivered with shock and pounded upon the Dicen's corpse. "Get up! Get up!! What did you do to my bloodmother? What did you do to her?"

"Calm down, General." Kute wheezed, "Now is not opportune."

"Friend Ygl, why not use jodepiece?" Gravelp inquired.

"I... I cannot."

"Why not, Elf?" Ding whispered. "Are you afraid to use it again?"

His remark, so cavalier, like he did not care for his Giantic friend. I understand me but hate his close friend? By the Divinity, he had changed through these ordeals. I would not give him the pleasure. "No... it is just I am not accustomed to so much power. Too much of it was used the other sunday..." Did he just smirk? "What is wrong, Ding? You have been acting strange of late, as if... as if, you do not seem to care what happens to any of us."

Kute wheezed, "You are a member of this Party, Dwarf."

Gravelp pulled Kute further upon her lap. "Stop. No argue. Kute attend now. Please, friend Ygl, use jodepiece if genie no come."

"What is going on out there?" Juna exclaimed.

I hesitated, studying the gem hanging on my neck, remembering all the pain encumbered upon me when such power was directed against the Demons and the Death Mist. "Kute, I cannot use all of the magic. I hope the small amount I will use would be sufficient."

"Okay..."

I kneeled to see if any blood stains drenched his fur jacket. To my surprise, there were none. My dagger opened his jacket's upper threads to provide me better proof. My piercing eyes bulged. "Kute... there are no wounds here."

"But... the poison... still flows..."

Strange. What the Dicen inflicted upon him was anything but gentle. "Hold still, Kute. If poison is in you, I am going to pull it out."

I thought about how Swen healed me and took my gloves off to allow my bare fingers to feel for the invisible wounds... telepathic contact was made with my vulnerable other-self floating aimlessly in the bluish-yellow void... the menthol coldness enveloped my hands...

Kute started to giggle before I could go further. His giggle raised to a laugh; then to a guffaw, prompting me to stop.

"What is going on?"

Concerned, Gravelp touched his cheek. "He gone insane with delirium. The venom. I-It must making him mad. Poor thing."

"No... no..." Kute chortled.

Ding rolled his eyes.

"What is going on?"

"I am sorry, General. I apologize for leading you on. You forgot I can heal already. There is no need to go through with this. No amount of Demon venom is going to hurt this Giantic Plant."

His deceit made me crack a smile. "You know, Kute, I could hit you for this."

"Ah, but you will not, my friend."

"Uhm, are we done fooling around out there?" I did not blame Juna's impatience.

"I am serious, Kute. I grow weaker with use of this power. I fear each use will be worse. Xurchon has finally weakened us."

Kute cupped my hand within burly palms. "Not so, General. Our strength and courage will keep us going. The God of Evil will have no luck keeping us deterred."

My genie chimed in. "*Listen to him, Ygl, for he speaks part of my riddle.*"

"*Swen, your riddle speaks of a sea of sand and a hidden green. Have you tricked us? A season could have been lost.*"

"*I have not. Thy mind Xurchon has swayed to make thee meet death out of his way.*"

"*But, it is the jewel's magic attraction I followed.*"

"*Many a decoy he has placed to baffle thee in this race. Lift the jewel to show the truth.*"

"*Will it affect me?*"

"The jodepiece will seek around to lead thee to where the Jode is found."

I lifted my piece. The gem dangled at first and then began to radiate its distinctive glow. In a staggered climb, the crystalline artifact rose to point farther toward the southeast, pulling and tugging on my leather necklace. "I... I cannot believe this."

"What you mean?" Gravelp spoke for the group since Swen and my conversation occurred outside their presence.

"Xurchon twisted Swen's riddle to fool us into coming here, my friends."

"Then, l-let us start out. C-Crumb sure bring trouble."

"Indeed I have, Mound." We turned to see the traitor with several Ogrean warriors at the primary archway sporting gravelly, body armor. Each one armed with either a pick or a club. Crumb's heavy form rested upon his growling kiradoura. Their armor shown loose, similar to Quirmean array.

"Crumb! You traitor to **sediments**," Gravelp challenged.

"Do you think our boulder will believe you when he sees that his **pebble** has accompanied these so-called messengers in the massacre of your own sediments?"

His foolishness bordered onto ridiculousness, annoying me. "Not so, Ogrean advisor, for those killed in this room are—"

"Ogres, Elf." He pointed behind us to where the Dicen lay. In the snaky Demon's place, the missing Ogrean bloodmother we heard about lay and next to her—her bloodchild. They had met their end-of-seasons.

The Party gasped... I gasped even more noticing the same strange tattoo on the bloodchild's nape resembled the marking on Squish's: a hood with a concave pockmark below with a dot on either side. What was the meaning of this?

Crumb smirked. "It seems like the meeting this **light** will have to be cancelled. Seize them."

The abiding warriors charged, threatening weapons at hand.

Gravelp twisted about, letting Kute's head fall on her lap. Her fists slammed down hard against the ground, the impact sending a riveting quake toward the small band. From beneath the warriors, the very grit and dirt exploded, catapulting their bodies toward the primary archway, away from us. Alas, this female sculptor's divine right, her gift from the Divinity, had been exposed. I understood why so many feared her hands and why she hesitated using them.

Her gift, her divine right: destruction. "Kute, get to feet. Fight!" Gravelp alarmed. This wonderful artist felt the need to brave this moment. She did not want herself, or anyone, held captive again.

Crumb's kiradoura attacked, glaring at Gravelp and extending threatening paws with a growl, expressing a displeasure at the Mound who hurt its master.

"Ygl, let thy humanity fly free to let the Jode's magic conceal thee."

Swen's unexpected wisdom granted me no opportunity to think. The defenses I placed against my jodepiece's awesome power lessened. In response to my exposure, a characteristic bluish-yellow light pulsated about me, covering the room within a sinister, cool radiance. The supernatural occurrence frightened the kiradoura who sensed a terrible evil's presence.

As my piece's power coursed through me, my compassionate spirit filtered within its facetted core bolstered me, restoring me. My partial humanity layered upon me, transferring some of my jodepiece's magic along the way. I churned like a spirit manifested—I became my jodepiece.

My genie continued, *"Power of the Jode spread out wide. Blanket the Party and Ogre in thy light. Let not Xurchon know where they are. Hide them. Conceal them. So, they may go far."*

Swen's chant seethed through me. The jodepiece's eerie radiance split, resulting in growing gaps among our distressed group, vanishing within us.

Juna's emerald dungeon melted away in the cool light. The bewildered Flower of fairies braced in the afterglow absorbing into her. With a rapid flutter of tired wings, she flew to our awaiting Party. "What is the matter? I heard that dratted Ogre, Crumb," she inquired in a shaky voice.

Demonslayer hummed and rattled against my piece's uninvited mystic intrusion.

Swen's billowy gases spilled out of the lamp with such content, she glided upward to the granite ceiling. "At last! At last! I feel the spell has been broken, leaving me one to be woven."

Her detached hands glided forward, gesturing, commanding her nebula to swirl around us again, a tinkling of shimmering runes accompanying... such sweet melody...

"Where are we going?" my Fairy friend asked me.

"Grab onto me, Juna."

Through the passing billows, I watched Crumb's personal sentries straggle up in confusion, fumbling for their weaponry.

"Seize them!" the advisor commanded aloud, his fists flailing at the bewildered warriors. "Do you hear me? Do not let them escape!"

Looking back and forth in fear, the unsure warriors wanted to follow the Sand's orders, yet a genie's sorcery proved just as formidable.

"Do not let them kidnap the traitorous Mound!"

"Swen?" I commanded.

As our group huddled together, Kute looked up and observed our genie illuminated by her heightened magic, my spiritual kindness shielding her. "There she is," he stated.

With my shared compassion dug up from my artifact, my piece's magic could not be employed since that part of my empathy had split six ways to camouflage everyone, leaving Swen as the sole spell caster. With a heavy sigh, I did not complain... a trace of my jodepiece flickered about her.

"Gases in the atmosphere, take the Party out of here," she chanted.

Again, the nebulous cloud spun round and round, faster and faster, yet not a scrap of Gravelp's rubble lifted. We could barely perceive our opponents. An Ogre rushed us, his eyes bulged with apprehension, but his dirty, thundering feet led him on. He leaped into the cloud imparting an echoing scream. The spinning vapors continued on their unnatural course.

Our footing disappeared from beneath...

A force within my jodepiece's essence prompted me to peer to my right in the gaseous domain. The same female, much like Swen, approached me from the billows. Winsome eyes fawned over me from the blurriness, beckoning, "Ygl, relieve me from this pain..."

Everyone turned in her direction.

"General, is this—?"

I raised a hand, signaling my friend's silence.

"... Answer my riddle; find the Jode." As the female spoke, her body melted into her gaseous ambience, her enchanting voice faded away. "Understand me... know me... the princess prodigy."

I shot an upward glance at the real Swen just hovering above us. Her eyelids not ajar, masking the bluish-yellow sparkles. Mystic energy spiraled around her outstretched hands. No, this genie could have not been that female in the nebulous billows, yet that female knew my name and the Party's goal.

"What was that all about?" Kute asked.

"I have no idea."

Juna affixed herself onto my shoulder. "Could it have something to do with Swen?"

"Maybe. She has been rather quirky. Like when she cries or shows signs of any emotions. I mean genies are not supposed to show any emotions, I do not think."

"Wait a moment—the legends, right?" Juna leaned against my neck, resting her head upon a pillow of crossed arms.

"The magic...?" Gravelp pondered, my shimmering charm mesmerizing her.

"The magic? Of course, my jodepiece's—"

"Your 'jodepiece'? The Jode?" Juna interjected. "Since when did you own that?"

"'The' piece's, General. 'The' jodepiece's. The Flower speaks truth."

"Just trying to keep it factual. Okay, I am way out of the loop here."

"Like you always do, Flower."

"Yes... yes, you are correct, Kute and Juna. My apologies. We have much to discuss. This piece's magic is now within every one of you. Before, only I could see that female within the gases but now—"

Juna interrupted, "Since your magic has spread, we can all see her. I love it. Yay!" Everyone giggled with her, enjoying the air of happiness she revived zipping about our circle of gloom. "By my wings, we can all see her. Yay!"

"Uhm, Flower, we could always see her." Kute tried being her realist.

"Oh wait." Juna paused in midflight. "Oh, yeah, we could... but not like this. Nuh-uh... No way! Not like this." Her credentials as a realist would not be taken away from her so easily. "Imagine magic in our hands."

I needed to set the record straight for everyone. "No, Juna, it is not magic in your command. It is not even magic in my command. A fraction of my humanity is within every one of you, shielding you from the awesome power of my... this jodepiece. In turn, we are concealed from Xurchon by Swen's spell."

"Our Swen wielding such power against a god?" Juna surmised.

I did not know how she could. Our genie had her own issues with the artifact.

Unexpected movement aroused in the nebulous gases. The first movement, a great gray wolf dripping saliva from a thirsting tongue. Behind the salivating beast trotted a pair of mares bearing larger sizes than any Quirmean stallion, and a lumbering kiradoura whose garlanded belly fur was a stretch of white with brown tips. "Look. The mounts."

Swen's gases withdrew from their rotating rhythm into lithe forms, twisting elegant wisps into the clear sky. Beyond the bewildered mounts, a barren land laid to view with little season to attest.

"Ouch! The ground. It is hot," I alarmed.

We boarded our mounts in haste.

"The Ty. We have returned to the Ty Desert," Kute remarked.

"And behind is sediments," Gravelp added.

There we situated, the Party of the Jode, in a terrain with almost no season, while a huge jagged wall loomed a mile northwest of us, a perceivable equal to the desert's width.

My chanting genie let her gases swaddle her. "Even when protected from his wrath, my mystic spells will cross his path. I cannot take thee very far. Stronger than mine are others' arts." Her nebulous cocoon slipped her within her boxy lamp's shelter with not a wisp trailing behind.

"*Swen...*" I wanted to share my discomfort with her about my confusing feelings for Kute and her.

"*Shush for me. We are more than three,*" she advised.

To my embarrassment, I could not disagree with her. If the group of us could visualize the mysterious princess through my shared compassion, then indeed everyone could delve into my thoughts' deepest pockets. I finally understood what my bloodfather, Scall, cautioned me about misusing my divine right. My mind felt naked to my comrades. The helplessness startled me.

"W-where we go now? Crumb b-brew many trouble."

"Where else, Ogrean Mound? To the Giantic estate is where we are bound." Oh, Interim. I just rhymed again...

"Oh no! My Ethnel. Oh, Ethnel! No!" Juna panicked.

Everyone grabbed their weapons, awaiting the oncoming threat.

"Juna, what is wrong? What do you see?"

She hovered behind Gravelp, pointing, shivering. "Her elbows... they... they are so ashy. What kind of hygiene do you **roots** practice over there?! When we get to the Treedom, I am going get you some opava butter lotion. We are not going to have any of that. Nuh-uh, no ashy elbows, Fern! No ashy elbows. Not while I am with **growth**. No way. We are going to put some lotion on that body of yours. Ashy elbows."

Famished, Kute licked his lips, not focused on Gravelp's dry elbows. "I do miss me some opava butter on a nice slice of bread. Oh yeah, opava butter..."

I steered Stonecrusher toward our southern route as Juna related her captivating tale of woe. We had much to catch up with.

Well... after she finished scolding Gravelp. "I would hate to see your knees."

CHAPTER 19: The Lake

Rykon Tower.

"That's impossible! Khun could not have resisted. The Jode's magic is more powerful."

"But, they have indeed, Rondo. I fear worst to come if we do not react early enough."

A faithful populace attended Quirm's official church every seventh day. This was not that day. In the main worshiping chamber, Emperor Rondo maintained his desperate discourses with a god whom he charged his heart to. "For sure—"

"Thy proficient army was repelled by Khunian harlots and beasts. Harlots and beasts. A grand army was repelled by females and animals."

Of course, Rondo never expected any of this to happen. The forest wasn't captured and secured for his sake. Why did these wayward Elves deny an act that would make all of Zaendara flourish in the future? How did they? Man absolutely had the means to share so much wealth. All any of these ignorant estates had to do was desist. How did they?

"Great Xurchon, you assured me that the Jode's magic was the strongest ever; it can only be succeeded by you alone. But how could Khun overcome its might?"

The handsome deity wouldn't answer.

Rondo realized something like this would occur. For the past days, he sat pondering the choice he made forsaking Istratos and Welna of the Divinity. This god had disclosed to him about the acclaim and love he would receive, if only the mythical jewel would be procured. Too much opportunity had been squandered, leaving nothing in his grasp except more grief. The rumor of rebellion made him more uncomfortable, accentuating his fear of failure and unreceptive of the love he so desired. This god, for there was no other, promised him the Jode could be procured with a divine interference more omnipotent than any other. An undeniable truth taught to the emperor at a young age when his father, Rykon II, blessed him to Istratos, the false thought... Rykon II, the absent father. A new chance must be taken. A new decision made.

"Xurchon, if god you may be, if Divinity you may be, why can you not procure the Jode?" Rondo almost regretted his inquiry, thinking it a protest.

Xurchon noticed his merit being tested. "Rondo, you must realize, no one questions my motives. A god's power is his domain and his alone."

"But it has been months and months since we have made the pact. You have nothing to prove... your worth to me."

"You dare say such words to me?" The question spilt gently, yet never departed from a tint of threat.

The son of Rykon II turned away from innocent cycs, his hand and legs performed their best effort not to befall victim to nerves, a balance must be attained and, "I mean to ask you why you have not done anything to those who have escaped?"

The wayward feelings returned again. Was General Ygl alive? Please let the Elf and Swen be... No. They must face the consequences. The traitors they are.

"I have. My Demons disposed of them well at Ty. They will not be a detriment to our plans." In fact, the deceitful visage knew not where they had gone. They had just vanished during the raid of Crumb's warriors. "I have told you where I sense the Jode to be. All you have to do—"

"That's not true."

****

"Eyes your." Cautious, Sama the Nixy teetered on rudeness, but she had become accustomed to Rondo's welcome, noticing the slight slant in his eyes.

"Of course they are. I'm of Vantenian descent. They are from the north. My grandmother was a Vantenian." The emperor gladdened his guest's distrust was easing. Mind you, she never left the comforts of his bedroom. Her beguiling Elvin appearance would've stirred much of the nobility; even moreso, the citizenry. Not even his brothers, Advisor Werkle and General Spenz, knew of her existence. Somehow Rondo felt the tall scaly female needed to remain a secret—his secret. Her innocence, quite appealing. He didn't want to hurt her.

His bedroom never changed. The countless pelts created quite a masterful vision of championship that never unnerved her in the least, however, her basin being replaced with a lagoon of his metaphysical rendering surpassed the pilose display. The potted ivy, no longer reposed upon the mantle, settled near his visitor, being fawned over, and Sama's left arm wrapped around the pot's base hoisting her head near the vines' canopy.

"You like that plant, don't you, Sama?"

She barely acknowledged him. "Yes, Emperor."

Rondo opened his palms as if parting the air. Bluish-yellow energy sputtered, allowing similar sparkles to roll along the lagoon's perimeter, generating fresh new ivies from the makeshift soil upon their wake. "I'm sorry we could not find your son... your... bloodson. Ryl was his name?"

"Yes. I would expect not you to find him. I doubt I can."

He enjoyed watching her swimming about, almost to the extent of observing a school of fish without tailfins. Something relaxing settled upon him, visiting her away from the fuss. A smile nearly crossed his face regarding himself as the visitor, like he really didn't belong in his own chambers. "You are a remarkable one, Sama."

She must be younger than him, but somehow she reminded Rondo of the mother Hethomes never was. Queen Hethomes, the scholar and athlete, who spent more occasions with his younger brother, Spenz, than with anyone. What was wrong with Rondo? Wasn't the eldest worth his mother's while, as well?

As of days before, he awaited at the bath's edge in all "his glory," his presentation never having the perceivable, desired effect.

He slipped into the pool. "Do you like the new gift I made you? Do I not take good care of you? Why have... can you not tell me what kind of Elf you are? Where you're from?"

Caught off guard, she waded away. "You are man wonderful. You know I do know not where I come from. I wish I knew. Why are you sad so?"

The Emperor hesitated. "You think I am sad? No one has ever entertained such an inquiry to me." His perfectly coifed hair and physique for a man in his fifties made him so sure of himself.

"I do mean not to offend you."

"You're not."

She found herself cornered. She may have been an inch taller, but her height did not sway her discomfort. "The lake..."

"What lake? Lake Ban? Gwion?"

"No. The lake hard on wall your." She nodded past his shoulder.

"There's no lake on the wall.... Oh... the mirror..." A rectangular glass hung above an oaken bureau adjacent to the window she'd stare out on occasion.

"Yes. Yes, the... mirror." She rose out of the lagoon approaching the glassy lake along the wall.

Rondo followed behind, admiring how her green hair draped upon her scaly skin, her gills flexing. They stood before the ornate glass, he behind her, just staring at each other. She turned to him, bestowing his temple a tender kiss; stepping behind him, her webbed fingers' sodden touch seeped hopeful wisdom into his skin. "Where there is a mirror there is love."

Her statement stumped the emperor. He tried to analyze the meaning, staring back at himself into the reflective beyond. He shook, not wanting to understand, too scared. "What are you doing to me, woman?"

Sensing his change in demeanor, the aquatic charge stepped away. "I... I... did not—"

"You've no right saying that to me. I love myself more than anyone. I've killed and maimed in the name of love."

"I-I..."

Rondo clenched her shoulders before she fell upon the large bed. "What are you? Why can't you tell me who you are?"

Sama shivered. "I do know not who I am."

An arc of bluish-yellow energy leapt from his clasping, engulfing her mind, causing Sama to convulse. And there, to his bewilderment, he saw it. It.

Xurchon never divulged to him this talisman's properties, the talisman dangling from Rondo's neck within a safe encasement—this jodepiece. When Xurchon invaded Ygl's psyche through the emperor using the jodepiece, Rondo always thought the God of Evil retained sovereignty over that scope of power, that divine right.

Telepathy? Rondo could read his charge's mind and envision thoughts she could not.... Telepathy... he could read minds?

****

"What?" Xurchon frowned, astounded.

"Because..." Should Rondo say he fears his new god's inquiries? Should he say his heart accepts what his mind cannot? "Because I need an opportunity to think this over."

"That is strange coming from one who wants to find the Jode quick enough to fulfill our pact. One measly defeat means nothing, Emperor, when thou hast a whole continent to rule over. The Ogres and Giants are soon to have their controversy. Then, we will make our move."

"Yes. Yes, indeed." Rondo maintained his breathing, protecting his thoughts with his newfound talent. *This must end. Why must I wait for something I fear I might not get? Why did the Elf have to die? Why?*

"I'll have my spy tell me of what happens. When word comes of their conflict's launch, then I'll send my forces to see that the results come in our favor."

"Good."

A reluctant whisper aroused from the chamber's entrance drifting with evil and myrfran-pine incense's scent, "My-my liege..."

"Rondo, I think Werkle wishes to have an audience with thee."

"Come in, Werkle. If you had word to say, you were supposed to stay outside."

The corpulent advisor waddled within the heavy white smoke toward his impatient superior, his gait an evident contrast from the elegant dancer on the huge bat instrumental in capturing Ygl and his comrades a while ago. "I am sorry, my brother, but a dire message was sent by messenger."

"Come on. Come on, tell me."

Xurchon intervened. "As your symbol and god, I require to know what you have heard, as well."

The meek advisor could not keep his attention off the virile god, finally turning away to a more welcoming gaze. "I... I believe, to my utmost, that the Lorel Elves begin to rebel."

Rondo bit hard on his lips' interior, his mind sought for an elusive answer. Why? Why must this happen? Could there have been an easier way?

Werkle continued, "At Skavir, the old man, Aman, who brought word to you of the sword, Demonslayer, lost his weaponry to flames set off by unknown assailants. Carts, traveling to and from the major cities, filled with weaponry, have been attacked and robbed by more assailants. I tell you, Rondo, it cannot be our own citizens."

"And, why not?"

"Thou speak for the Elves, Rondo?" Xurchon inquired.

Fear pierced its terrible sword into the emperor's heart. Hate and anger evolved with the anxiety. *What is wrong with me?* Rondo thought. *How could he be my... my god?*

"No. I do not speak for them, but against charges my own advisor had no conception of."

"Would thou like to send him there?"

Confused, Werkle blinked in the bleached entrails. "Where is there?"

Rondo didn't want his second younger brother delivered upon so perilous a search. "... All right. I concede, but he must be well protected."

"He definitely shall," the god affirmed. "Werkle, step forward. Thou hast been chosen a place of my choosing. It is where we believe the Jode to be, and if found there, it must be brought back to us immediately. Understood?"

"Y-yes, great Xurchon."

"Then, come forward." From normal size, the God of All Evil's hand enlarged, exploiting the ridges of an expanding palm. The Quirmean advisor noted the palm's conspicuous ridges converging and contracting into a vortex, a tiny bead of central light propelled into a splitting and a growing within. At first, a mahogany bark exposed within the portal, then more barks with a thicket of bushes emerged from the evading peripheries. "Go."

The short portly man waddled, his robes dragging, through the portal. The birds' twittering in the distance devolved into silence. Animals, small and large, scampered away into the underbrush. Life left no hints of any life.

None.

All had sprinted away from Werkle and the four Demonguards positioned behind him. The advisor became smug, considering the twinkle in the God of Darkness' eye... evil befitted him as well.

CHAPTER 20: Tungloc

✦

Ygl did not know what to expect during the autumnal onset underway, winter's snowy statement would not be too far behind.

He led a cavalry of six soldiers through Lorel's northwestern region. Many spoke of a monster skulking the parts killing Lorellians. He secured Steadfast, patting a soft fur as impenetrable as any dragon's scales, his precious unipegon in tune with the general's desires. No more loss of life would occur during this watch.

He hunkered a little deeper in his thicker cloak, knowing heavier clothing would follow soon along the way. Ygl never cherished the cold.

Steadfast's triple-toed claws crunched upon the russet and yellowing leaves with every slithering grunt. A crisp wind whooshed some of the leaves with orangey companions past them, daring his unipegon to take flight, but Steadfast did not take the bait.

His cavalry's mission this late day was important. The madness must end. Too many Elves were being killed. The monster must be found. Being the first general of his father's kingdom at nineteen did not sit well with Ygl, but he must do his best.

"General." His weary soldiers—such an annoyance. Three training seasons accumulated not enough a stint for a race of Elves who dwelt much upon meditations. "Our mates need us."

"Yes. That is why we are out here." The young general's unipegon loomed a foot higher than their horses, like riding a rhythmic hill. Steadfast snorted a couple of flames from an extended snout, searching left and right. "Keep your guard up, kin," the young general ordered.

"And, what about Thalla?" an older Elf inquired.

Ygl's patience was lacking. "What about Thalla? She is a grown female two seasons older than me. She can take care of our bloodson by herself. She thrived without me while the Khunians were training me. What does your mate do?"

"She meditates."

Figures...

"Why do we bother to listen to one so young?"

"*Because I am your general.*" He made sure his soldiers comprehended his telepathic anger.

"'General.' You can barely lead."

"Have pity on him!" his captain, Lyp, urged.

"*Pay attention!*" Ygl's patience waned.

Steadfast, grunting, bent forward in an instant, stretching his draconian form, scaled belly raking the ground, right clawed hooves extended; serpentine tail elevated... Welbern was already unsheathed.

Ygl's challenger screamed. The creature moved fast from the left, hidden in the foliage, almost camouflaged. Reptilian jaws, maybe two feet long with jagged teeth, attached to a five-foot-long neck, took a horizontal bite across his challenger's abdomen, pulling the older Elf off a startled horse. From the right, another creature executed the same attack.

"*Tridras!*" Ygl's telepathic sweep quickened. "*I will fight the left one. Everyone else make the other meet the end-of-seasons.*" Ygl refrained from thinking about his mother's death from another monster long ago.

Almost one story in height and width, the amphibious lizard's second head leaned in to assist ripping its initial victim apart. A splattering of blood and guts brushed against the graying skies and semi-naked trees. A third head catapulted from mid-hunch, ready to acquire Ygl for another meal.

Steadfast took flight with slender draconian wings, dodging the attack, cutting a path through the browning branches and unfading firs. Chipped bones littered about, mingling with the assemblage of decaying leaves below. Lorel's first general should have paid more attention than disputing with his soldiers.

The tertiary head spat a sour acid at the evading unipegon and rider, impeded by Steadfast's impenetrable hide. Ygl leapt off to dodge the putrid slime, lifting his thick cloak as a cover. Bubbling steam emitted from the acidic damage smelling like rotting tomatoes.

Ygl threw off his cloak and regretted not acquiring Quirmean shields. *"Be careful. They spit liquid fire."*

"How did they get here? They are not meant to be here." Captain Lyp maintained his spot.

Too late. Another soldier screamed as his sword arm fell off from the liquid battering. Captain Lyp shot two arrowheads in an attempt to defend the assailed soldier, blinding one of the plodding opponent's heads, but the other two heads slurped up the disabled soldier.

Fearless Steadfast's offense proved fierce against his adversary. The spiny knob at his tail's end smashed through the third head, tearing it asunder. Incendiary flames spouted from his muzzle, melting the water monster's second head. As he reared to deliver the final blow, a couple of waxen feathers floated from his draconian wings. But, Ygl gathered his psionic energy into a telepathic blast disabling the persevering head before his faithful mount's blow would come to fruition.

One tridra down. One more to go. Both unipegon and rider turned to assist the others, only to discover Captain Lyp the lone survivor from the amphibious ambush. Scattered body parts evoked sorrowful messages. The tridra's seeing heads carefully evaluated its two new opponents, reassessing a new stratagem. Its body's fattened girth toppled arboreal obstacles to satiate a conclusive meal, acid drooled from the blind head's ravenous jaws.

Ygl and company braced for new maneuvers as they evaded the toppling trees. Sleek Steadfast, hissing and slinking, circled around the bellowing tridra, completing the defense.

The Lorellian general observed a tree resisting collapse, a lingering sycamore, maybe fifty feet in height. The shedding tree rotated toward the passing tridra. The literal move startled Ygl, having never beheld an unhuman act so extraordinary. Wide spreading branches, heavy with leafy abundance, squeezed and tightened into sinewy limbs resembling arms and lumbering fingers. Strong hands, the bark sloughing off, clutched the defiant tridra's able heads, popping them in an instance. The blinded head shrieked in shock, spitting acid everywhere, forcing Ygl and Lyp to duck for cover unlike audacious Steadfast who spat crimson flames in return.

Earth rumbled! Earth shook! A cRaCk exploded in the crispness. The base of the tree creature's massive stalk split, revealing a mammoth pairing of fibrous soles three feet thick, rising out of the bedding. The fibrous underpinning, bugs and dirt tumbling, smashed the tridra on a calamitous track as if the amphibian resembled an uninvited cockroach.

The new intruder stared down at the surviving trio, his trunk, five feet thick, eclipsed the twin suns. The blotchy bark contorted to create something akin to a human face, a smooth light gray with peeling overlays exposed a greenish-white and yellow surface. Sporadic fronds popped amongst the natural leaves and blossoms. A fruity headdress of solitary bounty dangled. Fruits and blossoms that should have fallen off during autumn's onset. "These are my woods in this region." His voice, a thousand branches swooshing. "Do not return."

"*Steadfast.*" The young general beckoned.

Ygl's faithful unipegon slithered near the plodding behemoth, grunting. They stood facing each other for what seemed like eternity, unique wild beasts, studying each other... with a hiss, Steadfast kneeled upon the grasses, obedient.

"What is this?" Nervous Lyp stepped back.

"Hold." The Lorellian general's telepathy probed deep within their new adversary's mind, tickling their savior's vascular cambium—nothing... nothing, but tissue. "What are you?" Ygl inquired.

"Your divine right has no effect upon me, Elf. Who I am would be of no concern to you."

✦

CHAPTER 21: Spell of Demonsia

" How far do we have left to go?" Welbern sliced through a clump of dry weeds ten to twelve feet high.

"I do not know, General. Being like the rest of you. I was born in one estate and not given a map, but we will make it."

"Well, somebody better know how far we have gone or else this Dwarf is going to lose his temper." Sweat wetted Ding's ruddy face. When we fled from the Ogrean estate across the Ty, he steered ahead of us. Before we arrived to the Dark Plains, he had already left a nice path for us to follow. Panic gripped Ding; we were sure of it. And why not?

His tantrum annoyed Juna. "Oh, shut up, Ding! You are not the only one who should be mad."

"I lost my own **ore**."

"And, probably your own sense of mind. What is wrong with you? The others cannot see it, but I can. You have changed. Where is that pride you used to have?"

The weapons' hacking concluded her question. Our Dwarven thief grumbled once or twice, then fell silent. The panic stirring within him eventually ceased as the rest of us took turns sharing stories with each other about everyone's happenings on the remaining miles. Juna made sure she did not misguide our direction. She explained her innate ability to guide so well came from her knack to sense changes in the air.

"You had another dream, General?"

"No, Kute, a memory. Memories. Things I have forgotten are returning. Lyp was in it, Captain Lyp. Do you remember him?"

"Yes, the **twig** who was prisoners with me at Chrot."

"Yes, he was in it... and Steadfast."

"Your mount?"

"Yes, and a tree creature. I miss my Steadfast since Lorel's raid."

"Tree creature?" Kute's interest became more piqued.

"A tree but not a tree. Tungloc was his name."

"Talking trees? Now, you have lost it, Elf," Ding criticized.

"And, what of it, Ding?" I challenged. "Have you not seen enough? This was real. I know it, but he had to be of good intent because he killed a tridra."

"A tridra, General? That is a sea monster from the Nesia."

"Yes, in our forest. It makes no sense. Tungloc told us to keep away from the northwest region. And, we did."

Mystified, Kute nodded, impressed. "A creature with that much power? Where is he now? He would have given that mist quite a showing."

"Doubt it," Juna clucked.

"I do not know..." I resumed, "Tungloc should have lost his leaves... it was fall and he should have lost some leaves..."

Juna distracted me from my musing. "Well now, that is weird."

Gravelp let her cowl down, her hair was pinned up and braided through the middle with white opals. I saw no sign of that strange tattoo on her neck.

"Gravelp, do your sediments place tattoos on the back of their necks?"

"Some do."

"Do any of those tattoos look like some kind of face... with curves and dots?"

"I not looking at everyone."

"Okay."

"I... I do not know. Why ask?"

"I saw something. The same tattoo behind Squish's neck and the Ogrean **rock**?"

"Yes."

"... And, her bloodchild?"

"Her **stone**. She no have no **pebble**."

"Okay, yes her bloodson. Would royalty and kin, uhm... sediments have the same tattoos? Is it all relative?"

"Hmmm... no, well, yes, on occasion but that's unusual."

"What does it mean?"

"I... I do not know."

"General, what do you think it means?" Kute asked.

"Well, you know how the female was transformed into the Dicen?"

"Yes, she was possessed," Kute noted.

"No. No, she was not."

"What do you think?"

"Demonsia."

Everyone perked up.

"Demonsia?" baffled Kute asked for the group.

"Demonsia. Demonsia is more than possession. It is more than total control of any being. It is a total assimilation."

"Assimilation?"

"Yes, when you actually become Xurchon's offspring."

"No."

"Yes."

"That would mean—"

"Total loss of everything—mind, body, and soul."

"But you would have to—"

"Meet the end-of-growths, the end-of-shifts; the end of everything. But there would have to be an agreement made."

"An agreement?"

"Yes. Gravelp, do you remember how the Dicen spoke?"

"Yes, my dialect."

"The Demons who invaded my kingdom, spoke in Man's dialect."

"What are you saying, Ygl?" Juna became impatient.

"A pact was made. A pact with Xurchon."

"But those were Demons who attacked your estate." Juna settled upon my shoulder.

"Maybe some were, but... but others were assimilated kin through Demonsia. I am sure now."

"We have cults among us?" Juna began to realize. "That would mean there are factions in our estates disillusioned about the gods and goddesses."

"I think they preferred to be referred to as the Divinity, according to Ethnel."

"Yes. Yes, the Divinity. You are correct. I forgot. There you go rubbing it in my face again. It really is not fair you get to see my god when I never have." My Fairy companion picked at her cobweb boots' tattered webbing.

Kute remained determined. "They will have no such control over my Treedom."

"Stop with your believing, Kute. Reality is just a lie," the Flower retorted.

I needed to change the conversation. "Gravelp, do you reside in a pink home?"

"Home? Oh, cavern. Yes, cavern is pink. Why ask?"

"I can see it all over your outfit."

The Ogrean Mound shivered at my remark, lowering her head, covering the pink opal ring she bore with her other hand.

"I knew that explosion earlier in the sunday was real. Was is not?"

"Y-yes..."

I rode next to her, touching her hands. "I do not mean to alarm you, Gravelp."

She refused to respond to me, twisting her body farther away.

"Gravelp, you did not take the lamp, did you? You were too busy escaping to be concerned about it."

"Leave her alone," Ding growled to me from the rear.

"Okay, then I am going to ask you, Ding. Did you steal Swen's lamp from Crumb?"

No answer.

Gravelp whimpered, "It-it all my fault... all m-mine."

Kute rode to her other side, clasping her hands as well, his lighter tan contrasted with our darker hues. "It is okay, Mound. No one is here to hurt anyone or judge."

She choked a bit. "We-we h-have orphanage at m-Mountaindom for misplaced stones and pebbles. A lot of s-sediments no like idea, but we serve everyone. They b-believe misplaced stones and pebbles should fend for selves because that how learn, b-but me **boulder** and rock disagree. I go take care of orphans, show I care because no one respects my divine right. Stones and pebbles respect and like me. Sediments start have more respect for me...

"Then, one **light**, I go check on the orphans while asleep and... and saw creature in rooms..."

"A creature?" I asked.

"Yes. Y-yes like Demon... Demon we saw. That D-dicen... Eating our bedrock..."

"Bedrock?"

"Y-you say 'bloodchildren'; we say 'b-bedrock.' Stones and pebbles make bedrock. The-the D-dicen eating our bedrock..."

Stunned, no one knew what to say. Kute clutched our hands tighter.

"Our bedrock being killed by monsters." Gravelp tried not to weep.

"... By my wings..."

"I am sorry, Gravelp."

"Everything will be all right, Mound."

"All right?" Juna the Realist made sure her reputation did not tarnish. "Kute, stop lying to her. She just witnessed a massacre."

Gravelp continued, "Dicen saw me; attacked me but I too scared... should have focused my divine right more..."

"What happened, Gravelp?" I inquired.

"I... I destroyed orphanage... and... and rest of bedrock... I killed bedrock..."

"It was not your fault."

"... Squish was there."

"Squish? Crumb's mate?"

"Yes. She there; saw everything... she no do anything. I got blamed for bedrock's end-of-shifts, and she no say anything. That is why I upset. She no say anything and sediments fear me more. Me boulder and rock more upset with me. I j-just k-keep away from everyone. Better that way."

"... Your bloodmother and bloodfather..." I did not know how to reply to so heinous an act. No one knew. Why would Squish not come to Gravelp's aid with this confession? In effect, the matter would have been resolved easier.

From Gravelp's left rear, another hand touched her other leg, not too far from our clasping—Ding's. His imposing knotty hairs masked rare concern on his ruddy face. In response, her other hand clasped his.

"Kute, may I speak to you?"

"Yes, General."

"In private."

I led the mystified Giantic Plant to an isolated area twenty-five feet away from the Party, leaving Gravelp to Juna's maternal instincts.

"What is wrong?" he whispered, his sweaty chest at level with my face, the twelve-foot weeds acted like a fortress against the searing sunlight.

"I feel Ding must have stolen the lamp."

"So what. We have the lamp. Ding is thief, a very natural act in finding it and bringing it to us."

"I think Gravelp may be covering for him as he may have enabled her getaway. I could see the same pink particles on him."

"Why are you saying this, General? We are together again and we have a wonderful female as a new ally to the Party."

Our ally. True, she dealt with undeniable issues at her estate. Nonetheless, my friend's new attitude toward the artistic engineers moved me. "You no longer regard her kin, her roots, as 'barbarians'?

"Why, no. A bit slow maybe, but I can see my roots got them all wrong."

"A beard."

"What?"

"You called her a 'beard.' What does that mean?"

At first taken aback, Kute produced a broad smile, retracting his underbite. "The Mound is a beautiful female with a misunderstood spirit, but that was in jest."

"What is it?"

"A 'beard,' to put it plainly, is just a female a male marries to hide his orientation."

"Oh. What would it be for a male?"

Kute thought for a moment. "Oh, I do not know."

I stepped closer, depositing a nervous kiss upon his chest, his musk satisfying. "Could I be your 'beard'?"

He did not know what to think of me, the air between us becoming thin. He sensed the jodepiece's linkage between us and recognized my earlier, desirous admission shared with the Party. "General, you would have to be female to be one." He chuckled. "Though, with a little bit of makeup..."

His remark, an annoyance. "Kute..." I scoffed.

"Look, the Party will keep your personal thoughts between us. I think we all understand we invaded them by accident. Do not let this concern take you over. We have much at stake here."

"I am not feeling concerned, Kute," I chided.

"Oh... do not get me wrong, you are a very attractive male, but we are all fraught at the moment, especially a Mound we left to have this discussion. I do not want to say anyone is being selfish here..."

"I understand."

He laughed off the tension between us. "A 'wig'! That is what we should call the closeted **seed**. A 'wig'!" He laughed further at his witty thought.

Like a pestering insect, Juna buzzed around our heads. "Uhm, what is going on over here? There is an issue on the other side over there?"

"We are quite aware, Juna. I figured Ding and you were handling it. How far do we have left to go?"

Our guide's wings lifted her high above the cathedral of parching grasses, one hand over her brow for a better view. She swooped down, flittering about me, laughing aloud. "Yippee!"

"What is wrong? Do you see it?"

"Do I see it? Do I see it? Look, my friends, through the grasses. There! Do you not see it?"

We peered through the slender gaps the thick grasses would permit us. Something became visible.

"Mountain peaks? What does that mean?"

"That means, General, we are near the Treedom, my estate."

"The Cory Mountains?"

"You live in a forest, the Mound lives in the Ty. What difference does it make for my roots to live here?"

I felt terrible about my ignorance. Where someone thrived did not matter as long as they had a home there. "How many miles, Juna?"

"Oh, about three I would say." She beamed with pride at the Party's success. New powerful allies would be underway.

"Well, what are we waiting here for? Come on, let us move before the Ogres' threat arrives," I ordered.

Kute peered into the weeds to either side of him. "Wait, General. I fear the few miles between will have to be met with precaution."

"Why that?" Gravelp asked. Her kiradoura and Redfang growled.

From bushy eyebrows, Ding glared. "Keep low, Redfang."

Uneasy, Crater and Stonecrusher moved about, grunting.

"Intruders," I noted.

"Calm down, Hogar's Beard."

"Worse, General. Remember what is said about this plains' residents. Wickedness thrives within, and if my theory is correct, Xurchon plans to acquire the denizens' aid."

Sharp forest-born senses spotted the grasses rustling not far away. Blue and red auras slipped quickly from my line of sight. "But we are hidden from Xurchon by the jodepiece's magic."

"Then, these beasts must sense his unholy presence," Kute remarked. "And must know their obligation to such an insolence. This is nothing we cannot handle."

We raced forth on our journey's final track as fast as we could. Kute and Mound Gravelp gained distances while Ding and I cleaved any fallout from the cleared path. Juna stayed sentry on Kute's crown, ready to enact her divine right. Patches upon patches tumbled. The thick adjacent grasses rustled with more intense season. Brave Kute and nervous Gravelp held their clubs firm, swinging outside of their mounts' range. A painful sting shot up my arm signaling me to let go, but I knew if I relinquished, our ambushers would be granted a chance most dire.

Deep throated howls and trebled screeches rang everywhere, recognizing the chase.

I could see the Cories better now, emerging larger in our frantic advance. Shaped fertile pastures, so different from any I had ever seen, staggered high along the slopes. Movement, figures, shuffled about those fields, jumbling into pathways cutting between.

I anticipated Welbern would glow, producing another sadistic laugh. My blade's shine would emit a familiar amber flame scorching the weeds from existence. A hopeful energy would explode within the brilliance resulting in seared victims screeching in horror.

Winged assailants flocked out of hiding, counteracting my wish, their onslaught producing ashen skyways.

"Welbern. Do not fail me."

A magnificent plumed bird with chain-linked arms and legs led the assault, an icy breeze in summer comprised of wyverns, harpies, bats, winged squirrels and monkeys. All screeched and screamed their hatred of the Party and what we held in our possession.

A weed-schlepper patched down and rammed its blood-sucking snout into my sword arm. My eyes connected with a quartet of pale ones as gangling limbs dug deep into my skin. Twice my blade punctured its small body; it would not budge.

"Welbern, where are you?"

Was the jodepiece inhibiting my blade? I focused a telepathic blast upon the schlepper with my reserved psionics—the creature fell off like a frozen corpse.

Kute swung his bulbous club, trying to keep the winged assailants at bay. "They are holding us back. The other beasts. They are coming closer."

"Quickly, Gravelp—" A winged monkey leapt upon me, biting my wielding shoulder; I grabbed a hold of its furry neck, throwing the bestial eyesore against a mini-sphinx. The gory wound throbbed with my gushing blood. A quick bandaging with my cloak restricted further damage as I switched to my other sword arm.

"Welbern?"

A seven-foot creature with a lion's head, a goat's body and a spitting serpent for a tail bounded through the parched weeds at Gravelp. The Ogrean Mound, too busy fending off two weed-schleppers and a flying squirrel, failed to notice the danger.

"Gravelp, behind you! The chimaera!" I warned.

She could not hear me but an enlarging Kute did and he rushed over to help his "beard."

"Oh-ho-ho! Have we got some issues here?" Kute jested.

Hogar's Beard bounded forward. The kiradoura rolled into a ball like an armadillo, bowling in the hybrid's direction.

More winged creatures impinged upon me. So many...

"Welbern...?"

Juna buzzed past Kute's ear. "Kute, stop with the jokes. Grow up!"

"I am, Flower. And, quite large," he teased.

Strategic Juna darted about, striking the creatures before they expected her multiple shots. Her gift, more powerful, brighter. Many had fallen from her flaring light's searing touch. She veered down to assist Kute and Hogar's Beard when she glimpsed Ding falling from a pair of doglike beasts' attack. The canines' paws and hind legs appeared human; the head and neck, serpentine.

Redfang leapt to his master's protection, wolven fangs drove one beast down by its elongated neck. With a crackling bark, the other monster attacked the wolf's vulnerable opening.

Juna's wispy wings propelled past numerous bestial assailants to Redfang's aid. A sizzling blast struck a goosebat that thought Ding's neck a nice mark while another blast seared the second canine's hind legs. The yelping canine faced Juna with vengeance, blood coating brownish-gray fur. Juna veered around to attempt Redfang's success, four quick blasts of her divine gift pummeled the rabid creature's throat. Zooming Juna did not bother to check if the beast's wriggling form met a final parting.

My jodepiece surged within me. I realized if I could feel the surge, then the others would sense my piece's mysterious being jostling for position. My psionics maintained at full capacity, a paramount duty for my Party's safety.

Swen's chanting... I could almost hear it.

"Welbern. Where are you?"

I cut down as many creatures as I could, but my defenses became overwhelmed awaiting a rich laughter or amber flare-up... nothing. Not even a weak shine flowing up my blade... too much... my telepathy tried maintaining everyone's safety... too much...

I swung my blade, and swung my blade, and swung my blade. The Plains' denizens did not care, for to them my act made their prey a better challenge.

"Welbern..."

Gravelp's fists slammed down against the ground, her divine right vibrated about her. Earthen explosions hurled to strike or bury.

"*Welbern.*"

Kute swung a strong arm upward to knock a catlike creature off as he enlarged further.

"*Welbern!*"

The ground rumbled. A horn blew.

I screamed and screamed, collapsing upon my knees holding my head... the pain too much... too much... "*Welbern, I am so sorry. I did not mean to infect you.*"

Another winged monkey pounced upon me, tearing at my back. "The sword. The sword," it shrieked. I gutted it, tossing the monkey off me with my blade, but my grip weakened with the turmoil.

A pair of harpies swooped down, snagging Welbern. "The sword! The sword!" they chorused.

Juna set the initial harpy ablaze with a pommeling white light. What concentrated power! The second harpy snagged my blade—Kute's foot-long fist knocked the winged beast down, deflecting my blade thirty feet away.

A mini-sphinx charged toward the spot, roaring, finding itself disposed by Ding's axe.

"Your stony hide does nothing against Gore's diamond tooth," the Dwarven thief spat.

I attained Welbern and swung Demonslayer in full arcs, cutting down much of the enemy with my able arm. Many assailants attempted to keep their distance from Demonslayer's hungry thrusts, noticing the Khunian zeal in my eyes and my bandaged shoulder. Anger rattled my body.

The skyways cleared as a Giantic cavalry on colored pegasi pursued the aerial denizens. The Dark Plains' inhabitant's plan failed, their evasion tumbling the grim grasses. Throughout the field, the guffawing Giants' raid rang triumphant, razor horse hooves and sickled lances trampled grassy clods and susceptible beasts.

Within their raid's midst, I lurched in fatigued triumph, slicing and gutting passing beasts with Welbern and my dagger. The end-of-seasons simmered around me. The end-of-seasons thrived all around and I never grew sick of it, an odd behavior for a Lorellian—the price I paid being Lorel's first general. No wonder my kin, meditators, admired me with such shame.

The Dark Plains' denizens tried to retaliate with heads and tails tucked in low, or heads and claws held high, some beasts did not like the idea of the Giants ruining their play period. In the sky, a small aerial battle reigned as wyverns stormed the winged cavalry. One of the dragon's five-foot relatives snatched a hulking Giant's sickled lance from his grip. The warrior's reddish pegasus swooped around in an endeavor to confuse the miniature dragon, but the scaly head followed the winged stallion's path—a stream of crimson fire blocking the route. The Giant held firm to his reins as his mount reared. He vaulted from his startled mount onto the wyvern's neck. All the way to the meadow below the duo fought to steal the other of its season. Some of the rescuers noticed the struggle and sped their steeds to their comrade's aid with aggressive force. Resolute, evil creatures countered them. Despite the opponents' efforts, the hulking warrior disabled the wyvern with an instant skull crushing, thrusting the beast and himself upon another unsuspecting wyvern. The reddish pegasus followed along, clashing with other beasts.

"Though we lose for now, Elf, our numbers still remain unmovable deep within these plains," the harpy cackled.

I ducked fast, avoiding a spikey stick wielded in her talons. A bit of dizziness overtook me, maybe from blood loss or my psionic toll. I regained my stance, adjusting my blood drenched cloak, steadying my shoulder.

Within her wings' plumage, the beautiful female harpy sneered. "Do not think you can dodge me. We know it to be you who must expire." The desirous evil swooped again, jabbing with her thick stick and talons.

Unnatural heat coursed through me. My blade, at last, chose not to yield. An initial giggle partnered with an anguish cry. I could sense two new forces battling each other among the bellowing, my jodepiece versus Welbern...

The harpy's stick almost gouged my neck.

Welbern quivered in my grasp. *"Fight it, Welbern! Do not let my jodepiece win!"*

Chiming runes... Swen's sweet chanting...

A familiar heat coursed from Welbern's hilt though my veins. With clenched teeth, I glimpsed up through dirty, sweaty beads, checking the desirous avian's next descent—the spear's point inches away.

I thrusted Welbern upward with a mustering strength. The smelly harpy squawked her mistake as quivering Welbern sliced through her exposed bosom and spike's wood. She slid off her impalement onto the grasses beside me. Her alluring face flopped upon a limp wing. Her shadowy hair's mass, her pillow. Her nurturing chest heaved a final breath, allowing bloody, blue droplets a smooth path to stream. I could not understand how such beauty could yet be so evil.

The Dark Plains' ambush foiled. The winged assailants' lessening force turned away in eager flight. Pressed-down weeds shown paths where many a large horse jockeyed, trampled spots where many a struggle had taken place.

Ding and Gravelp rested among the strewn forms, tending to themselves and their mounts. The Mound fanned a shoulder burn probably from the chimaera. Ding tied a stick onto yelping Redfang's hind leg.

Not far away from them, I noticed the weeds rolling apart in a rippled fashion. I staggered closer, peering at what lay within—a gigantic white horse peppered with brown spots, bloody blots and a foreleg twisted beneath his bulk—

"Crater…"

For a moment, as I neared the carcass, I could have sworn Steadfast, my lost unipegon, lain there. My heart beat faster for hopes of a false image. With a swift leap, my sword carried me; the landing beside Crater, light. The Party's valued member, his end-of-seasons raged too much for my Lorellian heart to bear. His fur felt so soft against my forehead.

"Ygl, wake up!" Juna chirped inches from my ear.

"The General is fine, Flower—aAaRgGgH…"

"Ugh! What have you done, Elf?"

The Party irked from sudden pain. My groggy guard allowed my jodepiece's entity to slip through… I increased my psionic defense, protecting them.

"No, he is not, Kute," Juna retorted.

"The General will be fine." He cradled me within his bearskin vest's wrappings, my back's gashes felt like stinging needles against the hairy fabric. Sheathed Welbern lay across me. Ardent Stonecrusher carried us to a vast opening trailing into the Giantic estate as we trekked across a mile length pasture, a spacious "moat" stretching south toward the Dwarves' **Grand Diamond**om.

Chanting… Swen's chanting increased; her runes… shimmered as if decked with millions of tiny bells.

"Are you all right, General?"

"I am fine, Kute. What happened?"

"You fainted upon Crater. Do not weep. Crater was not the best of horses, but his courage and loyalty surpasses his weaknesses, which is why I brought him along to be our provisions carrier."

I stared at my friend through tears, his underbite overshadowing much of his features. "Do you not care about the seasons?"

"'Seasons'? Growths. Of course, I care, but you must remember, General, we are at war."

"Is this what so civilized a race as yours can ever dream of, Kute? War? Do you not see that we all meet the end-of-seasons for a cause?"

"I am sure we do, but this is a game we play. War is always a game. My belief is the greater the cause, the better the game. So far, my experiences with you have been of great joy. The search and fight over so infamous a gem as the Jode would bring prestige to the Giants. Now, do not think this is why I have chosen to aid you in the first place. Indeed, I sensed a great trouble in the air when the Flower and Ding entered my **trunk**'s **hollow**. I want to give all the aid I can provide in stopping Xurchon, General, even if my growth is the price. After all, this is one of the most glorious events I have ever faced in my growth. Might as well make the best of it."

Two beliefs clashed: my sympathy for the season while Kute believed the opposite. But why should I feel so upset and personal when my dire acts clashed with my beliefs themselves? I hated myself for what I had done these past sundays, committing a sacrilege against my kin's simple beliefs. The Khunians had indeed influenced my kin and me with something in common. If I could promise to not kill again...

"General, I will follow you all the way."

"Thank you, Kute."

Throughout the overrun field, most Giants trailed behind our Party. Others approached us from other directions. Another Giantic company detached from the grouping, assisting the few warriors injured from the battle.

The hulking warrior who disabled the wyverns approached astride his reddish pegasus; not even gray Stonecrusher could rival this warrior's magnificent mount. The warrior, more massive than in the sky and double every warrior's size, imparted intense strength from his bronze-like armor. "Whoa, Slab. Hold.

"Lo, Plant Kute. We welcome you back."

"And I, the same to you, Thorn, to my roots and to our trunk. How does the Tree fare?"

"Trunk": bloodfather. This spokesperson must be Kute's bloodbrother.

"He did not mind your leave earlier, for it is obvious one such as you can take care of yourself, but many cloudnoons have transpired since the parting. He is not himself of late." The bloodbrother's semi-transparent visor, reminiscent of the Quirmean captain's, hid his eyes but not the sweat streaking down his roughened jawline or the concern in his voice. The accompanying Giants shared his bloodbrother's concern with tilting heads.

"That would not be unusual for our stoic trunk, Thorn."

"Thorn"?—general. His bloodbrother, my equal.

"You misunderstand, Kute," the Thorn continued. "He struggles with something he refuses to allow anyone to see. He broods in the Hollow Royale never speaking to any of us, but we know he is in great pain. This cloudnoon, he still ruminates even when the alarm had spread of these beasts' attack. Praise Lolung-Cor, we arrived momentarily to save you and your companions." The Thorn's massive hand, the size of a medium pot's lid, flicked his bear-skin cloak over his wide shoulders. A cotton tunic covered his breastplate, the sleeves attached to bulky bracelets.

Juna buzzed by. "I could have told you that."

"I did not know, Flower." Kute remained stoic.

"That is because you look at everything so rosy, instead of seeing what is in front of you."

"Flower..." The Plant turned his attention to his bloodbrother. "We are sorry for bringing this."

"No, it was not your bringing of the evil beasts. These past cloudnoons they have terrorized our mountainsides attacking many of our roots. Leaf Dionjor has taken over but he does not seem to be the same neither."

"How is that?"

"He incites division within our ranks and roots. What we have tried to implement has been halted."

"Stop, Umbala. Stop. Enough. Enough."

I had never seen Kute so abrupt. And... and to speak somebody's name? I did not think my friend had ever done that before... wait, I think Kute addressed Ding by his name but rarely and not enough to make me remember.

Kute continued, "Everything will be all right, Thorn. Where is the Tree now?"

"I already told you. He presides in the Mount Royale awaiting your return in the Hollow Royale."

"I will see our trunk, then. If Trunk is sick, I will take control now. Please, have the rest of your warriors stay at the Cories' border. Any sign of danger, please ring the alarm."

"Come with me, Party of the Jode—"

"War?" Umbala interrupted. "Is this what your secret mission was for? To bring so glorious a prize?"

"No, Thorn Umbala." I felt a duty toward our Party and this war. A contract I should uphold, and not my friend. "Yes, war could be a heroic reward, but this is the sickest reward you will have in all your growths. Xurchon proves a threat to all races' tranquility."

Disbelieving mumbles rumbled...

"You say this Xurchon is real and plans to rule our estate?" someone asked.

"Is your god, Lolung-Cor, real or a thought in your dreams?"

... More mumbles rumbled...

"He is, but—"

"Oh, quiet. If the legendary god dares bring anything against the Giants' might, we will stand ready." Umbala's honor beamed with much needed relevance. I hoped his hubris was acceptable enough to resist Xurchon and the Ogrean might. "And, who are you to speak to us in such a manner?"

"The General is this Party's head, Thorn, and your peer," Kute advised. "The God of Evil brings grievances and pain beyond belief if he should conquer us. As the Elvin Thorn has spoken, the god seeks to steal our tranquility by throwing our estates against one another. Already the Ogrean estate plans an assault, but not of their own will."

"We wage war. We have done so before," Umbala responded.

I interjected. "This is not a threatening stance, Thorn Umbala. Do you not see what the God of Evil plans to do? The god desires your mighty estates to clash and destroy each other in an effort to make Man's rule more relevant. We tried to stop this from happening. Success was not there."

"The General is correct. The Mound... the **Fern** saved the Party of the Jode from being intertwined by the skillful trap set by a traitorous root and so the Fern is an invited guest to this estate. Is this made clear?"

Wandering eyes examined the hooded Mound with disgust. Ding stayed by her side. She pat Hogar's Beard to keep him from growling. A rider approached Umbala with the lance he lost in battle. I could not help but notice his was unique from everyone else's, double-headed and bearing streamers.

A frantic multitude gathered upon the Cory's distant fields, picking the food they planted. I could be wrong, but some of the crop did not appear so ripe, though hard to see from our perspective, even with Lorellian sight. Earthen behemoths, these mountains—hundreds, maybe thousands of feet high, dwarfing Lorellian mountain heights.

"Roots!" Thorn Umbala commanded, his sickled lance raised high. Slab's reddish wings spread wide as the pegasus reared. "Hail Kute! The Plant has returned!"

Everywhere the cry echoed. More joyful shouts echoed all over the Cories. I touched the jodepiece hanging from my neck, keeping my psionic defenses solid. This small jewel had caused so much trouble, its potential, fearsome, but this grouping did not need to see all that power. We could endanger ourselves to Xurchon's wrath despite Swen's protective spell... No chances must be taken. I stared at my friend cradling me like a bloodchild, admiring his drive but too tired to admit anything. "Well, Kute, shall we be going?"

"Of course, General," he whispered with a caring timbre, turning to his contingent. "Thank you, roots! Your loyalty is indeed strong. We must ride to see the Tree. Build your defenses throughout the border. If any sign of the Ogres become evident, you know what to do."

... A rhythmic rolling of tall grasses. Only I could hear the distinct sound over the raucous noise... singular in nature yet sounding like a hundred ants marching... hiding in the plains... marching in one direction, eluding everyone... I tried peering over Kute's bulging bicep, but fatigue and pinching wounds won. The creatures, however, lost this sunday. Stay hidden.

He steered Stonecrusher again to the Cories' entrance, a huge gulf between mountains requiring a platoon of twenty to forty guards to replace the planters on the highlands' fertile green on both sides. Flags upon triangular flags dotted these treeless mountainsides, unlike the Ogrean pennants that remained localized at the capitol. A fibrous tumbling of fruits and vegetables detailed these banners. Steeper the mountain peaks extended as we traveled closer to the animated entrance. Joyful cheers escalated with the returning pegasi cavalry. Los and Num's heat irritated little in this region.

Kute maintained a confident smile waving at the building crowds, but I could sense his awkwardness with the moment's irony. He must have felt terrible about the awful predicament he led his kin into, yet they welcomed him with rowdiness. What irritated me most was his unwillingness to reveal his feelings. Oh, how annoying this feeling called pride. His heart, too set on the mission and probably his bloodfamily. Where did his positive attitude go?

Deep thuds. Gravelp caught up with us, steering Hogar's Beard, the kiradoura's thick claws lessening the space between. "Friend Kute, what signal you say about? No see. How big estate know Ogres attack when sediments separate wide?"

Steely glares sought the Mound's face, seeking the motive behind her question and receiving innocent curiosity.

The fine ground sloped, plunging a bit as we arrived across the spacious gulf. Along the Cories' lower inclines, Giants awaited cheering aloud, and waved more thick spears and sickles in the air.

"Do you see yonder hollows above, Mound?" Kute's deep voice could scarcely be heard within the joyful uproar. High above the warrior Giants' heads, a number of dark caves dotted beyond the entrance. Beside these caves, a tiny Giantic band rallied, some being female clothed in fashionable outfits. Fashionwear hoisted by small shoulder straps, dappled with light furs and quirky patterns with matching leather strapped boots. The male's fashionwear, thicker, bolder. Whose feet would Crater's hide have the honor of covering? "There we hold great numbers of huge stones, what we call 'boulders.' I know that means something different in your dialect."

"Gravelp see..."

My straining eyes raked upward on these steep rises of land, the summits and alpine levels thrived with the pegasi riders' comings-and-goings. I did not know how long we trekked, but the Cories' bustling bosom welcomed us with delight. Injured Redfang became Thorn Umbala's passenger on Slab. Ding perched in front of Gravelp on Hogar's Beard, a reluctant bloodchild.

Faces. Happy faces. Joyful faces. Flags. More triangular flags. Such allegiance I had never seen before anywhere celebrated an esteemed prince's return home. My Lorellian senses could not handle the strong sounds echoing everywhere from the rice paddy fields to the western orchard lines to the homes. Yelling. Bellowing. The Giants' voices were quite noticeable, indeed. Giants came trickling down from their mountain homes, their "hollows," the farther we traveled just to touch or grab their missed Plant. I hoped they did not pull him off Stonecrusher. Few took notice of the rest of the Party.

"Please, my roots, let me through. I must see my trunk."

"He is loved by so many," I muttered.

"Of course," Juna startled me. I did not realize she rested upon my opposite shoulder, nestled within my hair's curls. "Kute is an ugliot."

"An ugliot? What is that? Another race of Giants?"

"Nope. He is so ugly that he is hawt."

"Hot? He burns?"

"No, silly. Hawt. H-a-w-t. He is just too attractive for his own good. Untouchable."

"Hawt?"

"Hawt."

Hawt. Despite his impressive underbite and awkward eyes, Kute's charisma did overshadow these flaws, if one referred to them as such. I knew I found him quite attractive. He grew on me in ways I could not imagine. So did Swen...

Thalla... I apologize. How could I be looking at others when your end-of-seasons happened not too long ago? I... I had no right to think this way. None. None whatsoever.

The crowd's force pushed us farthest into the estate where the Fairies thronged thickest and the mountainous pressure lessened. A jolt of dizziness overcame me from a pure air's sudden surge. Pure air—as if I stood on one of those summits. A spring breeze carried the plantations' scents. Though somewhat ripened, they still smelled miraculous. I could almost taste the fruits and vegetables. Why did Man's fields not smell this way? And this regional area should feel warmer from Los and Num's presence, but logic had given away to a more temperate environment.

More flags. And different flags, not too far in the distance from a few caves. With colorful splotches streaking as if the vegetative designs upon them exploded... odd.

Trendy Fairies soared from fields bustling with food and peaks forested with caves, each sporting the same pair of wasp-like wings as their Flower. Except for their garments, anyone could have mistaken some for ethereal Sprites or the darker skinned Pixies, but countless shared Juna's pale complexion. Some spiraled downward, creating a wreath around Kute's head. I could not, would not, shoo them away, understanding their merriness. Their bright colorful formations weaved about with splendorous rhythm.

The very air... so dizzying... so intoxicatingly pure—a wondrous welcome.

... Almost too wondrous...

A cherubic female Fairy, about the size of my longest finger, buzzed before my nodding face, staring, sizing me. Her little hands attempted to suppress charming giggles. "You are cute."

This compliment indeed deserved a grin and pleasurable laugh. I tapped Kute's shoulder. "Kute. Kute?"

His caring stare, a reassurance. "Yes, General."

"Juna. She is not here."

He studied the bumbling faces, searching for a crystalline headdress. "Do not worry, General. Knowing the Flower..."

"Where is she?"

"Up there." Maybe ten miles high, a lone mountain loomed, embellished with a wide array of unusual flowers. No fruits. No vegetables. An irregular extension of terrain separated it within a hilly cluster's midpoint. "Mount Royale."

CHAPTER 22: Dandelions & Flytraps

A sedimentary outcropping three miles high.

Ood, King of Fairies, observed the mass assemblage. As he pondered on a dandelion's puffy top, few tears rolled down his cheeks. His designer Aphronior chiton and tights matched the dandelion's nuance.

He had not seen such a spectacle since the revolt. Like busy bees departing momentous hives, his citizens amassed, agitated bees rocketing about, joining the homecoming. Not a single residence remained occupied with a Fairy, large or small. At these alpine heights, intolerable to most Giants, the Fairies thrived with the pegasi riders who traveled down from winter's snap, but no matter the season, no layer from the stratosphere bothered any Fairy who passed through the freezing degrees like milk on cereal.

"Ood?" Juna grasped the iron porringer brimming with porridge, running her finger along the rim. "Where are you?"

The Fairy king glided into the cave, beholding his extravagant wife clad in a shimmering bodysuit split below imitating a cerulean dress with ruffled hems. Satin slippers replaced her boot's fashion. A cobwebby mask and arm sleeves retained her signature style. A definite improvement compared to her arrival, except her fertile form was still blemished the same. The set of stringed crystals that pinned up her braided buns now spangled about her loosened tresses with sparse silky tassels—her headdress transformed to an exquisite hair dress.

"Are you going to revel with the crowds? I am sure you are famished." Puzzlement clutched the king when he spotted the dagger tucked in her satin belt.

"We are much too old for such frolics."

"Are you serious, Juna? We are not **twigs**."

"Well, we are close to it. Plus, I am wearing a belt. This porridge should be enough. You should go. You look so skinny. I see you are wearing Aphronior. You could not find something better?" she criticized.

"I do not think any of that was appropriate to say to me, Juna."

"Well, I did not."

A floral array carpeted Juna and Ood's lair from top to bottom with garlands of lush strawberries and mini-apples. Upon the balcony's terrain, multiple gems studded. These gems, a Dwarven trade-off for Giantic harvests, refracted Los and Num's light, painting the surroundings a rainbow of hues. Not much furnishings were seen in this or many cavernous homes since no one in the estate cared much about building. Some wickerwork abounded, constructed from weeds or bits of things found wherever possible.

The Fairy king disregarded her attitude. "I am here, my sweetness." His white tasseled shoes landed lightly next to her delicate toes, sensing tension. "They have arrived."

Juna rubbed her free hand on the wicker chair's rim. As a Fairy queen, she needed to maintain a form of graciousness, but every so often she would find herself acting so infantile. Graciousness be damned.

"Habits are hard to break," germane Ood stated.

"What do you know about habits? Oh, wait, you are an expert at staying **hollow**."

"What is wrong? Why do you act so frightened? I did as you asked. Nobody knows where you have been. They only know a disagreement had occurred between us and you would not speak to me until we had come to terms—which obviously is not too far from truth.

"Kute would have objected to this form of publicity, but we know you. Do we not? Ethnel knows, the strange happenings the Giants have been experiencing... your dagger?"

The queen hesitated, rubbing the petite chair, ruminating for something more to criticize about him. Through watery eyes she noticed the dryness in his skin, touching him with delicate fingers teeming with power—oh, he was crying as well. A gem's tangerine sheen illuminated them. "You should really wash your face more often."

"The dagger, Juna. Never do you carry one unless—"

"And, who are you to tell me what I should garb myself with or not, Mr. Stay-at-Hollow?" she continued criticizing.

"You chose to go out there. To adventure with Kute and—"

"And so I did and it was great! Better than being with you."

"That is it! You will not go back out there again. You—"

"Oh, here we go again with expecting your permission."

"Do not change the subject, Juna. What happened out there?"

"You never want to go out with me. We are stuck here always, and I think I have a right to change the subject of anything I do not want to speak about." She stomped with every syllable.

The porringer crashed upon the floor.

With a wispy flutter she jetted into the adjacent tunnels, weaving through the various forked passageways, all the while disregarding her husband's urgent calls from the gem-lit room. Juna darted over their designer Thoreus rug, woven from a caterpillar's molting, into a shady tunnel curving upward.

Earlier traumatic events she experienced returned to haunt her: the weaving tunnels resembled the Dark Plains' obstacle course, her shrieking predatory hunters replaced her husband's calling... she trembled, trying to maintain her course. Her diaphanous clothing almost crashed against the wall.

... Peculiar... some fruit appeared spoiled.

The importance behind embarking on Kute's journey was never in doubt to her. Something was urgent about it she could not delve to understand, but someone had to go. Kute knew beneath her churlishness lay a wise mind ready for purpose. To her astonishment, heralding became an unwelcomed bargain. The stress, unwelcoming.

A light fizzled from above, a bend passed; the tunnel's outlet came into view. Nova violets swayed in the breeze upon a small, grassland precipice jutting out, and a private balcony of sorts. She fell onto the grassy protrusion, whimpering. From the cave's mouth she could admire the majesty of the kingdom's northwestern estate; a **bushel**, a duke, no longer oversaw a section. A spattering of kaleidoscopic flags dotted all mountain ranges with the traditional.

The crowd below caught her attention. Somewhere amongst that crushing band of citizenry, a prince trudged on with an Elf, an Ogre, and a Dwarf to attain the Mount Royale. Juna knew Kute's fortitude in speaking to his father deserved much credence, but her confidence never waned as long as her fretful companion's innate character did not paint such a positive outlook. Kute needed to stay honest as well as her, Juna the Realist.

"There you are." Ood caught up with her on the bedrock structure, his chiton's panels flapping. "Do you know how difficult you are? You pull me in with your antics just to keep biting and biting at me until there's no more of me left. I will not tolerate it. Do you hear me? I will not."

"You are not allowed here. You know you are not," she snapped, still ambivalent about embracing her cherished honesty.

"My Flower..." A small group of Fairies caught them off-guard. She wanted to snap at them too, but weariness won the gambit. A male spoke for the group sporting a yellow tunic with lime-green ruffles as a trailing midline. His long, gloved hand held his mate's black gloved one. "We apologize for our intrusion. We were going down to celebrate the Plant's return when we had seen your appearance. I tell you, we are happy you came to terms with Tree Ood. All the Fairies were worried."

Juna composed herself. "... Thank you. That is very kind of you to state... Please do me a favor and gather all the Fairies to the assembly room once the festivities end. I have a proclamation to make that all must hear."

Bewildered, the male Fairy initiated a quick bow for the group before they flew away. "Yes, my Flower and Tree."

"You are brave, my sweet Juna," calm Ood stepped farther out of the tunnel's shadow, his chestnut hair's straw highlights tussled in the high-altitude breeze.

"I always know who the jerks are."

"How?"

"Because I am always the most attracted to them," snarky Juna stated.

"I guess you lucked out on this one."

CHAPTER 23: Tobacco

Nacar, the Treedom's capital.

Mount Royale and the surrounding mountains' shade was a relief from the unbearable Ty's pounding heat. The kin's crushing flow had steered us up a rise of land onto a grassy trail. A mile and a half onto the mountainside, a Giantic phalanx of fifty guarded the trail, long spears pointing outward in the direction of the surrounding agricultural landscape, saluting a Plant's return.

A striking male Giant strode to him upon the purest white pegasus, triangular shield at hand, another strapped upon his back with a battle staff and sickled lance. Maybe twenty seasons older than Kute, my friend gave the clean-cut silver-haired male certain favor. Something rang different about this Giant—no yelling, no screaming. He remained calm and would not keep his serene gaze off my friend.

"Kute, who is he?"

"That is my shield bearer."

Kute turned to address the parade. "My **roots**, this is the end of the road for you." As he spoke, the cheers diminished to a slight. "I must now go converse with my **trunk** about my journey's happenings."

His kin paid no mind to his desire, too excited about his arrival; prompting the guarding phalanx to act before our passage. Lances barred the frenetic parade from our ascent. Despite the crowd's tremendous pressure, the phalanx's barrier held.

Our mounts galloped around a bend's ledge—sharp lance heads pointed threateningly at us from the widening path's opposite end. A secondary phalanx of forty guarded a jutted cave embellished with the most splendid greenery nature would provide. A curtain of striped-blueberry vines fashioned the cave's door; other fruits and vegetables garlanded the thirty-foot archway. This rough platoon did not appear welcoming, in formation like an impassable wall. They reminded me of Thorn Umbala, not a hint of joy on their hewn faces.

What a mess...

Kute's palm swung out, warning. "Hold, companions. These guards seem to not approve of my arrival."

Behind us, a squad of warriors wavered from their resistance against the enthusiastic parade.

"Stand aside, guards, I am here to see my trunk."

The unwelcoming platoon's stern faces regarded each other. "We are under orders not to let you pass," one remarked.

"Why... why, that is preposterous. I am his sprout. Let me in." Grunting Stonecrusher trotted toward the menacing lances with Hogar's Beard and reddish Slab following. The shield bearer, not too far behind.

"Move!" Umbala threatened, but they would not.

"Wait, Kute."

The Plant raised his palm again. Stop. *"What is it, General?"*

"Let me see if I can scan for your bloodfather." With fortunate ease, my free thoughts drifted through the apprehensive platoon. I restrained myself, at first, sensing the unexpected evil inhabiting their minds. Kute glanced at me, sharing the same psychic rapport.

"W-what that...?" Nervous Gravelp asked. Our Party sensed everything.

An opening emerged within the rapport. I did not bother blocking it, sensing it was of a noble grace. *"Help me, Plant..."*

The plea sounded weak, but surprised Kute caught the essence. *"... Leaf..."*

I traced Kute's urgency down the psychic stream to the voice's origin. The harmful entity, sensing my telepathic assault, projected tons of infernal foulness at the Party's thoughts. I maintained the advantage.

"General..."

"I know."

"This is not possible," Kute objected.

The rear phalanx tried impeding the parade's approach around the bend. We glanced at everyone with confusion.

"What wrong, Ding?" Alert Gravelp rubbed the cool shell coating Hogar's Beard, easing the tense kiradoura, clutching the Dwarven thief.

"Do not ask me, Ogre," Ding retorted, readying Gore. "I am not gifted like the rest of you."

A screech erupted from beyond the vine curtains. *"Aa ThHhOoUuSsAnDd CcUuRrSsEsSs UuPpOoNn YyOoUu AaNnDd YyOoUuR DdIiVvIiNnEe RrIiGgHhTt, EeLlFf."* A lanky, double-headed Demon bounded out of coverage upon a nebulous equine. The first head belonged to an elder Giant, a small clear gem held his thin gray beard's tip, his lengthy, emerald robe dangled off the steed's rump. The second head manifested the stork-beaked Demon.

Anxious Gravelp squeezed Ding closer, "Great Falvanch!" the thief struggled like a cranky bloodchild.

Leaf Dionjor could not fight the ensuing demonsia. "G-guards! Attack them! They are spies from the Ogrean estate!" A gnarled finger displaying a pair of melted rings pointed at us. Sleek boots kicked the nether hide faster.

The platoon could do nothing but obey.

"General..."

"Y-you do not need to repeat yourself, friend." I slid off my friend, the southern wind tickled my wounds.

"I am sorry. General, why can they not see the Demon?" Kute grabbed a shield from his bearer, readying his club against the onslaught.

"Magic is against us."

The oncoming crowd halted in awe at the siege. A plump female screamed when a sickled lance deflected off Kute's club. Pricking lance heads nearly slid Hogar's Beard off the path's ledge. The defiant kiradoura would not dare rise for fear that it would lose its passengers. Ding followed my lead and leapt off to parry with the lances.

"Stand down!" Thorn Umbala commanded, handing Red Fang to the shield bearer's possession with a massive sweep, careering between Kute and the assaulting platoon. The wavering squad behind us rushed to defend their Plant's honor.

With elegance, I bounded upon an opposing warrior's lance and kicked him in the face before somersaulting over him, minding my wounds. *"Kute, try not to kill them."*

"General. Use your magic. The Demon gives my warriors pernicious skill never warranted before. I do not want them to meet the end-of-growths."

The Demon cackled. The Leaf expressed grief.

The crowd mauled upon the possessed platoon, but none were able to attain the Leaf. A phalanx warrior that did reach him turned to attack our allies. The Demon possessed all that came near it!

Stonecrusher started kicking his razor hooves before wounds could succumb him, his hefty wings hoisted him above everyone, riderless. Umbala leaped off Slab into the fray's center knocking many over, his strength, immense. With a mighty punch, he knocked ten assailants down, disabling them.

Hogar's Beard reared up with nervous Gravelp clinging, his bear-like claws swiping.

From behind us, a couple of those motley-colored flags unfurled, infuriating some of the mob. A squad of our allies turned in an attempt to suppress the flags' existence, resulting in another massive fight on the precarious trail. Kute, seeing the new ruckus, grew to an approximate height without hurting everyone on the ledge; however, there was not enough room. The crowd below performed their best effort to cushion the fallen.

The dashing shield bearer raised his battle staff.

"Stop! What are you doing? Leave those roots alone," Kute implored.

<Hum...>

Welbern?

An evil essence lingered within my psychic field. I barely dodged the Leaf's lance as I dashed beneath his mount. A sudden chill pulsed through me as Welbern arced toward the scaley right side.

"NnOo!" My adversary tried dodging the blade known well, but Welbern would not be cheated its prize, kissing the demonic side with amber flame on the following sweep and slicing through the thick lance. "XxUuRrCcHhOoNn,

SsAaVvEe MmMe. DdEeMmOnSsLlAaYyEeRr DeFfEeAaTtSs UuSs. TtHhEe RrOoOoTtSs KkNnOoWw." A plume of amber smoke and entrails spilt from the incision.

The Giantic onlookers shook their heads as if they had experienced a nightmare witnessing the Demon no longer enshrouded.

"Look, my roots! A Demon!" Kute signaled.

With the Demon's psychic spell disrupted, the warriors charged the abomination.

In defiance, the cornered Demon's gnarled hand choked the groggy Leaf's throat while trying to smother its smoldering torso. "None shall come near me." The defiant horror pulled on the nebulous mare's reins. "Not even the Cories' power can help you as long as this worthless trash is within my grasp."

Why did my jodepiece's magic become useless? Swen was too scared to use her magic alongside my artifact, believing my piece would drain her, making her evil. Fraught Welbern would not be able to react quick enough to stop the Demon while struggling against my... the jodepiece's essence. My spiritual link maintained minimal control thriving within the piece, too busy protecting my mental faculties. Everyone's troubling predicament was my fault.

... A movement behind the fluctuating doorway... a weighty roseate figure resided within, behind the striped-blueberry vines...

Hollow cackles echoed throughout the Cories' range. Opaque eyes lined with feathers and scales sought skyward. The puzzled Giants gawked at their bewildered visitor. The Party's stare wanted answers from me—I shrugged my shoulders.

Sweetness' trace gently tugged my psionic field. *"What is it, Swen?"*

"The entity of the Jode made that laugh, thy advantage could be its gaff. Only Plant Kute would know the ideal to make such a threat seem real."

The stork-faced Demon rasped. "Xurchon, is that you?" Its nervous mount, appearing more brown mare than nebulous beast, began to pace.

Kute studied my gaze as if something lay hidden he never noticed. His tired rugged face studied the Demon...

I shivered. Someone found interest in me. I could feel their presence. Their stare's eeriness pierced deep...

Ding turned away. Now, since when was Ding so concerned about me? Okay, granted the fight in Chrot, but that was another matter altogether.

"Master Ygl, thy memories the Party knows, for far into them has gone thy soul." Swen's voice, a sliver in the sending.

I tagged onto her clandestine transmission. *"What are you saying? Do they know everything about me?"*

"From prior the day thou started to walk to many and many other thoughts."

After her answer, I sealed my thoughts from everything, clutching Welbern's hilt tightly. I could not believe they violated my privacy without my permission. Everyone else did not bother me, but Ding stoked my concern. Ever since the beginning he had shown a dislike toward me and the Party, yet he still chose to partake in this mission. Whatever he withheld from us, friendship alone could not undo. Who knew what secrets he pulled out of my mind he would use against me.

I gulped. The Dark Plains' denizens bled too much out of me...

Kute's blonde beard shaped his smirk. "Demon, that is not your Xurchon."

"Do not trick me, Giant. I know my master's voice when I hear it." Welbern's amber flame ate throughout the creature's searing scales gnawing up its torso toward the choking arm's pit—and, not a lick of flame touched the advisor.

"Can you?" Kute challenged. "Demonslayer's bite slowly steals your **growth**. And you think your mighty god is coming to save you? No. That is the Cories' power ringing out its victory over you. You should have not come."

"Liar!" A clawed hand throttled the Leaf's throat tighter. "See if your mountains can help now. Xurchon said there was no such thing."

Dionjor's side was exposed to the weedy curtains. The hidden figure's position, unclear.

Tobacco? I could smell tobacco.

I advanced. "If you believe such a lie then I do not think you would be stealing the horse-creature."

Xurchon's bloodchild steered his mount my way, averting its attention from the creeper curtains. "Why Elf, you do—"

A sickled lance's bloodied point pierced beneath the unwanted visitor's right chest. The logical Leaf took the attack's advantage, pushing the maddened creature off him and racing his uncovered mare to awaiting arms.

An ebony pegasus with gray flanks trotted out the cave, transporting a disgusted Giant almost the brawny mount's size. Both glared at the Demon while the Giant puffed from a crude pipe. Maybe forty-eight seasons in age, the Giant and his pegasus displayed an endless arrangement of black braided hair and beards studded with gems, a blending with no origin. Of great width and proportion, the Giant puffing on pipe of fine tobacco seemed a superb match to Mountain Smush. No doubt. Tree Erosc entered the fray.

The ebony pegasus gnashed hefty teeth at the struggling Demon, pawing razor clawed hooves at the intruder.

Erosc's red eyes glared beneath his stately brows' mysterious shade. "What is the meaning of this transgression? This creature... where did it come from?" His eyes, a red moons' pairing, surveyed the crowd for an answer, meeting with his bloodson's blue. "Sprout, you know? These starnoons you have left my side to go on this expedition. Was it you who brought this misfortune?"

Everyone expected an answer from my friend who stood solemn within his kin's enclosure gaping at the unwanted visitor. The air did not feel comfortable, yet smelled so pure if air could.

"It is true," the burning horror shrieked. Amber flames grazed near the heaving chest, flickering higher and quicker as a scolding for such a lie. "He has brought the end to your Treedom. The Ogres come to war with you." Clawed hands dug farther into the blessed soil; the long neck stretched as far away from Welbern's caress possible. "Listen to Xurchon..." Demonic words gurgled with blood in a welding throat.

I almost smiled at such torture. Let your end-of-seasons be slow and very painful—what you deserve.

"Allow Xurchon's words to guide you... He is the way..." the creature gurgled. Before Welbern could finish devouring, our unwanted visitor vanished in a bitter wisp taking the terrible essence with it. The ground lay pure.

Purposeful, Erosc rode forward, his narrow, red moons sized me in hopes of remembering me. Mound Gravelp fidgeted. The Giantic Tree did not like her strange behavior prompting the other Giants to criticize the outlandish guest mounted upon her low-growling kiradoura.

"Are you of Giantic blood?" Erosc seemed to twitch on his saddle, evaluating her dark pigment.

"By legends, **sediments** and I related to you."

"The Fern means 'roots,' Trunk," Kute clarified.

The onlookers mumbled louder, spreading the news. Many began to fret at Gravelp, yelling at their king for orders to have her imprisoned. Guards advanced toward the Ogrean exile. Ding and Hogar's Beard stepped up their defense.

Kute grew ten feet facing the advancing guards, booming. "No one will lay hands upon this Ogre."

Thorn Umbala, the shield bearer and I joined Slab landing next to them with injured Redfang baring menacing teeth. I had never seen Kute so angry. The guards withdrew. The angry crowd silenced.

Erosc stopped to examine the two of us again. His eyes' redness, a halo edging around a dark gray—the ruddiness, frightening. "You dare threaten your roots, Kute. They welcome you with elation and you speak to them in this way? You go out to explore Zaendara in hope of finding races such as these, leaving your roots and I behind to be menaced by the Plains' creatures. I have felt much grief these past cloudnoons."

Thorn Umbala interjected. "You gave him the permission, Trunk. Kute—"

Mound Gravelp, quivering, held her club high for all to see, mystifying the Giantic king.

"What is this?" Erosc queried.

"We-we share same c-club," she answered. "Club b-belongs to Ogrean royalty. WH-why?"

"Yes. Why, Trunk?" Kute supported her. "Why do I own a club from their estate when we have never met?"

Erosc shook his head, exasperated. "I... I do not know the meaning of this? The Fern is to be under our protection until we get to the bottom of this matter."

Leaf Dionjor trotted next to their Tree. "Yes, Plant, many a strange thing has happened. It was not until your trunk fell silent on his throne did I begin authority over the futile plagues offending our Treedom."

"Would that include the plague you placed against our community?" Umbala challenged Leaf Dionjor.

"... I did sense the Demon trying to control me. I prayed for Lolung-Cor and Pyty's aid... it did not come."

Erosc took a puff from his briar pipe's long shoot. "What I wish to know, Kute, is why this war with the Ogres? Where did this Demon come from? And, where, by all that is mighty, are the Divinity?"

My jodepiece's sudden piercing made me twitch. Kute glanced at me for an answer as I fiddled with my piece. Did the piercing hail or defy evil's god?

CHAPTER 24: Dear Daddy

Northern Lorel.

The frightened squirrel scampered around the birch, sustaining its bushy tail ever so high from the intruders. The rodent remembered when Elves used to mill about this part of the forest... the tiny head reacted to the next infrequent rustle, an arrow struck the branch the squirrel bounded from. Scampering up the bark faster, the skittish squirrel evaded yet another one.

"We both missed it, E'alor." The lean, built female laughed to her leaner companion.

"That's bad for you, Jonas. You're better than me."

"Well, my arrow did come closer."

The inseparable friends jockeyed their horses farther under the lime canopies discussing the past days' events, very cooperative with each other since youth. On the recent raid of Lorel, they tracked the Quirmeans with a few followers. They continued in the northern region alone these past days because Jonas wanted to search for more Elves, hearing a whimper by a pond, but found no one. She never listened to anyone's decisions despite being such a nationalist at heart. E'alor and she had become excited about their new environment. Being raised in Gablen's city life, they never got the chance to experience the forest. Today, they broke away to explore—and to plan.

"Did you hear any more word of the Elvin rebellion?" she muttered.

"It's getting stronger. That's all I know. They are getting ever so enthusiastic about freedom." The horses traveled to Lorel's outskirts facing a minor township fifteen miles away. "Their population is so small compared to us. They don't even match up to a fourth of Quirm."

"It is spiritual tenacity that keeps them strong," Jonas replied.

"They're meditators. They don't believe in spirit." E'alor rolled his eyes.

"Don't forget what happened during the raid on Khun," she countered. Jonas knew very well how the tenacious Khunians resisted with everything in their archaic arsenal—and they were female. Her zealous heart's beaming at such news shocked her. She wondered if she could master similar bravery someday against her father's erroneous ways.

Nonetheless, Xurchon, Quirm's new belief system, weighed heavy upon her. Her people. Her country was in danger, and she knew it. Jonas' followers and she must remain hidden in this region believing in no god or goddess in case Xurchon considered detecting them. *"Believe in yourself and you will succeed..."* She thought to herself. "Yes."

"What, Jonas?"

"No-nothing, E'alor."

"Maybe Khun will be the extra strength Lorel needs to give our empire quite the shake."

"I sense a cruel war coming our way, my friend. One I believe will destroy many lives." She didn't like the idea, but if war became real, then she'd face the mishap boldly. Her brother's mishap should be avenged and Rondo's reign must end—no matter the circumstances.

"Don't worry, Jonas. If we lose, then we'll do as the Elves have been doing—"

"Die trying." Jonas' eyes shut as if trying to block out the phrase. "You're right. We've no other choice. After all, we have to show the Elves who's better at this game."

They laughed.

"Come, Princess. We've a rendezvous to complete."

The friends galloped back into Lorel's waiting foliage.

CHAPTER 25: Jumbling Bananas

" Opava butter..." Kute drooled as he slid a slice of wheat bread into his mouth, chewing with delight upon the buttery mixture. "It has been too long."

The homecoming merriments continued through the night with no reveler fancying leaving Mount Royale's banquet hall. Overgrown grapes spiraled like purple and white stalactites from the hundred-foot ceilings, dripping luscious orbs like oil on a slick from the fruity chandeliers to greedy fingers. Hops-laden beer spilled from gilded chalices. Entrenched bonfires scattered about, grilling a meaty assortment dangling from ten-foot poles.

At the gala's head, Gravelp and Ding sat at the Giantic royalty's master table to King Erosc's right, with Kute next to his father. The royal family's remnants joined them to Erosc's left, minus Queen Fabia and another empty seat. The stoic, shield bearer aligned behind Kute's family with other shield bearers. The Party members did not bother changing clothes, except Kute, who sported a flimsy attire. Hogar's Beard lay next to Gravelp, accommodating her nervousness.

A smaller banquet table positioned to the master table's south with a presiding trio of quieter personages. Hats exhibiting wide floppy rims overshadowed the personages' faces.

Boisterous Kute bellowed over the ruckus. "Mound, eat your meal before it gets cold."

She blinked between Ding and him. "Your horse? Y-you cook?"

"Crater? Of course. My mount met a superb end-of-growths. He should be honored like all warriors. Eat."

"... You eat your... sediments?"

"Of course—"

She batted her eyes again.

"—but only if they met the end-of-growths in battle. There goes the honor," Kute affirmed with confidence.

"B-but why?"

"Do you not see it? Their end-of-growths sustains our fervor. It rejuvenates us. It is a gift they provide to my **roots**. The gift of battle. Eat. What an honor." He hugged her, pecking her head. "You are so beautiful."

"You think?"

"Of course."

Awkward Gravelp hesitated at first, but she did not want to offend Giantic custom. She bit a little piece, appreciating the absurd spices added, assuming the central pyre must be Crater's. "Ygl okay?" she asked.

"Yes. Yes, the General definitely needs his rest with those nasty wounds. He fought well this cloudnoon."

"Hope he fine."

"The General should be. The **chloro**s are providing a special tea with their medication. How was the opava lotion? Did it feel nice on your skin?"

"Smooth. Tell Flower Juna 'Thank you' for me."

"I will. In its solid form, opava provides a different effect.

"Trunk, I guess Stem will not be partaking in the festivity?"

King Erosc focused on the corn on the cob churning in his teeth. "You are twenty-five growths old. You know your stem... I do not understand why you came back."

"I was bound to, Trunk. I do not understand—"

"**Stickots**!" A disturbance. Shouting. Chalices spilt over, beer streamed across steel tables. A group of Giants pushed four others to the opposite end of the hall. "Get out of here, stickots!"

Giants on the other side protested with supporters, defending the foursome. "Plant! Plant!" the dissenters yelled.

Kute rose slower than Umbala. "What is going on?"

"What 'stickot' mean?" Gravelp patted her growling kiradoura.

Kute's shield bearer sidled closer between his master and her. "'Stickot,' Fern Gravelp, is a gay slur."

King Erosc grumbled. "Know your place, Shield Bearer."

"The Shield Bearer is mine, Trunk," Kute defended. "What do you mean, Bearer?"

"The LGBT are not allowed to sit with the heterosexuals, Plant. They are segregated to the other side." His firm whisper, smooth.

"...Well... I do not see what the problem is..."

"You believe gay roots should be separated from their hetero friends? Even at your hollowcoming?" his bearer asked.

"... Well, I do not... but I-I do not see the problem. We are all here having fun. Are we not?"

A gay Giant threw a punch landing hard on an offender. A fight ensued, the dissenting sides folding upon themselves. General Umbala shifted nervously. Kute froze in confusion. Ding laughed.

Erosc sucked on his cob. "Do not move, Umbala. Allow them their fight."

Gravelp intervened. "Y-you allow this, Plant Kute?"

Ambivalent, Kute glanced at a frustrated Umbala. "Trunk...?"

Umbala clenched his fists. "Trunk. What you do is wrong. We must have order. This is Kute's celebration."

"What did they expect, Sprout? They do not act like either of you. Their audacity..."

Gravelp mumbled, shocked at the disastrous affair. "Segregation? Cannibalism... Me barbaric?"

Altruistic Kute stiffened between his father and guest, his mind's wheels spun in constant flux from the critical messages pouring in. As if in automatic, he grabbed his startled shield bearer, depositing the debonair Giant before him, the riot growing wilder in the background. He studied the bearer's silver crew-cut, angular jawline, and passive gray eyes.

"Wh-what are you doing?" the bearer muttered. "What is wrong?"

The Giantic Plant clasped the urbane bearer's face with open palms...

"N-n—" the bearer tried stopping him.

Kute leaned in with puckered lips.

"No!" The bearer flipped him onto the table, a clean sweep.

"It is preposterous what I am hearing these cloudnoons." Erosc strode down Mount Royale's cavernous halls lined with apricot aromas and metallic furnishings. Kute performed his best to catch up through the streaming creepers wrapped around iron-cast torches coating the walls. "Kute, you are twenty-one?"

"Yes, Trunk."

"You are of age to be my Thorn. You are a good warrior. Be like Sifya and know your place. She is a master seamstress."

"Sifya has destroyed too many spinning wheels of late."

"You know Aphronior is taking her under a fellowship?"

"Really? Well, good for Sifya. A superb designer one cloudnoon."

"She could make a nice cape for you. Damn those Dwarves and their issues."

"Yes. The Grand Diamondom is having quite an unrest over there."

"There are hollows that need more of those torches they forge. Damn them! Maybe we should go and take them over. I will not barter any more grain with them."

"Oh-ho-ho, Trunk! Let the Dwarves have their moment. I am sure their roots will work out their issues."

Erosc beamed. "Look at you. You and your pragmatic thinking."

"I only want the best for everyone. Dionjor is your Leaf."

"You would definitely make me a fine Thorn, then. Speaking of which..."

Leaf Dionjor approached from the lower hall. His emerald panoply's frilled breastplate resembled a falling frond. "I am sorry, Tree Erosc. He is waiting in the foyer."

"Yes. Yes."

"Who is coming, Trunk?"

"The Bushel of the North. He has come to share new crops with me. He farms the best tobacco, a new one, tangy flavored.

I do not know how he does it, but I need that crop so my divine right can duplicate it."

"And, their coffee." Kute agreed.

"Yes. Yes, we definitely need that for the hangovers. Now, back to these strange roots we are supposed to meet—"

"Trunk, roots are roots. Let them be—"

"No. I will not let this be, Sprout. How can someone be so preposterous? To call yourself something different from anyone else? It is unheard of. Dionjor, where were we supposed to meet them?"

The royal family entered Mount Royale's spacious foyer. A grandiose display of the estate's plantations matted the auspicious area. A mixed group of twenty Giants awaited their king. Several embracing in some form or another.

Dionjor gathered himself. "They call themselves LGBT: lesbian, gay, bisexual and transgender, Tree... Ahem... here, Tree. We were supposed to meet them here."

Kute spotted another person, an aloof male, resting fifteen feet away from the courageous grouping on a promium couch covered in furs. Promium, the strongest metal in the estate, could only be used for shaping broader items. The dignitary laid a parchment upon an end table. An opposite end table displayed a large conch shell. A hat with a wide, floppy rim overshadowed the visitor, though an adjacent brazier's flaming uncovered a face blushing with modesty.

Kute gasped... the Northern Duke had indeed arrived.

The meeting between the LGBT and King Erosc did not go well. He found it hard to accept two persons of the same sex loving each other, feeling it would lower the troops' morale and weaken the military. However, Prince Kute and Leaf Dionjor encouraged him to accept the faction in order to maintain their estate's clout with the Dwarves and Nixies.

The Northern Duke had no choice but to partake in a meeting coinciding with his, also joining the call for inclusiveness. Erosc relented, but relegated the openly LGBT citizens to the position of shield bearer, which met much resistance that year. For example, the bearers refused to partake in any tourneys, therefore closing the events down. In reprisal, King Erosc decreed LGBT unemployable. No plantations were allowed to hire these disobedient scoundrels. None did— except his closest friend, the Northern Duke.

"Kill them with kindness," Kute advised. "They are the majority. It is a new growth and I do not want to see you or they harmed."

He admired the duke's plantations, the largest in the estate. The northern Cories flowed closely along Inner Earth's equator, granting the duke's many crops wondrous prospects. Kute knew his advice carried fault against the reputable notable's knack for civil disobedience. The duke's refusal to wear armor ruffled him little because Kute knew he could affect change.

The enigmatic duke studied his kind visitor's revealing face. In return, playful sunshine unmasked the notable's facial aspects beneath his floppy hat's umbrella rim. Upon fields buoyant with passion fruit, cool breezes bounded from the Nesia Ocean brushing them, carrying the western plantations' peppery scents.

They kissed. Deep. Passionately. Nothing; no one could see them hidden amongst the jumbling banana trees, the coffee and nutmegs. The positive duke toured paranoid Kute around the northern region. They surveyed the Forest of Khun's emerald treescape as the duke related a plan to journey within the neighboring estate to acquire lilies tasting like brown sugar. To Kute's astonishment, this amiable dignitary was quite ambitious and defiant to King Erosc's authoritative doctrine involving independent travel: nobody journeyed alone. Nonetheless, the couple strolled through the tobacco plantation cultivated on the region's leeway side where cooler temperatures and more privacy reigned. Mint plants discovered in the Ty desert were brewed with the tobacco for a special taste. The duke prided in his achievement. Kute marveled at the dignitary's impudence—such direct action.

He did it. The Duke defied King Erosc. No one did. In contrast, the Duke simply wanted better things for the estate he knew Kute's father would not permit without conquest. Bothered, the Duke almost regretted their kiss. Kute promised to keep their secret.

Hand-in-hand, they stood in the wheat and barley fields farthest west, admiring one of many steel statues erected throughout the region. The thirty-foot monument in this field resembled Kute's father. Kute knew the duke had to negotiate with the Dwarves for these metallic masterworks, a concession indeed to drive King Erosc's irc. The compassionate prince, however, did not report these items to his father.

The Northern Duke's betrayal still did not settle well with the Giantic king. How could his closest friend harbor those repugnant people? A lesson must be taught. When winter approached, Erosc's divine right coupled with Advisor Dionjor's gift kept the kingdom's crops alive—except the northern plantation's.

"Let them struggle..." Erosc stated.

The following summer, the duke's employees harvested the fields like any other in the Giantic estate, and they flourished. The phenomenon astounded Erosc so he took a cavalry with him to the northern region. The noble dignitary led the skeptical king throughout the plantations, disclosing a project in progress with the bananas' ashes, another Dwarven negotiation best kept under wraps. No hand-holding. No kissing. Oh, the duke would not dare. Erosc did notice the royal statues erected and felt a bit disturbed but rather flattered. However, the large fruity monuments were a quirky touch. Why have such disturbing aesthetics?

He leaned against an oversized plum in the tea fields when he overcompensated his strength upon the structure. The plum moved, revealing a slightly dry boundary beneath. Astounded, brawny Erosc lifted the weighty plum aside to find sixty tons of wheat buried in an underground steel silo. Flabbergasted, he ordered all the fruity monuments destroyed and the hidden grain burned. Hellish bonfires razed along the mountainsides as if Inner Earth experienced sporadic indigestion.

How dare the duke negotiate alone with the Dwarves without consent and hide this grainy treachery from him? How dare him.

That winter, the disappointed king enacted his same punishment: the northern region remained barren. When spring arrived, the Northern Duke's workers returned to their plantations—not a single harvester fatigued.

These wintry punishments partook no effect whatsoever? Unsettled, King Erosc returned to the northern region with a larger cavalry, and Kute participated. The king's cavalry searched high and low for hidden grains. They searched in the burned pits. They searched in hidden caves. Nothing was found. Finally, they arrived in the stark wheat fields, his metallic statue looming like an unnerving aristocrat. He almost teared up staring at the grand edifice—then, he wondered... After growing forty feet in height, he lifted the thirty-foot wonder to notice nothing underneath. Just solid ground, no grain-filled pits. He replaced the alloy statue and turned to hug his close friend; and with a wave of hand, the austere ground presented an eerie yellow glow. Wheat. Long slender stalks of healthy wheat sprung from the earth to greet Los and Num.

Proud Erosc tapped the statue's vertical panels; something fell out—something granular. He could not tell at first because the wind caught the item. He glanced back at the stoic duke whose overshadowing hat hid any emotion, and he glanced back at the panels. With his gifted strength he tore at the alloy panels, bending them further to find more grains, wheat grains, trickle upon his leather boots and with the wind, getting snatched in his bejeweled beard. In an angry fit, he ripped the panels asunder, drowning within a granulated sea.

From the granules Erosc bloomed to a twenty-foot height, maintaining his senses, glaring down at his stoic betrayer. "Destroy all these statues. Burn all his fields. All of them." The maddened king ordered.

"Trunk. You cannot possibly mean that." Desperate Kute attained his father's height.

"Yes, Sprout. I do. Let the other Bushels see the price to be paid for betrayal. I want to see the twin suns' flesh embracing these mountainsides. Burn them."

And, the pegasi cavalry did. Throughout the night, coronal flickering set the northern territory ablaze, resembling a halo for the Giantic estate.

This horrific action concerned the other dukes but raised much of the populace's sympathy. Protests stirred throughout the kingdom all spring and summer; by midsummer, the northern region raised another triangular flag replacing the normal flora printing. Instead, the tumbling flora exploded upon the fifteen-foot flag in a kaleidoscope of colors, a defiance.

"What is that sound?" King Erosc tried dining with his family. His daughter, Princess Sifya, ran late for breakfast. A boisterous racket on the roadway beside Mount Royale reverberated louder and louder. The males proceeded to investigate from the hall's veranda. Multitudes upon multitudes of Giantic folk paraded upon the roadway past his citadel, protesting his treatment of the northern region, confronted by counter protesters.

Kute's initial enjoyment watching the mixed multitude became replaced by concern, for he noted the defiant flags spotting the parade.

Erosc muttered obscenities he kept his family from hearing.

When the largest, polychromatic flag arrived, Kute's concern turned into apprehension. Upon a bleached pegasus, Powder, the Northern Duke traversed, never appearing worn-from-tear in his ashen, designer garb embroidered special for the occasion. His floppy hat turned ever so at an obtuse angle, leveling toward the family's veranda nearly two miles high—his quiet eyes engaging his lover's.

"They threaten civil war, Tree," Dionjor advised, regarding the indistinguishable pairing amongst the colorful hoopla.

Erosc's anger could not be contained any longer. "Slaughter them all. Let them meet the end-the-growths. Slaughter them, and may Lolung-Cor and Pyty have pity."

Bisexual Kute could not let such a travesty occur. He would not forgive himself... Too much. Too much unneeded pain had been placed upon citizens who wanted to do nothing but love. He struggled hard. How would his father react to his disclosure? His desire for his father's treacherous best friend? "... Trunk..." Kute struggled with his words.

"Slaughter them all!"

The iron door swung open before anyone could depart, slamming against the earthen wall, almost knocking the solid door from the Dwarven rafters. Kute's sister stood at the ingress, twice her size; her ample breast reduced to muscle.

"Sifya?" confused Erosc queried.

"Trunk, my name is no longer 'Sifya.' Call me 'Umbala.' My name for now on is 'Umbala.'"

＋

Kute awoke on his bed, a premium frame swathed in animal furs. A squadron of four guards guarded his shackled shield bearer at his bed's foot. Umbala sat by his side. "Wh-wha' happened?"

After reminded of his body slam, Kute insisted on being left alone with his offender. "The Shield Bearer is a conscientious objector. The Bearer does not believe in fighting. There is nothing to fear here."

General Umbala obliged his brother and left with the squadron, closing the iron doors.

Kute slid to his bed's side, clutching the superalloy edge, staring at the torchlight dancing upon the bear-skin rug. "I... know who you are."

"How could you ever forget, Plant?" the bearer probed.

"I understand the General now—memories are returning to me. Ones I never thought I had... I... I did not mean to offend you."

"What were you thinking?"

"I was not... but I will not apologize for trying to kiss you in front of everyone."

Stunned, the bearer shifted a little. "You... offend me..."

"I believe in you."

"You believe in yourself more than me. I am not you."

"We are a more diverse estate."

"Look around you, Kute. Remember what happened at your hollowcoming. Your hollowcoming. We are being segregated."

"Is that not what you wanted when you raised your flag?"

"... That flag was meant for visibility. To show our roots LGBT will not hide anymore."

"But, you are hidden? Are you not? The 'heterosexual' hero who came down to save the cloudnoon."

"... You had no right," the shield bearer shifted a bit, uncomfortable, looking for the right words. "You did not start change for the LGBT roots. I did. You took advantage of that rise to come out yourself, yet you expect me to be like you."

"I thought you'd be grateful, at least. I believe in the best you—"

The dashing bearer continued his measured critique. "You capitalized upon the shoulders of others. Raising your status. You are fraud, Plant Kute. That is your shame speaking, you know. You wished you were down there with the crowds... with me..."

And, there it was. Guilt. Guilt. Each generation wished it could be like the other. The bearer, older, affecting change, yet frozen with fear. And, younger Kute whose innocence blinded him to further that change. Fear stifled one while ignorance the other.

Kute grabbed his shield bearer, kissing him, deeply, passionately. Blond whiskers brushed against silvery stubble, moist mucosa searching deeper upon the other. For a moment they embraced alone, separate from everything... everyone...

The bearer glanced downward, away from him. "The sad thing is I still... care for you. After all that... I still do."

"And I care for you."

"No. You do it for the glory. You always do."

Kute turned away, wanting to explain his wish for a better world. A jumbling banana fell upon his open palms. He clutched the quavering fruit whose evading vibrations unpeeled it. He had Advisor Dionjor cultivate sporadic clusters about his room like sacred chandeliers. He wished he could span the distance between the clusters and he, revisiting that blessed day long ago. Now, he understood his advocacy at Khun—his attempt to mimic his lover.

Things could only get better...

"What is my name, Plant?" the older Giant's voice, calm, sweet. "That is the least you could offer me. Who was I?"

Kute struggled from the confession. "... You are Shield Bearer."

"What is my name?" the calm bearer pressed.

"You are..." Kute struggled against his shame. "The Bushel of the North..."

Stunned again, the Northern Duke repeated himself. "What? Is? My? Name, Kute?"

The Giantic Prince hesitated, the dancing torchlights mesmerized him or maybe he wanted their dance to transport him away, from everything... "... Alduur. Your name is Alduur."

Alduur caressed his lover's face, the jutted jaw's stubble, so familiar. "I quit," he whispered.

"You cannot. You know what they will do to you," Kute insisted.

"I will take my chances."

Kute stiffened. "... You are my shield bearer. Know your place."

CHAPTER 26: Binary

66 Gracious Tree and beautiful Flower," in the great assemblage, many regarded the winged emissary. "The Giants are preparing for war."

Fairies alike debated over the subject, their clamoring voices saturated the echoing cavern. Some loitered amongst the plant life, their colorful apparels camouflaged well with their silent companions. They almost occupied the cavernous lodging past its upper limit, surrounding a small waterhole akin to a large lake to their tiny populace.

Juna and Ood observed the attendees from a pebbly pedestal jutting upward from the waterhole. From the far reaches of the assemblage's dark patches, to the winged groupings scaling the hedges; to the late arrivals encircling the open ceiling, Juna observed thousands of concerned faces who reciprocated similar looks. Los and Num's rays provided ample brilliance.

"We must start moving to the front lines with our allies." Stated Ood.

"I know," Juna mumbled to her husband. Her hopes that the Divinity would appear and stop this nonsense had gone past her particular threshold as well. Believing belonged to Kute.

"You did your best. They know you did. This war is not your fault."

Juna fingered her dagger dangling for her glimmering body suit as she pondered a rematch with Gasma.

Ood resumed, "Shall we begin?" His affirming hand grabbed her nervous fingers. "You can always stay."

"And miss all the excitement? No. I already tried to hide from the responsibility once. I am as much a leader as you. If they and you go to fight, then I do as well." Somber Juna looked at her calm husband with a hardness.

He did not return the gesture. "I know."

Their unfolding wings fluctuated like iridescent flowers, hoisting them above the assemblage. The couple quieted the clamor with dazzling white and black power exploding from their clasping hands.

"Well, what are we waiting for?" Juna yelled in the echoing cavity, reminding her of Chief Mitral's divine right. "Do we sit here and let the Pixies provide a fighting edge over the Giants?"

"No!" a middle-aged female in a ruffled collar remarked, darting up with clenched fists. "Great Flower, we will fight our ancient foes."

"Then, go to your hollows and grab your weapons. Hide your sprouts and twigs. If ever a moment in your growths you believe in your heritage, let it be now. Stand proud my roots. We will be victorious. By Ethnel, we will win!"

In unison, the clasping hands' surging explosion rocketed upward like a comet as if saluting the stratosphere. A blinding stream of flashing power blanketed the Cories' summits. From the Assembly Room's zenith, with a windy gust preceding, the assemblage erupted forth.

"Come, our roots! Come together! War!"

CHAPTER 27: Choice

✦

The Forest of Lorel.

Thalla arranged her tools. A bottom step had broken earlier in the day, and she gladdened no other issues arose with the spiraling stairs crawling up the sequoia. A solitary trio of sequoias comprised the Majestic Treehouse, a triple-tiered structure constituting satellite tenements spanning throughout. Since age ten, she knew the daily importance of inspecting her royal bosses' wooden constructs. Rot or insects could damage the wood; rain could rust the metals. Her father and she made sure not to build the stairs any higher than eight feet to prevent accidents. Hammers and nails. Hammers and nails. Seven years later, the workmanship made her company and her grateful. Layer upon layers of flowing braces compounded the interior sets.

Meditation? Who could bother with that custom? Not her. She needed to use her hands for something—anything.

"Well, I can see you are wrapping up? Am I wrong?"

She yelped. Who could that be? That voice, familiar... "Ygl?"

He stepped out of the sycamores' shadow, a little taller, leaner than five years prior, his musculature more sinewy in his royal attire. A knapsack hung over his shoulder.

"Oh my Achal, Ygl!" She ran to him, but hesitated.

"What is wrong?"

"I... I am sorry, my prince..."

Ygl perked. *"It is all right, Thalla. You can touch me."*

She did, and how they hugged tighter than twine, laughing louder than shattering plates. These two strangers who met once before his military training. The prince and the builder.

He whirled, laughing, holding her, pointing at the lowest, largest tier bridging a mile wide. "Look at them up there. All that meditating they do in there, all those open windows, and not one can see their prince has arrived home," he mocked.

Thalla giggled. "Inner Earth would quake and they would not realize it."

"I knew I liked you." Prince Ygl stated.

He walked over, admiring her handiwork with the broad staircase. "You do good work." He tapped the tough oak.

"Quirm has provided us with a treatment to maintain the wood's health. You know Khunians would never help."

He hesitated, absorbing her comment. "Yes... you are correct. They love nature too much and believe in hard work. That is so different from Lorellian ways."

"They like to fight."

"No. They like to protect. Protect nature."

"Protect nature. We need nature to survive. Silly."

Ygl clenched his teeth.

Thalla continued, "And, look at you, Prince. Back in your wonderful clothes."

"Yes. Methelo brought them to me when I could no longer wear their armor."

"Oh, I forgot they are so small and pasty. It amazes me how we are so related."

Ygl's lips pressed together; he rubbed the staircase, seeing some unfinished work. "Thalla, have you ever wondered how we thrive?"

"Well, no. Not really."

"... Man has everything, yet we struggle." He clenched the wood.

"Well, that is season." Playful, she stepped behind him, noticing her incomplete work, touching him.

"No, it is not season!" Angry, he snapped, swinging, hitting her.

Surprised, Thalla collapsed, the tools scattered from her belt. "Wh-what did I do?"

Nervous, Ygl stopped, tearing up. "I... I am sorry. I did not mean... They are very rough there, in Khun."

"I do not know what you mean."

"I am no longer your prince. I am now a general."

"I do not know what that is."

"Blasmle, their male Leader, told me something. He kept repeating it every sunday..." Ygl fretted, clutching his rich fabrics, gazing beyond the trees toward Khun. "... What am I?"

Thalla rubbed her lip's corner, wanting to change the subject. "I am all right, thank you. Do you know what a millimeter is?"

"A caterpillar?"

Thalla could not restrain her giggle, examining the staircase's hidden damage. "You need help. Come help me fix a bridge after this. It will be good for you."

"I missed you..."

Thalla paused before approaching closer, trying to mask her giddy demeanor. "May I touch you?"

"I... I do not know..." He gulped with shame. "... Yes."

She caressed his cheeks, staring into his eyes. "... She and I are no longer together."

"She... was your mate..."

"Bloodchild, you are so gullible. I was not being entirely truthful. We were more like lovers. Come on, who gets married at twelve?" She noticed her joking was not affecting him like she wanted it to. "Ygl, whatever that mean Elf told you over there, I will always care for you. We are all flawed. All of us. You are worth it. Oh my Achal, you are so worth it."

Ygl tried restraining his tears.

Thalla leaned in—

I gasped. Her kiss meant so much to me. I opened my eyes. "Thalla... Swen?"

Swen's lower eyelids flitted upward, her nebulous gases framing her contoured features, her silvery hair's swirling fibers added to the frame as she floated away.

"Was that you? Did you kiss me?" I asked.

"Thy memories come to the story, revealing all that is buried."

"How... how did you know?"

She did not, or would not, answer.

I could see my room through her gas' gaps. Kute had me placed here. This infirmary of rock, furs and metals.

"Would thou like for me to heal thee?"

"N-no. No. Kute provided me a tea that seems to be working. I think he gave it to everyone else. I just seem to be taking a little longer. It has a strange taste to it.

"Swen, I am torn. You see my memories. I do not understand how, but you do... I miss Thalla so much. I do. I really do, but, I am so torn."

"I understand. Things are not planned."

"I love her. I do, but..." I fell to the ground, quivering. The guilt overwhelming. Swen's runes encircled me, shimmering in the nebulae. One drifted past me similar to the "hooded tattoo" I saw behind Squish's neck but with a medial line slashing through it... I gasped again, "Swen, that rune..." She did not answer, leaving me adrift in pause. "I do not know how I am feeling. It is like something is awakening in me I do not understand. My feelings for you are strong, and even less though for Kute. Nonetheless, they are feelings. Strong feelings. I had never felt before... for strangers..."

"Thou does not choose love. Love chooses thee above. All else does not matter; all hate becomes the latter. Rebuke thy hate. It's not too late."

"Hate? I do not harbor hate for anyone. I admit I get angry, but I do not have hate."

"Master Ygl, remember Limbus, thy son. It's never over beneath Los and Num. Spirit rises to the surface—"

"'Integrity is born'..." her first words she stated when she escaped her strange lamp. They just came to me like they belonged to me. Like an instinct.

"Courage be thy shield." She continued.

"'Truth be thy sword.'" I found myself approaching her, searching within her cosmic eyelets... I leaned in to kiss her, her nebulous gases curdled around. I touched her cheek.

"No. Thou cannot touch..." Her displaced head floated aside. Her runes shimmered as if casting a spell. She noticed her magicks did not affect me. "How?"

"Maybe I was."

CHAPTER 28: Rarle

N acar, the Giantic Kingdom's capital.
Throughout the narrow streets, the war-bustling crowd worked their way to the Grand Entrance. Bronze armaments and mounts clanged against one another leaving little space for the frustrated populace to stand. Back and forth in their homes the warrior-farmers exchanged items with their spouses to assist in the security of all they held dear. More Giants marched along the mountainsides with their mounts to avoid the tight traffic below. The bouncy intoxicating field swayed relentless to the great flow of a race gone mad with wrath.

A vast shadow veiled the fertile land. Curious eyes peered upward, watching the Fairy multitude's soaring ascent to the clear skies. The colorful cloud dissolved, splitting some allies to go to the frontline while others acquired more weaponry.

"The Treedom is very active this cloudnoon. Never have I witnessed such a spectacle before." Erosc turned from the Hollow Royale's terrace. Shadows bounced about on his throne room's walls; trophy kills from the Dark Plains hung between the iron torches projecting from crevices found. "All these growths have gone by... Could peace be a cherishment even to me? I rule over mighty roots, yet even we have a gentle side." His stare, strong; unapologetic. He keeled a little as if fighting pain.

"Do you need any assistance, Tree Erosc?" I asked.

"No. No, thank you... Eagle? Is that your name, Thorn?"

"Yes. Tree Erosc, many others are in need of aid." The trendy tailors provided me with a long sleeve vest with mesh netting running down the left sleeve. Leathery slippers popped below pants modeling a grape vine design. A leather side-satchel contained my boxy lamp.

"Thorn Eagle of the Lorel Elves, my estate must come first." Tree Erosc's ebony robe ruffled against his weighty throne studded with vertical, striated jewels.

"No, Trunk, all estates must come first," Kute advised. His shield bearer lined against the wall with the other bearers. Gravelp abided near them, still wearing her customary silks.

"Is mine not? By Lolung-Cor, are you insane?" Erosc challenged his bloodson.

Kute rubbed his chest where he received his wound at the Ogrean Mountaindom. "So many things have been happening these past cloudnoons, Trunk."

"As I can see," Erosc remarked grudgingly to Gravelp.

"My sediments no motivate selves." The shy princess massaged her kiradoura's head.

"Who is your traitor?" Erosc interrogated.

"Crumb. Our Sand," she answered.

"Like Leaf, Trunk," Kute interpreted for her.

Erosc grunted. "We are fighting a war that has no exact pretense. This is preposterous and ridiculous. Precious blood is being spilt on my land for no reason."

"How is Stem?" Kute asked his bloodfather.

"... Stem is all right. She is as she always is. She has awaited your arrival as well. I would not doubt her tardiness since what has come to past."

"We will rise above what has come," Kute justified.

"It is not your fault, Sprout," Erosc comforted Kute.

"I know how Stem must feel."

"Stem is all right. You have always been one filled with too much love."

"I am sorry, Kute. Who is your 'stem'?"

"The one who bore me."

I could only sympathize. I remember my bloodmother, Rarle, again. Her hair and eyes carried a bright luminance. Neither could match her heart. She nurtured young Methelo and me whenever our bloodfather embarked on Khunian visits. One sunday, my bloodbrother and I took care of each other, left alone to our own devices. A great snake-creature, much larger than any I had ever seen, rose from behind a bush, slithering its hungry body in our direction. A strange liquid dripped from its jaw's corners, ichor from fanglike fingertips bubbled over like purplish pus—a Dicen, but my ignorance won that sunday. Methelo clung to the tree's bark we rested against. I armed myself with a thick branch. The Dicen paused... Protective Rarle responded to Methelo's cries. We had never seen our bloodmother's animalistic side coming to her bloodchildren's aid. The creature and she fought a great battle for a Lorellian not trained by Khunians. I joined in trying to help my bloodmother, her soon-to-be general... The Dicen met the end-of-seasons with my bloodfather's assistance. Rarle's season eventually ended because of poisonous wounds. Sundays later, I left for my Khunian training. Funny, how these forgotten thoughts returned to me... Yes, I understood and sympathized with Kute's feeling for his bloodmother, his "stem." Nonetheless, I wondered if my wild instincts were traits from my bloodmother or could the jodepiece have some sway?

"Trunk, how did a Demon possess Leaf when they fear the Cories?" Kute asked.

"I believe Dionjor traveled alone into the plains. He used to do that for moments of silence."

Meek Gravelp approached. "My sediments great number."

Erosc's red eyes locked onto her, examining her. "Are they? May I ask you, great Ogrean Fern, why you tell me this?"

"Be-because w-want help you."

"You do?"

"**Twig**, I will not tolerate the way you react to the Mound," Kute intervened. "She has helped the Party out of good faith. The war we hold is against Xurchon. The Ogres are only pawns."

"Pawns which must each be defeated. Remember who you are speaking to—Sprout." Erosc challenged, noticing Kute's insult.

"I am sorry but they have been tricked. We must acquire another means to end this war. Remember our clubs." With Kute's claim, Erosc eased a bit, rubbing his lower jaw.

The shield bearer observed my friend closely, and if I could mistake his noble gaze, I could almost imagine a jealousy he entertained at Kute's words. I knew this because even I felt a bit jealous at the prince's unexpected assertiveness, or did my jealousy derive from the attention Kute received from his imaginary paramour?

"I am sorry, Sprout. They must meet the end-of-growths."

"No," gloomy Gravelp quivered. Hogar's Beard rose to nuzzle his owner. "It true, Plant Kute. Sediments not hold back. Fight to last."

CHAPTER 29: Convergence

The Dark Plains.

The brown-hued grasses paved an absurd lot: tree grass, rock grass, blade grass; air grass... the territory always had a way of reshaping after certain damage into deadlier obstacles, garnering the grasses their namesakes. Travelers tried plundering through and got lost in the process. Many of these grasses matured so high, their development would attempt to block out Los and Num's rays, especially the thick tree grass.

On this starless night, the plain had already reshaped using the flying squirrels' carcasses as fertilizer, a fine course to have on menu. A friendless sentient, the Dark Plains never discriminated upon its next meal. Everything was regarded as the same since being abandoned a century or two ago.

The weeds rustled, a couple of trolls jogged through snickering. The weeds rustled a little more, a small breeze swept through—ceasing. The weeds began to rustle further, appearing to stretch higher for the naked skyways, their fibers beckoned, and leaned north; even the cumbrous tree grass tilted fibril filaments northward.

The Plains' denizens chittered and chattered, howled and spattered with sympathy. Oh, the glee and indignant wonder...

Across the weeds' topmost layer, the Death Mist trundled. With eager fleetness, milky tendrils crawled above, meandering throughout austere blades toward a desirous destination.

The jarring chorus multiplied louder and louder... wilder and wilder... Oh, the joyful renewal of a rematch with the Giants.

The creatures' numbers submitted greater and greater to their Almighty. So much greater did their numbers increase than the meager skirmish at the Cories in days past. The scandalous moment rang nigh. The mountains' power would soon be tested and proven wrong. Could the air contain such sycophancy for Xurchon, a welcomed figure?

The mist rolled and rolled...

And rolled...

CHAPTER 30: Convergence 2

Kyblore Island.

Isoris' gills fluctuated a little heavier, the slits expanding. She awoke lazily upon a moist moss bed in her grotto, her visions flitting past her, dreamy bubbles tickling her face's temples. She raked her scaly fingers through the lagoon a foot below, the caressing water curled up her camouflaged arm. "The visions get stronger," she thought. "I cannot deny their authenticity."

Being the Nixies' queen carried much weight these days. Her visions would help her people procure better fish to hunt—maybe a clearing bearing fresh fruit, but her visions seldom traveled past the Urvan Sea. When they did, the visions felt so vague as if their relevance did not matter.

From the mossy entrance into her home, a ripple widened into the lagoon. A wiry shadow streaked across the depth. The queen's immediate instinct recognized the figure advancing. "Tatenu."

The Nixy caller popped out of the bluish-green, treading backward into a glide, her webbed fingers played a titillating game between watery treads; her glistening scales melded well with the surroundings. Tatenu shared the same divine right as Isoris, creating quite a strong bond between them.

"Hail, Tribune. How goes third **Ocean**dom your?" Isoris asked.

"It goes fine, but sense danger much. The Dwarves have not arrived for trade for a while, and I have never met with the Giants despite overtures to the Dwarves for a forum. The quicu are restless."

"I take it omen your was like mine?"

"Hence visit my, Ocean. Could Numr'c be trying to tell us something?" Tatenu could barely see her invisible sister in the camouflage. A contour here. A contour there.

"About a raincloud falling from the sky and flooding across some pasture hideous?"

"You know there was power much more within mist that, Isoris."

The queen chuckled. "I know, but why even bother to think it was the Divinity sending us a vision? We have seen evidence no of them. Why would they want to send us visions such if the Divinity were true?"

Alarmed, Tatenu swam closer. "Isoris, as much as I agree with dictum our to 'Forever be joyous,' we must never forget we have rights divine our because of Jeble and Numr'c. Especially, you. You have the gifts greatest."

"That is why you are the Tribune, Tatenu. You are to set us aright even though many are starting to disbelieve."

"But how, Isoris?" She hoisted herself upon the mossy patch, her barely visible sibling reposed curling amphibious legs inward. "**School** our no longer seems joyous so. **Great pearls** many ago, school our stopped loving each other. Things are not as they used to be. Rahor says we do not hunt out of respect to the creatures sea. The dolphins have told him the creatures sea have complained of attacks dastard upon them out of self-indulgence, and not necessity.

"You have power much, Isoris. Only through you can we present visions our to school our, and through you, influence them."

Queen Isoris knew these points' truth. Rahor, Tatenu, Hapinset and she were the gifted children born by Rain, the former queen, to administer the Nixies and commiserate in this existence. "Are you glad bloodmother spawned so many of us? More than public our?"

"Why would you say that? It is a right divine unique. Ordained by the Divinity. The public respected privilege her."

One day, Isoris desired to consummate with a husband, a **chosen**, out of curiosity. Yet, underneath the twin moons, Nus and Anul, her urges seemed to have accelerated. Five tunneling indentations mauled over the carpeting algae as Isoris' webbed fingers slid upon her sister's hand, up Tatenu's arm. "Tell me. Have you seen visions any of the Divinity? I never have." she whispered.

Tatenu pulled away, diving into the lagoon. Watery rivulets dripped amongst the ferns. "There is something afoot here, and I will get to the bottom of it," she remarked after resurfacing. "You know right divine your has effect no over me. And, you know I am faithful to **bonder** my."

Isoris ignored her advisor's complaint. "Maybe you should have Rahor look out for that visitor strange, the Nixy without scales or gills. I am sure he is the root of problems our."

Tatenu remembered well the sporadic dreams entailing the strange guest. Who was he and what was the strange crystal dangling from his neck? Maybe Isoris surmised correct. Maybe they should remain vigilant for him. Better yet, vigilant for Isoris as well.

CHAPTER 31: Munch-Munch

Mount Royale.

My goblet's murky liquid imparted a rosy color mingling with the dark tint. Coppery flecks dispersed whenever I stirred my finger within.

"Go ahead, General, drink the elixir. It is good for you," Kute encouraged.

"I have never had a drink like this. It is different from willowberry tea."

The drink did not taste bad, even had some sugar in it—a gritty swallow that seemed to heal my wounds well. I did not have to worry about using my jodepiece whatsoever. Very fortunate.

"Who has the better drink? Khun?" The moment my friend asked, his buffed general sauntered into my quarters. Gravelp and Hogar's Beard followed with Kute's shield bearer. "Lo, Thorn. How fares the border?"

"No sign of the Ogres, but I am sure their arrival is imminent. Our border is quite secure," Umbala answered.

"Good. Of course, General, you know I invited everyone here for a meeting of the minds."

Gravelp nodded in acknowledgement.

"To answer your question, Plant Kute—"

"Please, General. No formalities. We have traveled far and hard. There are no lines between us."

"Thank you. Well we do not have the drinks Dionjor concocted and they do not heal as quickly as the elixir has healed me."

"That is good to hear, General. Unfortunately, Redfang is not healing as fast as you. He does have a problem consuming it."

"I guess Ding is trying to work with that?"

"Of course. Oh, the Leaf did not concoct it. I did." Kute's wink mystified me.

Uncomfortable, General Umbala spoke. "Please, everyone, the matter at hand. The question is what are you going to do while we war with the Ogres? Obviously, they want our little diadem. Personally, I do not think they can pass our forces, but in the event they do, what do you plan to do, General Eagle?"

"I just do not know, Thorn Umbala. The Dwarven estate is definitely an impossibility." I knew we would encounter this luckless scenario and this was an answer nobody wanted to hear. To Interim with it all.

Gravelp grunted. "'Seems we trapped in corner."

"We are very well trained in the ways of war," Umbala replied. "A good offense is the best defense, I say."

Kute's eyebrows wrinkled. "Thorn, are you saying we should outright invade the Dwarves' Grand Diamondom? Can we do it?"

"It is worth a try, Kute."

"It is too risky," I insisted. "Believe me, up against Man's mist, we are no match—not while Swen and I hide the Party from Xurchon's omniscience. Not before we can find the Jode. Umbala, you have never felt that mist's power. We have. And, it took everything in our arsenal to fight it. We have been hampered because of it."

"What other alternative do you think, General Eagle?"

"There is always the Nixies." A deep voice as rich as the topsoil flouring the Treedom's plantations filled the room. Blackened Erosc asserted himself within his ornamented braids, quite a vision to consider, and a thick sickle-lance at hand, war-ready. Dual streamers dangled beneath the sickle and lance heads.

"Nixies?" The name escaped me.

"The Dwarven thief reminded me about them. They could be a possibility," Kute added.

"Are you sure, Trunk?" Umbala questioned. "They inhabit Zaendara's tip. We have never dealt with them directly. Their commerce always arrived through the Dwarves."

My interest was piqued. "Commerce? I have never heard of the word."

"Fish, kelp, shells..."

Kute's brief answers still confused me. "What do Nixies look like? And is commerce like sharing?"

Everyone, except innocent Gravelp, gasped at me with disbelief. Ogres would be just as ignorant as me, no doubt. The idea of inescapable war bothered her more than simple questions; nonetheless, I needed to ask.

Kute emitted a booming laugh. "Oh, General, this is what I love about you. You are just as inquisitive as I. I love you dearly because of this. You are truly my friend. Is sharing something you have done with your neighbors, the Protectors?"

"Well, on occasion, yes. We are all Elves, but we had a treaty with Man that allowed them passage onto northern Lorel for an exchange of items."

"This is not the system we go by here. We have learned to trade goods on certain cloudnoons with each other. The Dwarves have what the Nixies and we desire, and the same. We trade goods. It is quite a system. Unfortunately, we Giants never travel.

"As far as I know about Nixies, according to the Dwarf, they look like you except have scales and webbed hands."

"Is that so? I have heard of such a sighting."

Impatient Umbala interceded, "Interesting, General Eagle. So what are we going to do?"

"I just do not know. We certainly do not know if the Nixies' estate has been overrun. That is something worth looking into."

I surveyed the room's interior as everyone pondered. The Giants' homes seemed rather similar to their trendy outfits. All furnishings, once again molded with fashionable metals, even the bed's frame. My bed's material had some kind of material within raising it above the metal framing within a type of fabric—very unusual but efficient. Much like Erosc's throne, jewels were embedded. A strange star, probably confiscated from the Urvan Sea, rested upon a side table, a striking difference. Fresh fruits and vegetables garlanded the room, overflowing into a hallway graced with flowers attached to one another, or some grain—a running motif throughout

Mount Royale. Hence, a probable divine right granted by their Divinity.

Gravelp clutched a shiny big apple from above, smelled it and bit down, hesitated, and enjoyed her new experience.

"The Nixies is the route we shall take," I concluded. "But how are we going to get there? For sure, the Dwarven skies will be surveilled by Man. My jodepiece will only protect us from Xurchon."

"Ding will have the answers you crave, General Eagle. We will provide you with a pegasus or two," Umbala instructed.

"Or two? You are not coming along, Kute?"

"No, my friend. My place is with my roots. Flower would tell you the same if Flower was here."

"Uhm," Juna's shrill voice popped out of the garland. "I am already here, Kute." A male Fairy fluttered down with her, quite an endearing couple, very regal.

"We were listening," she smirked.

"I am Tree Ood, her seed. Thank you for bringing my earth back to me safely."

"It is an honor, Tree Ood. Believe me, your earth holds her ground very well. She was as much a guardian."

Juna blushed, hovering closer to her mate. "Well, Ygl, I do not think I have heard kinder words."

Ood blanched. "... Uhm... my love... my, my wind..."

Noticing her error, Juna blushed more. "Oh, by Ethnel, no one is ever better than you, my seed." She hugged him, moving her finger down his cheek. Their union, a lustrous floating bud.

"So, you are staying as well, Juna?"

"Yes, Ygl. It would be foolish of me to leave my Ood's side again."

"That leaves Ding, Swen, and me. I guess you are staying too, Mound?"

Gravelp shook her head with an attitude reflecting her final bite's approval, her right cheek puffed out like a squirrel packing nuts. Her first apple. She rubbed Hogar's Beard's shelled spine, easing the kiradoura's tension. Her club strapped on a provided satchel. Erosc still eyed it, mystified.

Odd. I noticed Kute was the only person with a shield bearer in the room. "Gravelp, I am sorry you are in the predicament you are in."

"This hand **shift** dealt," she relented. "No choice. We, all, in same predicament. H-Hope in end."

"And so, the Party must split again," upbeat Kute concluded. "Good luck on your journey, General. May Pyty's sickle of sustenance sustain you." His massive clutch shook mine.

"Thank you... my friend." The deepest sorrow flashed through me. This may be our last meeting. Maybe this was why I delayed my answers. I just did not want us to split again. I had lost most of my bloodfamily and felt just as crestfallen as Gravelp. I did not want to lose this "bloodfamily" neither. Oh, how treacherous and evil Xurchon plotted to create such an environment.

Limbus... Swen, you were so correct. I must never forget my own bloodson. How could I be so selfish? Nonetheless, what must be done must be for the good of Zaendara.

"General..."

"Yes, Kute."

"The Dwarf may be my friend, but please remember, the Dwarf is still a thief."

"... Okay..."

Gravelp plodded forward, placing her hefty hands on my shoulders, opava butter lotion sifting up. Mutual tears welled upon her eyes' gritty lower lid. "May... all Divinity be... you." She understood my pain.

This experience with an Ogre shown new to everyone. Such emotion. Such pain. Gravelp and her kin were not the barbarians we had thought. How could barbarians create such beautiful, haunting sculptures and a breathtaking estate?

I clutched her closest hand. "You are as much a member of this Party as anyone else, Gravelp. You know that?" I affirmed.

Taken aback at first, she nodded with quick support and a slight smile. Kute nodded in agreement. Juna covered her lips with gracious fingers, satisfied with my leadership.

Her empathy did not escape Tree Erosc. With rattling, bejeweled hair, he approached the saddened princess. "I do not know how this will end. We will get to the bottom about those clubs. However it does, I will not hesitate to proudly call you my sprout." He waved his sickle-lance to the room. "Glory to war."

Umbala raised his weapon. "Glory to war and Lolung-Cor."

"And Pyty," Kute concluded. His shield bearer remained indifferent, the battle staff remaining in its sheath. "We will win."

Juna clucked her tongue. "Kute, being psychic is not your divine right."

CHAPTER 32: In the Still

The Dark Plains.

Avian grasses chirped at an unusual arrival who did not represent a small party proclaiming or a lithe mist crawling. No, this visitor was much grander. Much heavier. The grassland shook with their calculated approach.

King Smush did not like haranguing with the notorious grasses so long—weeds so resistant. True, the Ogres had ventured within to search for food with the Pixies on occasion but never so far. Their campaign against the Cory Mountains evolved into a sluggish process. Smush's earthen gift could have parted the plains, creating a huge path; nonetheless, his powerful divine right was limited, he needed to reserve his energy. Thank Falvanch, they brought enough sustenance.

Common sense dictated he bring Crumb along despite the various stomach issues his eldest son seemed to have. Almost every day, Crumb and he would cut a trench through some territory with their combined might. The army ripped and tore the grassland prairies apart the rest of the way. They would not be deterred.

Queen Squash stayed at the Ogrean estate to preside over their citizens, the arduous mission did not suit her, her distinct divine right an equal to Smush.

Not a foul denizen could be seen or heard during the solemn march. Maybe these creatures had never seen a sight so magnificent, though Smush knew the plains would not be so intimidated. One afternoon, his army marched through another familiar area, however, these cluster of clearings beheld peculiar markings. At first sight, the clearings appeared ordinary in the dense prairie, but at each cluster's center, half-eaten monsters and animals' carcasses were littered speckled with bones.

Still, no denizens could be seen. No manticoras. No werewolves. No harpies. No flying squirrels; yet pieces of them cluttered the ground. Even foreign animals left elements of their demise. Rotund, russet bushes besieged the clearings' perimeters, seven feet tall.

Tentative, Smush's strident gryphon squawked. The king softly rubbed his mount's feathered head. "Calm down, Dune." They traveled through.

Pixy First Queen Gasma dashed beside his right cheek, her small size measured half his sculpted face. Her tannish locks with blondish flecks bounced upon arrival. "Mountain, there is much hesitation among your men. This area makes the mounts skittish." Her bosom peeked through her red vest.

"See no danger, First Lady Gasma."

General Punok cantered next to his father upon his grand gryphon, replying, "Pillager very restless. Danger near."

Crumb tagged behind upon his growling kiradoura, Patch.

"Punok, what you say?" King Smush inquired.

"... First Lady, can you check see what ahead?" General Punok requested.

The seven-foot tumbleweeds rustled.

"We are already ahead of you, Crag Punok," Gasma responded. "Some of my **sediments** are checking." Her quartet of wings rocketed to the clouds, meeting her husband, Guisarrio, at midair.

"What, Gasma?" The Pixy King looked spiffy in his leather pants and short jacket.

From their aerial position she directed Guisarrio to observe the mass procession passing through from one clearing to the next as if by osmosis. "Do you notice how those bushes seem movable from east to west but from north to south they defy movement?"

The east-west bushes rolled back to their original positions blocking traffic, perplexing the queen and her king. The Ogres, oblivious to the obstacle, bumped into the vegetative impediment, pushed a little and trudged around it.

"Look," shocked Gasma stated. "Some Ogres are being enclosed by the bushes." She gestured into the air, her fingertips summoning particular particles to combine at her command. Liquid molecules culminated upon her hands, evolving into irregular aquatic spheres. With an outstretched hand gesticulating upward, she combined the spheres' power, blasting a geyser high enough for the other Pixy kings and queens to behold.

As she awaited her council's arrival to her signal, Gasma turned her attention to the briared fences blocking some Ogres' progress—especially the royalty. General Punok, already ahead of Smush and Crumb, swiped at the bushes with his stony club, the mace head knocking them aside. King Smush took hawkish Dune aflight to survey the happenings.

The bushes General Punok swiped rolled near and practically over him. From the bushes' underside, root-like teeth emerged, a roaring hiss emitted from the exposed gap reminding Punok of the steamed baths' spouts at his estate. Faithful Pillager, manifesting his namesake, gnashed at and attacked their briar assailant before the voracious weed could devour mount and rider. The gryphon's power, mighty.

In abrupt response to the bush's roar, the other brown bushes rolled over and pounced upon their prospective prey. The frantic Ogres, caught off-guard, flailed aback. Some weapons caught their mark, others, too late.

"Liongrass!" Advisor Crumb yelled.

"Weapons!" King Smush commanded in the busy general's place.

The Ogrean general leapt into his adversary's gaping cave of an orifice. Pillager, with wings spread wide, bounced back, pouncing upon his master's hunter, tearing at the briared derma with sharp talons, paws and beak. Mace-club in tow, Punok tore at the hundreds of raptorial teeth that broke upon his invulnerable skin, ripping through the upper palate. Death's multiple scents did not escape him. The liongrass bellowed in pain from the internal and external assaults.

Other Ogres did not fare better as the carnivorous weeds' mangled teeth minced hearty prizes while tumbling and tumbling upon more and more Ogres. Prickly skin sought to scratch and puncture prospective meals into submission. Once partially satisfied, the beasts' fibrous maws opened to get hold of another Ogre as chunky tidbits spattered out.

Liongrass enjoyed the killing more than the consuming—a proper rival to the King of Kills. For sure, the land had unexpected fertilizer.

The Pixy council's sextet gathered in the imperfect storm's epicenter. Gasma directed the closest members. "Zeph, Hoodia, Guisarrio. We must go in pairs where the Ogres need us. They need our divine right. Go! Ethnel be with you!"

As they parted, they made evident the Pixies' alliance was not halfhearted. Every location the Pixies swarmed, a vulnerable area the Ogres could not reach fell to their brand of mercy. This adversary would rue the day it attacked the wrong prey. Pixies dive-bombed between the spines of the tumbling terror's prickly hide, stabbing the exposed layer with blades dipped from the Ty Toad's acid. Unfortunately, the spines had spines on them, shortening some tiny fighters' lives.

"Aim for the eyes!" First King Guisarrio instructed a messenger as he veered toward an adversary. The messenger jetted in the opposite direction with the added directive.

The tumbling terrors' eyes exposed quite small, hidden in the thorniness. Only the Pixies could detect the oculi, their ally's advantageous opportunity. Guisarrio found his target staring at him from within the bristling hide. He knew, like him, the Council's members beckoned the air's wet fabric, blasting their respective aquatic energy at their optical targets, causing imbalance.

Hoodia's innate talent created water bubbles, which seemed harmless, but coupled with the fact the Council loved to bathe in caustic chthonic salts ever so often made her power a deceptive surprise. Cautious Hoodia directed her fizzy blitz so as not to affect her allies—the bubble burst caused a stinging injury and if that did not work, an onslaught stream of acidic bubbles followed.

Unlike Hoodia, Zeph and Starrm controlled gas. Zeph further transformed into a gaseous state that seethed beneath the tumbling terror's eyelids, penetrating the fleshy region. Vicstusi zoomed nearby, blasting sparkling barbs of ice.

The liongrasses falling susceptible prey to these assaults roared their displeasure and tried to get away, but advancing Ogrean clubs and picks met them.

"Oh no, you will not..." Cocky Gasma savored the most kinship to Ethnel's gifts, she probed for that elemental part moisture cherished most. With immediacy, her flesh melted away with hydration's onslaught. Watery beads soaked into her form, morphing her features as she billowed larger... and larger...

A bewildered liongrass attacked the enlarging First Queen. Watery Gasma expanded her amorphous form, engulfing the tumbling terror. The liongrass struggled and resisted in a losing battle of wills as the Pixy seeped into its threading membrane. Farther and farther she dug, sucking every bit of its moisture... the weedy beast roared... her task completed, she released her hold, separating from the desiccated clump. "This is the gift of Ethnel, beasts. You have messed with the wrong sediments!" she sloshed. Spiny particles flaked off her.

Angered, King Smush gave no quarter for this intrusion, exploiting his divine right to the highest degree. With his bulky steed, Dune, he pounced upon another and another of the fibrous furies. Punishment must be dealt. None could penetrate his invulnerable skin as he smashed his vibrating fist through his fibril foes. His silken cloak flailed in the wind with each offensive, a quartz crystal keeping it attached. The carnivorous herd trembled in pain's significant wake.

Another fibril fury tumbled at frightened Crumb. Growling Patch reared down, allowing the advisor to call upon his gift. The liongrass hesitated... alone in the clearing staring at the Ogre... sniffing the area within Crumb's nearness. Its carnivorous brethren either fled from their strategic mistake or were torn to shreds in the counter-massacre...

This Ogre smelled different—engorging the frenetic creature with respect.

"Crumb, what you do?" King Smush yelled down upon Dune in flight. "Monstrosity meet end-of-shifts."

The liongrass sensed not to attack this prey of preys reeking of a familiar smell. Crumb knew the grass recognized him. He did not want to kill the creature—an undesirable crossroad.

Sloshing through the sky in her hydrous form, aquatic Gasma did not perceive the situation Crumb's way. "Crumb..." she warned.

The liongrass hissed and roared, noticing itself surrounded and spun around, and rolled toward the encroaching forces. Its thorny hide dug deep into the ground, preparing an escape, earthy chunks spat here and there.

Crumb, torn between two allegiances, fought his anguish. A duty for his king and brother; the other to a god he worshipped greater than any other. To ally with Xurchon meant a new era of enlightenment for Zaendara and his people. This era would rain justice unto the Giants for the grievance they performed against his people ages ago. But what Crumb feared more than anything: to deny his king their gods; his people, their gods.

The pain... too much to bear.

Yet, there must be justice. Crumb's trembling hand pointed to the ground. The grasses wavered. The earth shook with the tectonic budges. Tears welled in the advisor's eyes. "... Forgive me..." he muttered.

The tumbling terror rolled and bounced... rolled and bounced... and bounced high above the Ogrean army, spinning against the gryphons. Eager spines extended as far as they could.

From beneath the bouncing barnacle, an earthen lattice broke from the continent's womb, forming a grassy palm, stretching around the spinning quarry, enveloping the liongrass. In vain, the liongrass bellowed, retractable spines poked throughout the sentient entrapment, engulfing the beast, thorns and all. The earthen hand retreated into its continental abode, stealing its unwilling quarry.

Days following, the Ogres and Pixies continued their ponderous trek, maintaining vigilance with every step. A platoon of gryphon riders ventured a distance outward, surveying the landscape with more distrust. Skeptic Pixies roamed closer through the weeds ahead. Needless to say, no signs of the liongrasses' ilk resurfaced. Whether the Dark Plains was neutral or not, this territory would be more Xurchon's friend if that moment ever arose.

During the night, while others slept, some regiments maintained sentry. The silence stirred eerie to many, for not once had anyone encountered any of the plains' denizens.

This predicament did not bother Crumb. He knew the matter's fact as he spent those moments contemplating. Contemplating his choices. Contemplating what would happen next. These following days had not been easy on him. Nonetheless, justice must be served to the Ogres. His job as their advisor would lead them to it. Damn his sister for her insolence.

General Punok maintained lead with these treks, riding upon alert Pillager's strong spine. His greatest need: protect his father more than anyone; not that the most powerful Ogre needed protection whatsoever. The gruff general should have taken much credence in this fact, but his innate knack of being an overprotective son outweighed his rank.

The Cory Mountains' jagged peaks loomed the closer the Ogrean host seized upon their destination. No clouds bordered the majestic summits populated by triangular flags, though many a cumulus floated above Smush's forces. The plushest green coated every mountain's surface, colorful, prolific fields dotting.

First King Guisarrio zipped around Punok's head. "Well, this is different from the plains."

"So different from Mountaindom." The general's voice, a volcanic explosion.

"Well, it is fair to say, Crag, we have not spotted any of the enemy ahead."

"Thank you, First Lord, for stating obvious with due respect." Punok glanced over his shoulder, not far behind solemn Crumb straddled his kiradoura, Patch... "Solemn?" Punok asked himself. For sure, odd behavior for an outspoken advisor.

The invulnerable general twisted back, wrapping his cloak about himself, a trophy kill's skin, a chimaera. The dragon-tail made a nice belt. The lion's head, a nice helmet.

Horns. Blaring horns, many resounded from the vastness. The general gripped his clubbed mace tightly, his thumb rubbing the kiradoura-claw head. He knew his race detested battle, preferring more interest in creating beauty than destroying it. Those blaring sounds, an unheard-of racket in their realm, indicative signs of what was to come. More horns blared across the Cories' expansive summits, almost substituting the missing cirrus.

With a bass squawk, Pillager elevated General Punok higher for a panoramic view. "Hold ranks! Hold ranks!" As his order spread throughout the legions, he noticed a dotty swarm rising above the mountains, moving from peak to peak, reminding him of Kute's Stonecrusher. Punok murmured, "Gravelp, we have arrived."

Across the front lines, the Pixy Council shot aquatic spurts from their relative gifts, echoing his orders. Of course, First Queen Gasma's spouted the largest.

A rumbling commenced upon the land. Punok glanced back again at his older brother and father. Neither had an answer. The rumbling escalated louder, but did not seem to progress closer. The Cories' peaks revealed invariably-sized specks rolling down from them, initializing from the outermost summits. Once the plummeting specks disappeared from Punok's sightline, the next innermost peaks produced yet another set of plummeting specks rolling down the fertile slopes. The calamitous operation continued with the rumbling and the horns climbing to crescendo as the displays culminated into building endpoints. Before the spectacle concluded, the floating dots disappeared. All was silent.

King Smush rode mighty Dune aside Punok and Pillager. "What think?"

Punok thought for a moment. The gryphons' flapping emitted a wonderful zephyr with the spring freshness. "Appear led us to area for battle. They dam other entrances. Smart. Preplanned."

"What we do?"

"We regroup, Boulder. Make plans. They ready. We be ready too."

Farther at vanguard, awed, Gasma studied the spectacle, dull insectoid wings keeping her aloft. Her body's lower half transformed into an aqueous state, water splattered in the subtle wind as she reared. Her hair drooped like a waterfall. The moment would be nigh. "The war begins." Her giggle tinged with some concern, she licked her slippery lips. "This will be fun."

CHAPTER 33: The Mous

Ding and I exited the Dark Plains. A contingent of three Giantic guards and Thorn Umbala accompanied us pulling a pegasus each and carrying thick, steel lances. I guided a purplish pegasus named Claybreaker. I did not know Ding's pegasus' name. Grumbling Ding did not like the idea of leaving his best friend, Redfang, behind. Even moreso, traveling with me on the same mount.

The plan required leaving as soon as possible through the shortest route to the Mous Strait. A few sundays worth of nourishments had been provided as well. Welbern strapped handily on my saddle. Gore glistened well on Ding's backside. Roaming through the Dark Plains was inevitable. Thank Achal, Kute provided us with escorts and needed to stay behind for obvious reasons with lonely Gravelp. Our good-byes turned out short and heartfelt—probably the Giants' custom. War's glory seemed to outweigh everything except farming, however, a general escorting a general garnered a nice compliment.

In comparison, my kin would never regard the Giants' tradition. Khunian Elves were a closer match to Giants with their daring females. Nonetheless, my friend's camaraderie to the strait would have been nice replacing Thalla and Limbus' absence, friendship's warmth being customary to Lorellians—nothing better. Restful departure, a way of thriving with our seasons. Celebrating season. Celebrating meditation.

I had grown accustomed to him. To Kute... and to Swen.

He laughed when I apologized for kissing his stomach. "I have a nice stomach," he stated with a wink.

My guilt, never-ending. I had no idea his shield bearer was his actual lover, an awkward relationship indeed. And why should I feel guilty about my attraction to Kute? Thalla was bisexual and never hid it from me. Something had awakened in me during this ordeal. Why should I feel guilty? No reckoning should affect me...

Ding, on the other hand, I understood little about.

Our group trekked the tan grasses' manicured field up the hill headed for the cliff we knew overlooked the Mous. Umbala advised to make the remaining journey on foot once exiting mountainous cover. I agreed. Anybody could spot our aerial route. Once over the Urvan Sea, we should be safe.

"This is where we leave you, General Eagle," Umbala stated, shifting his lance from one arm to the next. His reddish pegasus shook its head uneasily. "Remember, they want your blade. Guard it."

A clinking on my saddle: the beaten lamp hung onto a thick link whose pearly luster harmonized with the early sunday. I rubbed my finger along a groove of many etching my lamp. What use would Swen be? With her power too tied up protecting our Party from Xurchon's awareness, her constant chanting drumming louder and louder in my psyche... my divine right too occupied protecting everyone from my jodepiece. Like a marriage, she would be my new wife. I hoped Limbus would be fine with that.

Now, I understood why she chanted so much when she first appeared: protection. She had begun protecting us... but these current chants carried a different timbre. The telepathic waves, a different taste.

And, who was this princess prodigy warning me in her gases? What riddle was the prodigy speaking of? And Swen's rune? Why did it look almost like Squish's tattoo?

"Thank you, Thorn Umbala. You will make it back safe, I hope?" I asked.

"By Lolung-Cor, we will."

Ding and I proceeded alone. The sunday shown too beautiful to dwell upon our gloom. "I am sorry about Redfang, Ding."

My potential ally trod silent for a moment, muttering, "It was not your fault, Elf. We were defending ourselves. He is safe with the Giants."

"Thank you for your assistance."

"I am the only one familiar with the Nixies. There was no other."

"Your help is appreciated."

"You make it sound like I had a choice."

"Ding..." My Achal, why be so stubborn? What type of season had he seasoned?

We reached the cliff's edge. The Mous' tides raged, the waves zipping between cliffs, dashing upon the reefs, swirling back. Umbala and his squad waited thirty feet behind us. Northeast, up the Mous, out across the vast Urvan, the sea's vastness flowed so calm compared to the gusto occurring below. Somewhere out there beyond the Ty Desert's influence, Kyblore Island, the Nixies' main estate, flourished, according to my thieving ally.

Ding struggled getting onto his mount.

I assisted. "Ding, maybe it would have been wise to have your mount kneel first?"

"Oh, drat you, Elf." He nervously hugged his pegasus, lugging his right leg over, exposing his rather fat rump. "I never asked for this beast in the first place."

"I am sure the Giants tried to accommodate you," I teased him. For sure, my notion held truth because the winged mare's fur, a rusty-gray, was as close to Redfang's coloring as Kute could get it.

"Gaah!" Ding still hugged his mount's neck. "... Oh, Redfang..." he mourned.

I rubbed the comical thief's back. Who knew Ding had a soft spot in him? "Are you ready?"

He rested for a moment. "May I protect myself."

I laughed, walking back to Umbala's squad. "May you protect us both."

✛

In a turquoise robe, a bloodied Elf, female, postured battle-ready beside a roaring fireplace. Khunian, but not Khunian because she did not sport their traditional ware. The fervor in her large eyes and gritted teeth matched the nearby flames, reeking of purpose.

Demonslayer was wielded in her clenched hands before her.

✛

I vomited upon the ground, quivering on all four. Who was she? And, why was she wielding my blade? When did a

Khunian possess my Welbern...? I fought from whimpering as best I could. Oh, bloodmother, my apologies, endless... I had awakened, yet I had not. *"D-Ding... I think I-I hate myself and I do not know why."*

"Pfft. Oh, Elf. There is no one who hates you more than me. Now, let us get on with this. I am ready!"

The Giants laughed at Ding's dilemma. I found Umbala's bronze boots in front of me.

"Do not worry, Ding," the massive Giant encouraged, "Slateripper is a fine mount," concerned Umbala stooped to me, his hand on my nape. "Are you fine, General Eagle?"

I glanced at him, welcoming a chiseled face absent its helmet. "I am fine, Thorn. Kute and you must have your **stem**'s eyes."

"Why do you say that?"

"Well, Tree Erosc has red ones. Or, well, kind of red."

Umbala grunted. He pulled me up, supporting me to his Slab. "I am glad you are fine. It appears Kute's blood was of some help."

"What do you mean?"

"Oh, something he was testing. In your tea? Since healing is a part of his divine right, he hoped his blood would help with your wounds. Apparently, his blood does not seem to work entirely on animals, but do not worry, our **chloro**s will be working hard in fixing the wolf. But, do not tell Ding, okay?"

"Yes. Yes, of course." I almost vomited again at the thought of those coppery flakes being Kute's blood.

An assortment of horns blared in the far south. As the escalating, metallic sounds rumbled behind us in our direction, the Giants' alarm system mirrored the aggressive strait's buoyant waters. An avalanche of boulders echoed their answer, tumbling down from the farthest southern peaks. In response, another avalanche released from subsequent peaks, with each avalanche following one after the other. Boulders upon boulders. Rocks upon rocks. Stones upon stones. The rumbling grew louder as the spectacle approached our gathering, blocking all entrances to the Cories.

"You must leave, Eagle, as well as I," the concerned Thorn remarked, replacing his helmet. He hopped upon Slab's spine. "By the way—"

"Yes."

"You must be seeing the twin suns' glare. Our **trunk** does not have red eyes. Guard them, warriors." Pegasus and master soared off to the building barricades.

Nervous Ding rolled up from Slateripper's mane, nodding in agreement. His mount reared and pranced in place, spreading rusty-gray wings, and hurtled into the air, razor hooves flexing. Importance weighed heavy for him to lead since he knew where to go.

Beyond my uncomfortable friend, I surveyed vast Urvan, the golden glittering waters appeared so much calmer considering the direction of travel; but I knew our new journey was just beginning into new territory I doubt my guide knew anything about either—the irony not lost upon me.

Slateripper soon dipped within the deep canyon with her Dwarven rider wobbling a bit in the leathery saddle. "Oh, protect me," the thief yelped over the rumbling avalanche.

SHtuCk! Howling screams packed with anger trailed blood-spray on both sides of me. I lunged into a forward roll, turning around, grasping my blade... Welbern? Oh, Achal, I left Welbern on the saddle's sheath!

Before me, writhing ten feet in height, a salivating Dicen stared, its fanged nails shredding through the warriors securing me, holding its struggling trophies high. Bone shredding through metal shredding through bone. The ichor from the nails' curved fingertips bubbled over like wound-pus.

"General!" Kute soared in on Stonecrusher. Umbala shadowed behind him alongside the shield bearer. "Get out of there!" my friend warned.

The dark Dicen cast its defeated preys aside, making a gambit at me with bulging eyes and a thick tongue wagging.

I ran and ran and ran. Claybreaker seemed so far away. All the while the Dicen's punishing talons dug deep holes into the dogged space between us.

"Claybreaker!"

My purplish mount raced in an instant to my aid, but I could feel the Demon's bitter breath closing in. The terrain's rumbling raged greater.

I lunged with all my strength as Claybreaker's spine surfaced beneath me. I held on. A dripping talon sliced through my outfit with Claybreaker barely ahead.

The terrain rumbled further, but the rumbling was different than what I anticipated. The cadence different, coming from another direction. As we careened over the precipice, the tan grasses exploded beneath us, tossing demonsia's latest victim to the Mous' rabid embrace.

On the Demon's nape: that dratted symbol—

"Squish... that was Squish...?"

Mound Gravelp waved to me upon faithful Hogar's Beard, blowing bountiful kisses from her distance. Her divine right's destructive route extended from her spot to the explosion. Trendy Giantic robes dressed her, though she did not reject her pink opals.

The airborne cavalry swooped past her, Kute waving.

A draft whistled. I touch my hurting side, pursing my lips. Blood.

I think I heard Swen sigh.

Soft winds... I must meditate soft winds.

CHAPTER 34: Epilogue

Hidden underground, Ogrean catacombs kept a safe distance from the sulfuric baths' caustic fumes. These stony masterpieces should never be hidden; however, the dead needed their privacy. What privacy? No one understood. Nonetheless, the deceased rested. Until tonight...

A couple of days before the Ogres marched against the Giants, a heavy figure stumbled into the granite crypt at the stairwell's base grasping his belly, the only item evident from within silken mantles. No streetlamps lined these catacombs, instead replaced by torches set in six-foot towers. No sentries guarded the venerated area, too busy protecting the estate from whatever elusive specters stalked the citizenry. No screams seeped down here where fiery, destructive motifs shared a likeness to King Smush's royal pillars' design.

The visitor stumbled through the intricate halls, granite coffins coating the honeycombed walls, until he reached a vast room set in mauve marble. Torchlight gleamed from the metamorphic limestone revealing flat, oblong slabs in horizontal rows.

At the marble field's other end, a lone slab established itself separate from the aged predecessors. Desert foliage formed a semi-wreath perimeter around the slab, eclipsing its base adorned with smooth looped notches accompanying familiar fiery motifs. The number of notches on the hem represented the slab's placement in this historical arena—a probable practice in monotony. At the slabs' centers, a different motif glared different from any in the estate: tripled arches overshadowing the silhouette of a wolf's head bearing big ears. The Ogrean version of heaven, maybe?

The shrouded figure arrived to the special slab, raising a trembling hand. At first, the slab rattled a bit before rolling over the emblematic wreath. A solitary torch provided ambience to the alabaster tomb beneath, sparkling agates peeking.

The shadowy visitor fell upon tired knees, leaning over the grave in an act of spewing, wheezing and wheezing, ready to cough something up... primordial fluid drooled; then, gushed from gut into grave as the figure's body heaved and heaved. The eight-foot pit glowed from the ancient sin's support.

A dark hand emerged, grasping the grave's edges, touching the visitor before crawling aside. The corpse's fingers trembled as they extended, transforming into curvilinear bone dripping with ichor.

"Welcome back, **mineral**. The others will be waiting." Crumb's monotonous whisper, a stone traveling upwind against a flood.

The adventure continues.
Catch up with the adventure in Part One:
"General Ygl and the Genie."
PJSELAROM.COM

About the Author

PJ Selarom, an Air Force veteran, is a lover of mythologies, inclusivity and comics. He ventures to combine these ideals in his wonderfully dark adventure of love, religion, and politics.

He resides in a treehouse somewhere in the country, taking care of his baby unipegon.

He can be reached at
PJSELAROM.COM/CONTACT